Lights
on the Sea

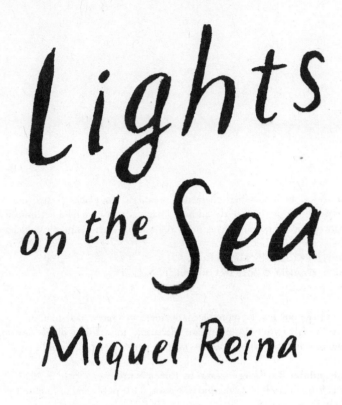

Lights on the Sea

Miquel Reina

Translated by Catherine E. Nelson

amazon crossing

Text copyright © 2017 by Miquel Reina
Translation copyright © 2018 by Catherine E. Nelson
All rights reserved.

Previously published as *Luces en el mar* by Espasa Narrativa in Spain in 2017. Translated from Spanish by Catherine E. Nelson. First published in English by AmazonCrossing in 2018.

Published by AmazonCrossing, Seattle

www.apub.com

Amazon, the Amazon logo, and AmazonCrossing are trademarks of Amazon.com, Inc., or its affiliates.

ISBN-13: 9781503903203
ISBN-10: 1503903206

Cover design by David Drummond

Interior illustrations by Godie Arboleda

Printed in the United States of America

To my mother,
for supporting me in everything I do.

Sometimes we need to get lost in order to find ourselves.

Anonymous

Table of Contents

Prologue

It all began with a bolt of lightning. Cutting through the stormy night sky, it crashed down on the roof of the most remote house in San Remo de Mar. The retired couple living there already knew it was to be the last night in their home. What they didn't know was that a lightning bolt would set off a chain of tragic—or perhaps miraculous—events that no one ever could have imagined.

But all this was still hours away. Whether they could have done something to change the course of events, or if everything was already predetermined with the arrival of the first drops of rain, was not something they could question at the time. As it happens, this story did begin with that lightning bolt, and certain details should be noted to understand how they came to be in that extraordinary situation.

Harold and Mary Rose Grapes, known to all as Mr. and Mrs. Grapes, lived in what was, quite possibly, the most special place on the whole island. Unlike the homes and shops that huddled together down on the beach, Mr. and Mrs. Grapes's house was located outside the picturesque town, at the end of an unpaved street, at the highest point on Brent Island. It perched defiantly on the edge of Death Cliff, right over the ocean.

On a clear day, the townsfolk could see Mr. and Mrs. Grapes's bright-yellow house from miles away, whether they were strolling the fertile hillsides of volcanic rock or sailing the small island's chilly waters. Either of those activities would have been ideal for enjoying the hot Sunday morning before the storm. The island's beaches, trails, and café patios buzzed with activity as San Remo's inhabitants took advantage of the rare warmth and clear sky. But as usual, Mr. and Mrs. Grapes chose to spend the day inside, enjoying, for the last time, those old walls that were their home.

An Uncertain Future

Mrs. Grapes spent most of Sunday morning packing up keepsakes, trying to decide which ones she could do without. As she was removing the last items from the wardrobe, a wrinkled photograph fluttered to the ground. She picked it up gingerly and, turning it over, felt a prickling sensation all over her body.

She sat down on the bed and took a deep breath before she dared to look again at the image she had hidden away years ago to forget the pain that was too deep. A man, a woman, and a boy, all smiling and hugging one another. Behind them, illuminated by the setting sun, was a partially built ship.

The photograph had faded, but Mary Rose could still picture the scene in full color. The man's hair was pitch black, and behind his glasses were eyes of the deepest blue, just like the boy's. Mary Rose felt a stabbing pain, and the poison of past resentments surged through her. She took another deep breath and looked at the boy's smile and his hair, which was the same shade of brown as that of the green-eyed woman holding him.

A tear fell behind Mrs. Grapes's oval-shaped glasses as she remembered the hundreds of afternoons they had spent at San Remo's old shipyard. Back then, they'd dreamed of discovering the world beyond the island. They had no fears, no ties, and no regrets. Now, thirty-five years later, Mary Rose didn't even recognize herself. When had she stopped being that woman? When had she allowed their dreams to die? The questions cut through her. And now, leaving this house and facing an uncertain future without it terrified her. She looked at the photo once more, then placed it in an open box and went down to the kitchen.

In the cluttered basement workshop, Mr. Grapes was working on one of his miniature ships. Shafts of sunlight came through the porthole windows. Here, moving boxes still sat folded, leaning against the washer and dryer. Everything was still in place. Dozens of old appliances lay scattered near the enormous cistern. The only space reflecting the impending move was the almost-bare pantry hidden behind a threadbare checkered curtain.

Despite his constant complaints about the cramped space, Harold spent most of his time amid that chaos. He enjoyed tinkering and working on inventions. But his favorite activity—the only one that could cheer him on the days he felt down—was building ships in bottles.

Using old bottles that he found washed up on the beach, he built scale replicas of historic ships. Those small marvels had previously been found throughout the house, but now they'd all been carefully swaddled in Bubble Wrap and placed in boxes. All but one.

Unlike the others, the replica that Harold now held was not in a bottle but in an old, squat mason jar. Inside, his most treasured ship sailed defiantly across a sea of resin. It was the first he'd ever made. This ship had no detailed ornamentation, no royal crest emblazoned on her sails. It was a simple seaworthy sailing vessel, a modest boat longing for great adventures. A model of the full-size ship Harold had begun building long before the miniature copy he was now dusting. A ship that never had a name.

Sometimes Harold could still smell the wood, tar, and sea that permeated the shipyard where he had worked as a young man. He could still hear his hammer strike the chisel as he packed oakum between the boards and feel the sun on his bare back. Harold remembered with nostalgia each of the real boats he had worked on: fishing boats, trawlers, passenger ships . . . The work was hard, but there was such joy in seeing a ship you'd labored over set sail for the first time.

And nothing compared to the love and care he had put into building the sailboat he now observed in miniature. A ship that had held all his dreams and had taken up all his free time. Harold set the jar down and sighed. Those dreams had sunk before the ship's hull ever touched the water. There was nothing left now but a bitter dream inside a glass jar.

A light tremor ran through his body, returning him to the gloomy basement filled with the smell of wax. The whole basement began shaking violently, and Harold grabbed the jar so it wouldn't crash to the ground. A few seconds later, the shaking stopped.

Harold huffed with irritation when he saw the miniature's mainsail had come loose and fallen onto its deck. He put on his magnifying glasses and picked up tweezers to repair the damage.

Mrs. Grapes's voice came from the top of the stairs. "Harold! Did you feel it? That was a big one!"

"No worse than the others!" he shouted.

"I'm sure it was! Thank goodness almost everything is packed, or there would have been a lot more damage." She came down the stairs as she spoke. "I'd feel better if you'd go check the guy wires."

"Sure. When I'm finished here, I'll go take a look. OK?"

"All right." And before returning upstairs, she added, "Lunch will be ready in ten minutes."

Even after all these years, Mary Rose had never gotten used to the earthquakes. When she reached the kitchen, her heart skipped a beat. The mauve-and-fuchsia hydrangeas that had graced her sturdy table now lay on the floor, uprooted in a heap of dirt and pottery shards.

The shattered flowerpot transported Mary Rose back to a time before this house could have existed in their wildest dreams. Suddenly, she was in their old apartment in town, hearing rain drum on the dining room window and watching lightning crash over the sea. A pot of hydrangeas had slipped from her hands and broken on the tile floor. A premonition had immediately filled her mind: *Something terrible has happened.*

Back then, Mary Rose knew the damaged hydrangeas were a bad omen. But nothing prepared her to face what she would discover hours later.

A burning smell jolted her back to the present. She ran to the stove, but it was too late.

While Mary Rose improvised a soup with the little bit of fish she had managed to salvage from the scorched dish, Harold used the time to inspect the guy wires.

He went down the steps of the back porch and circled around the house to the first of six steel cables that, like tethers on a giant tent, came down from the rooftop and were anchored deep in the rock underground. Harold had installed them years ago, when the foundation began to shift due to the unforgiving erosion of the cliff.

Harold squatted down in front of the guy wire and pushed aside the lush hydrangeas growing around it. But then he shook his head. In a few hours, they had to abandon the house. It no longer mattered if the guys were secure. So he stood up and went for a walk. He passed by grapevines he had planted with his father long before he and Mary Rose decided to build the house in that extraordinary place—even before he and Mary Rose had met. The vines used to cover the property, but they hadn't borne fruit for years. Choked out by the hydrangeas, the twisted vines were dry and bare of the fruit his family had once used to make grape jam, his favorite. Harold felt nostalgic as he gently touched a wizened branch. But, as with the cables, there was no use in worrying about the barren vines. The next morning, neither they nor the house would be there. Everything would be gone.

Harold continued to the end of his yard: the rocky edge of the cliff. From that spectacular overlook, he could make out part of the contour of the island and the immense sea surrounding it. In the distance, wispy clouds gathered on the horizon, but the beach still teemed with people. Near the cliffs, he saw a group of surfers fighting to stay on their boards. On the opposite side, where the mountains gently sloped to the sea, fishing boats were headed out.

San Remo was a small town on a rocky island in the middle of a cold ocean, so isolated that the rest of the world barely knew it was there. Life there was monotonous, and the locals were distrustful of everything: outsiders, change, and even their own neighbors. Like most of its inhabitants, Mr. and Mrs. Grapes never had set foot on ground other than Brent Island, nor had they sailed out of view of its shore. The piece of earth beneath their feet was their whole world, a tiny world to which they'd had to adapt and in which, like the flowers and vines around them, they'd planted their sorrow as deep as possible.

A gust of cold wind raked the yard and tore some petals from a hydrangea close to the edge of the bluff. Harold's gaze followed their erratic dance until they disappeared, swallowed by the abyss. Then he went back inside.

"Two hours of cooking wasted!" fussed Mary Rose as she served Harold some watery soup. "I wanted to make something special for today."

"It's just another day." Harold tried to sound convincing, but when he glanced up at his wife, he knew he hadn't succeeded.

"Everything OK outside?" she asked, changing the subject.

"Everything's fine," he answered, watching the pieces of burnt fish sink to the bottom of the bowl. "I don't think we need to worry about the guy wires, considering there will be nothing left to secure, come tomorrow."

Mary Rose took a spoonful of soup, and the burnt flavor spread down her throat. She drank some water, but the bitterness remained.

"I still can't believe this'll be our last night in our home," said Mary Rose.

Just as Harold was about to answer, the doorbell rang. Mr. and Mrs. Grapes looked at each other in surprise and, almost without a sound, carefully laid down their spoons. They never had visitors at this hour; they normally didn't have visitors at any hour. The doorbell rang again.

"Do you think they've come for us?" Mary Rose whispered.

"Ha!" Harold exclaimed. "I'd like to see them try to force us out before it's time!"

"Shhh! Don't shout," she said softly.

The bell rang again, insistently.

"All right already!" Harold exclaimed as he got up from the table. "I'll just remind them that, according to their blasted letter, we have until tomorrow morning!"

He stomped to the front door, while Mary Rose followed hesitantly a few steps behind. The bell sounded yet again, but the noise was interrupted when Harold opened the door. On the other side was the tall, thin figure of a man in an elegant gray suit that complemented his ashen complexion and gray hair.

"Good afternoon, Harold . . . Rose," he said, dragging out their names mournfully.

"Good afternoon, Matthew," said Mary Rose.

"What brings you here, Mayor?" asked Harold curtly.

"I'm sorry to bother you, but I just wanted to stop by. May I come in?"

Harold hesitated, then stepped back and allowed the man to enter.

Mary Rose made tea, and the three of them sat in the living room. The atmosphere was tense, and the mayor, shifting uncomfortably, spoke first.

"To be honest, I wasn't sure if I should come. Dealing with this situation hasn't been easy for me, but you must know that, first and foremost, you're my friends."

"We don't blame you, Matthew," said Mary Rose.

The man's eyes went hopefully to Harold.

"Look, Matthew," Harold said, fighting to keep his anger in check. "If you came to have us ease your conscience, you're out of luck."

"Believe me, I'm not here to make myself feel better. I know what it means for you to lose this house," the mayor started slowly. "I came for you, to see if I can do anything to help."

"Help!" exclaimed Harold. "Don't you think it's a little late for that?"

"Harold, you know city hall had nothing to do with the eviction," he insisted, twisting his teacup back and forth.

"But city hall did decide where we have to go."

"Yes," the man stammered. "I tried to get you something better, but your pension wouldn't cover the rent."

"And what about our compensation?"

"You know the land here isn't worth much—"

"So tell me what you've done to help us."

The mayor looked around the room as if he suddenly didn't know what he was doing there.

"Harold, calm down, please," Mary Rose intervened. "I'm sure Matthew did all he could."

"Oh, you're sure?" he asked furiously.

They were interrupted by a flash of lightning. Even the light fixture hanging from the ceiling was rocked by the shudder of thunder that followed.

"Even though you don't see it now," Matthew said as he watched the light swing, "I think that in time you will agree it was for the best. You may not be able to keep the house, but you will have everything else, including my friendship."

"Friendship?" Harold echoed. "The word *friendship* doesn't mean much on this island."

Mary Rose's teacup clinked against her saucer. She knew what Harold meant, but she didn't want to think about it. The memories were too painful.

"I should go," the mayor said, getting up. "It looks like a big storm is heading this way."

"Yes," Harold said, taking the last sip of his cold tea. "And we still have a lot to do."

Mary Rose placed her cup on the table and got up to accompany their guest to the door.

"I'll be here tomorrow at nine to help. All right?" the mayor asked.

"We'll be here," she replied.

Those were the last words Harold heard before the front door closed. He got up and slowly walked to the window. With the sleeve of his sweater, he wiped off the condensation and looked out. The beach was deserted. Thick, gray clouds covered the sky, and the wind off the ocean was beginning to blow in the first drops of rain that stuck to the glass like tiny insects. A few moments later, Mary Rose returned.

"I think you were very unfair," she said, joining him at the window. "You know Matthew isn't to blame for our misfortunes."

"But this time, he could have done something."

"It's not in his control! Or ours either! The letter was clear."

"The letter, the letter!" he moaned. "Curse the day we got that letter!"

Another peal of thunder made the living room light flicker.

"There are plenty of people in town who have lived in the residence for years, and they're perfectly fine," Mary Rose said.

"You know as well as I do that everyone hates that place. And we aren't old and feeble, needing someone to feed us like we're babies."

"Stop complaining, Harold Grapes!"

"I don't understand how you can be so accepting! Don't you understand what it means to lose our home?"

Mary Rose felt a knot rising in her throat.

"The mayor's right. This storm will be a bad one," Harold said, staring out the window. "I'd better close the shutters." He turned on his heel and left.

The House on the Cliff

Harold went upstairs to the second floor. He couldn't stand the way Mary Rose had seemed to surrender these last few months. It wasn't like her. And he couldn't simply accept the situation. This wasn't just a house. This home had been built with something irreplaceable.

Harold went from room to room, securing the shutters along the way. The rooms were now stripped bare, occupied only by the boxes that held decades of memories, furniture waiting to be moved, and a random assortment of items to be packed in the morning. Before fastening the last shutter, he looked outside. Sheets of rain swayed back and forth, pushed by the wind that was whipping up the waves along the beach. The gutters overflowed, soaking the hydrangeas in the garden. The rain was seeping into him too, slowly diluting his anger but soaking him in a heavy frustration.

Leaving meant more than losing their house; it transcended the material. It meant abandoning the only thing left from their happiest days, the scrap of wood that had helped him stay afloat, his only connection to everything he had lost. His life hadn't gone the way he'd wanted, but at least he'd learned to survive. Now, his whole world would disappear. His whole life would be crammed into a little room in a retirement home in the middle of the island. A barren place far from the sea, far from everything Harold had loved. Far from him.

He went to the dresser, opened the top drawer, and found the letter. He held it again in his hands, and the memory of that cold January morning flooded back. The morning the mayor delivered the thick ivory envelope.

"Good morning, Matthew! Come in before you freeze out there," Harold had said.

The man entered a little warily.

"Would you like to join us for breakfast?" Harold asked, closing the door. "We were just about to eat."

"No, no. I'll just be staying a minute," Matthew said, without removing his gray raincoat.

"At least have some coffee with us," Harold said, motioning for the mayor to follow him to the kitchen. "It's been months since we've seen you!" Like most of the islanders, the mayor wasn't a terribly social man, but he was the only person who had never turned his back on them over the years.

Mary Rose joined them, and the three sat down to a table laden with eggs, coffee, toast, and butter. The mayor was still wearing his coat. Mary Rose felt unsettled by his anxious demeanor.

"And what brings you out here?" Harold asked. "Don't tell me you're finally going to pave the road into town?"

"Well, no, it's not about the road," said Matthew.

"Of course, I can't imagine the mayor would spend money on something so practical."

Matthew responded with a forced, awkward smile. "I came to give this to you in person," he said, pulling an envelope from the pocket of his coat. "It's from the Central Government."

"The government?" Mary Rose echoed. "Is it important, Matthew?"

"You should read it yourselves," he said, laying it in the middle of the table.

Harold picked up the official-looking envelope and weighed it in his hand. He carefully cut open the thick paper with a bread knife and removed the letter. A large, fancy emblem graced the top of the letterhead.

"Central Government," he began reading aloud. "Commission for Protection and Public Safety—"

"Protection and Public Safety? Have we done something wrong?" Mary Rose interrupted.

"No, no, Rose. It's not that at all," Matthew replied. "I think it has to do with a study that was done on your property."

"A study?" Mary Rose was visibly upset. "Have there been people nosing around without us knowing? Matthew, what's this all about?"

"Honestly, I didn't know anything about it," he said, sounding to Mary Rose a little less than convincing. "About three months ago, three officials came to do research on the island. I thought it was a demographic study or something like that. I didn't think it was a big deal."

"But it was on our property? I don't understand!"

"Please let Harold read the letter," the mayor said, trying to calm her down.

Harold remembered the scene perfectly, and even though months had passed, he felt the same foreboding as he reread the letter:

Dear Mr. and Mrs. Grapes,

We are writing regarding the new Law of Geological Safety, approved by Parliament on the fourteenth of September of last year. The law stipulates that new construction along the coast conform to more rigorous regulations. Among the new standards, the law states that new construction must be built using anticorrosive materials and be situated a minimum of thirty-two feet from the shoreline.

Your residence, built before the new law went into effect, would normally be grandfathered under previous regulations. However, due to extraordinary circumstances, we are unable to exempt your residence from the new building codes. Below are relevant excerpts from a report by our committee of experts:

1. Land composition: the fragile composition of volcanic rock that forms Brent Island is much more susceptible to erosion than any other type of geological formation.

2. Lot and safety restrictions: at its closest point, the residence is situated four feet, ten inches from the shoreline . . .

As he reread that last sentence, Harold was overwhelmed by a sense of helplessness. Although it was true that the distance from the last step of the back porch to the edge of the cliff was less than five feet, it hadn't always been that way. In response, Harold and Mary Rose had sent in the original plans for the lot, showing that the house had been built more than sixty feet from the edge. It wasn't their fault that, over the years, the ferocious sea repeatedly crashed against the island and eroded the cliff, causing mudslides and eating away at the rock as if bent on making the whole island disappear. He sighed, looked again at the crisp print, and kept reading.

3. Morphology of the coast: the location of the residence is imminently dangerous. The residence is situated on a ledge, 111 feet above the water, a height that is not suitable for any human activity, particularly daily living.

In view of the above information, and despite dealing with a construction predating the indicated codes, the Commission is obliged to take necessary measures to ensure the safety of its inhabitants.

Therefore, you are hereby instructed to vacate your property on the eighteenth of July. Once cleared, the residence will be demolished.

Further details are forthcoming.

Sincerely,

Gregory Gray, Deputy Delegate of Public Safety

Harold let out a long sigh and carefully folded the paper. The letter held far more significance than simply requiring a move. It was a key that had reopened a cursed box. A box they had buried years ago in the foundation of the house and that now, like the rotting boards of a sunken ship, had begun to float to the surface again.

Suddenly overcome by a wave of anger rising from deep inside, Harold ripped the letter to pieces. He stared at the bits of paper that fell to his feet like dead leaves. Suddenly, an explosion roared overhead. A strange yellow light shot through the cracks in the shutters as the floor shuddered under his feet. He had never felt anything like it, but he knew exactly what it was.

Lightning Bolt

Much later, when Harold could piece together what had happened, he would remember the fear that paralyzed him for a millisecond as the word *lightning* resounded in his head. Then the house went dark.

"Rosy!" he yelled as he stumbled down the stairs. "Rosy! Please, say something!" He was disoriented, and his voice sounded strange, muffled by the ringing in his ears.

He made it to the front hall but didn't see anything. Under his feet, he felt the crunch of broken glass and wood.

"Rosy!" he yelled again, feeling his way along the hall to the kitchen.

As he bumped into the table, he heard a voice coming to him as if from far away.

"Harold, I'm here!"

"Rosy?" he said, tripping on a chair. "Where are you?"

Then Harold was momentarily blinded by light.

"Oh, sorry!" Mary Rose cried.

Harold opened his eyes again, and before him materialized Mary Rose in silhouette, a flashlight in her hand.

"I couldn't find you! Where were you? Are you OK?" said Harold, going to his wife.

"In the dining room," she answered breathlessly. "And then I saw the burst of light through the window! Everything just lit up at once. I don't think I've ever felt the house shake like that. I thought it was going to come down on us!" After a pause, she added, "Did you call me Rosy?"

It had been years since he'd used that name. Harold cleared his throat awkwardly. "I'm going to check on the electricity," he mumbled.

He groped his way to the breaker box by the front door. Mary Rose pointed her flashlight, and Harold began to toggle the switches.

"Nothing," he said. "The lightning must have hit the lines outside. I should go out and check."

"I don't think that's wise, Harold."

"You can come with me. I won't go far."

They grabbed a couple of umbrellas and went out onto the porch. Immediately, they were assaulted by the roar of the storm. Harold took the flashlight from Mary Rose, and they struggled through the wind and rain to the utility pole. Even though the flashlight was feeble against the storm, Harold could tell that the wooden post and electric lines had not been damaged.

"It must have struck farther away," said Mary Rose, pointing. "Look, power is out in town too."

Harold peered into the darkness. Only the flashes in the sky revealed the area normally marked by the little lights of San Remo de Mar. But Harold knew the noise had been too loud for the lightning to have struck so far away. His searching eyes fell on lumber jutting up from the abandoned shipyard hidden beyond town. He saw it for a fraction of a second, in the blink of a lightning flash. Few in San Remo even knew the island had a shipyard other than the one next to the port. It was in a remote area surrounded by sharp rocks and practically impossible to access without a boat. A shipyard already abandoned when he was young and which he had used to build only one ship: theirs. Since then, he hadn't set foot on that part of the island and avoided even looking in that direction. Harold turned away and looked again at the house. Water cascaded from the roof. He couldn't make sense of the fact that, in just a few hours, the only thing they had managed to rebuild from their broken dreams would be gone forever.

"Everything all right?" asked Mary Rose.

Harold nodded and started again across the soaked yard, circling around the house and trying to focus his thoughts on the task at hand. A strong odor brought him to a halt.

"Do you smell that?" asked Harold.

"Yes, it smells like . . . something hot."

With the flashlight, he began to scour the darkness that shrouded the porch, concentrating on the area where the odor was strongest, but he didn't see anything out of the ordinary. They continued walking, following the circle of light three feet in front of them until it landed on something unusual. Something seemed to swallow the beam of the flashlight. Mary Rose grabbed his arm.

"Please, Harold, let's go in. There's nothing here . . ."

But her words fell off as the pair noticed a strange vapor rising from the dark place. Beside the house, where one of the steel cables was buried, a deep hole was emitting steam. Bits of dirt, rock, and scorched hydrangea were scattered around the newly formed crater. The guy wire remained firmly anchored in the rock, seemingly undisturbed. Harold passed the light along the cable that ran to the top of the house. There, where the post that anchored the six guy wires protruded above the roofline, rose a plume of smoke.

"It can't be," Harold said.

He rushed around through the wet hydrangeas to where one of the other braces was secured in the ground. As he shined the light, he found another crater slowly filling with the torrential rain that continued to fall.

"What is it, Harold? You're scaring me," said Mary Rose.

Harold looked up and was surprised to see his wife's wet clothing. He too was soaked to the skin.

"Let's get inside," he said.

Once they'd shut the door, the roar of the storm diminished.

"The lightning hit the house," he said, peeling off his wet shoes. "Luckily, the cables acted as grounding wires."

"That doesn't make me feel any safer," Mary Rose murmured, her teeth chattering. "Maybe Matthew's right—it's too dangerous to live here. Leaving is the best thing."

At those words, the flashlight slipped from Harold's wet hands. It hit the floor and went out, plunging them back into darkness.

"I'm going to go change," he said.

The sound of his footsteps on the stairs faded, and Mary Rose was alone. She bent down and felt around for the flashlight. She turned it on again and went up after Harold.

Mary Rose entered the bedroom, but Harold wasn't there. One of the shutters had blown open, and she could see the dark sea beyond the cliff roiling furiously. She went to the window and secured the shutter. She used to like storms—the fresh, damp smell; the cold rain; the sound of thunder. Now, it all made her nervous. She shined her light around the dark bedroom. It had never seemed so gloomy. Moving boxes stood sentry around the room, awaiting their final contents. Soon the room would be completely empty.

As she turned to leave, she thought of the old photo of the shipyard she had uncovered that morning. Again, she was flooded with memories of those days long ago, before her life had been taken prisoner by the unexpected events that turned her world—and all her hopes and dreams—upside down. Mary Rose searched through the clothing where she'd packed it, but it was gone. Harold must have found it.

The Dream That Never Set Sail

As she opened the attic door, Mary Rose was hit by a strong smell of burnt wood. She looked at the central support beam that ascended more than nine feet to the roof. Black marks had been burned into the grain of the wood and looked like veins. She felt truly scared. The fear seemed to emanate from a dark corner of her soul, a corner scorched like the post itself. It was a fear she hadn't felt for years. Mary Rose crossed the big room, the floor creaking beneath her feet, until she neared the round window that took up most of the wall. Harold's silhouette was outlined against the glass, illuminated only by the bolts of lightning zigzagging across the sky and cutting through the storm clouds and falling with thunderous force on the sea. Fishermen had dragged the smaller boats up onto the shore, but the larger ships at the port were buffeted dangerously.

Beneath the cliffs, the waves rose even more violently, amplified by the turbulent winds that lifted them up to crash against the rock walls blocking their path. Mere feet from the edge of the cliff overhanging that same raging sea, their house boldly faced the elements. There were no obstacles to block the gusts of wind raking across the barren grapevines and the hydrangeas closest to the edge, tearing them from the ground they struggled to hold on to. The rain fell in torrents over the polished surface of the slate roof, gushing from the girders onto the yard below.

Mary Rose stopped a few inches from Harold and spotted the photo in his hand.

"I'm sorry I said that," she said quietly. "You know I don't want to leave either."

Harold sighed mournfully. "I know, Rose." He paused, watching the choppy sea that seethed around the island. "Do you ever ask yourself what would have become of us if it didn't exist?" He crossed to the center of the attic. "What would have happened," he said, looking up at the scorched beam, "if this were still a mast? If this floor were still the deck? If the portholes in the basement had never been removed from the hull?"

Mary Rose felt as though she'd been struck. She perceived in Harold a pain and fragility she hadn't seen in him in years, a pain that came from a place as old as the house itself.

"Of course I've wondered," she said, the words catching in her throat. "But what choice did we have? We did what we had to."

"Yes. And now what will be left of what we fought for all these years? Of the only thing that kept us afloat?"

Harold returned to Mary Rose. The rain crescendoed, a deafening hail that drove at the glass.

"I'm not afraid to spend our last days confined to a windowless room, far from the sea. What scares me is losing the only thing we have left from that time. The only thing we have left of him."

Another bolt of lightning touched down, and the house shook violently. It seemed the storm wasn't outside, but right in that old attic with them. With a trembling hand, Harold touched her face and turned her to look at him. His eyes were red, with hardly a trace of deep blue. There was only pain.

"I'm afraid too, Harold," she said. "But as long as we're alive, as long as we're together, those memories won't die. We have to hold on to them."

Harold lowered his eyes to the picture of the three of them smiling in front of their unfinished ship.

"I really try, Rose. Every night when we go to bed, after turning out the light, I hear the storm. I relive every second, every detail, and every sound."

Thunder shook the house.

Harold paused and then continued. "But when I try to remember his face, when I try to see his smile and his shining eyes—each day they're a little blurrier. His voice and his laugh are swallowed by the roar of the rain. And that's when I feel truly scared, Rose. I'm scared of forgetting. Of losing the memory of when we were happy, dreaming. I'm scared of knowing that the only thing that keeps us close to him is this house. This house that, come tomorrow, will be gone forever."

Harold looked up from the photo and into the tear-filled eyes of his wife. They both wept silently then, not daring to breathe, barely conscious of the storm battering the house that had once been their ship.

"I'm sorry I wasn't able to give you the life we wanted," continued Harold. "To be able to live great adventures together or to fulfill our dream. You deserved to be happy."

Mary Rose put her arms around Harold. "We deserved to be happy," she whispered.

Two Storms

Mr. and Mrs. Grapes weren't hungry for supper, so they each took one of Mary Rose's sleeping pills and went to bed early. The wailing storm filled each empty room of the house, drowning out their deep breathing and the ticking of the grandfather clock.

Outside, the yard was turning white, as if covered in snow. Hail shot down like bullets, mutilating the grapevines and the beloved hydrangeas. The deep craters beneath the six guy wires became shallow wells.

The hail beat down everything in its path in town also. It broke windows, dented cars, and damaged fruit ripening on branches. Only the oldest residents of San Remo could remember a storm as strong as the one lashing the island that night. A storm that had come thirty-five years earlier, when the house on the cliff did not yet exist and a young Mr. and Mrs. Grapes lived in a tiny apartment in the center of town. Harold still worked at the shipyard and Mary Rose in a florist shop. Just like this one, that storm had begun with a beautiful day, when the scent of flowers drifted through the open door of the florist, filling the streets with an intoxicating aroma.

"You're late," said a young Mary Rose when she saw the little eight-year-old boy run into the shop. "Your father's waiting."

"Sorry, Mom," said Dylan as he approached the counter, his brown hair mussed.

Mary Rose smiled, left the bouquet she was arranging, and went around the counter. "Come give me a kiss."

Dylan made a face, but dutifully offered his cheek to his mother.

"Don't worry. I won't keep you," Mary Rose said. She pulled a bag off the shelf under the cash register. "This fish is for your dinner, got it? Tell your father you're to eat it, not use it for bait."

Dylan's deep-blue eyes widened, and he smiled sheepishly. He was surprised his mother knew they did that. He grabbed the bag and ran back toward the door.

"Aren't you forgetting something?" said Mary Rose.

Dylan turned and saw his mother holding a squat, empty mason jar. He grabbed the jar and, giving her one last kiss, ran out of the shop.

"See you tonight, Mom!" he yelled as he disappeared down the street.

The hands of the grandfather clock in the dining room moved to mark midnight, and the chimes began to sound. Eviction day had arrived. And just as the last chime went silent, the gears of chance triggered by the lightning strike began to turn.

A sharp snapping sound burst from the craters around the bases of the guy wires, and as if someone had pulled the plug in a bathtub, they began to drain swiftly. After an enormous gurgle, the holes were empty, revealing new, deeper breaches. There was another cracking sound, and thin fissures began to open out in every direction, fed by the torrential rain that continued to filter down through them. The earth creaked and groaned as the cracks snaked across the terrain, surrounding the house like a ring of fire.

Finally, they reached the edge of the cliff. There was a fleeting moment of stillness, and then a powerful quake shook the foundation of the house, reverberating across the island all the way to the shipyard by the port. The shipyard in which, on that stormy afternoon thirty-five years ago, Harold had impatiently waited for his son.

The clinking of lunch boxes against the glass jar in the sack alerted young Harold to his son's arrival as Dylan dodged through the stream of sweaty men exiting the shipyard. It was the end of the work day for the laborers, but for Harold, it was time to start his second shift, the one he and his son eagerly awaited all day. Dylan quickly made his way to the dock, where his father was waiting in a small rowboat loaded with boards and tools.

"Sorry I'm late, Dad!" Dylan exclaimed as he jumped in the boat.

"No problem," Harold said, and playfully ruffled his son's hair with his strong hands.

"Looks like we can fish tonight," said the boy, showing the sack to his father.

Harold burst out laughing and began to row. Slowly they left behind the enormous dry docks on which massive ships waited to be finished and headed out to sea. After fifteen minutes of rowing, they'd left the port of San Remo behind, hidden by a high rock wall. Ahead, on the shore of a small cove, appeared the old, forgotten shipyard. They secured the rowboat on one of the dock's rusty moorings, unloaded some of the boards, and entered the dilapidated building.

Every time he passed through those doors, Dylan's chest swelled with pride. He couldn't believe he was helping build a ship, a ship that would carry him and his parents away to fulfill their dream. He had been helping his father for almost two years, learning the ins and outs of the trade. Each one of the boards they fitted had his fingerprints on it. In those two years, he had never missed a day. Even when sick with a fever, he'd been unwilling to miss a moment of the construction. This ship would take them far from the island to live anywhere in the world they wanted. He couldn't wait to call it home.

"How long until we finish her, Dad?" Dylan inquired.

Harold buckled his tool belt. "There's still a lot of work to be done, son. But if we keep going at this rate, and the sails arrive on time, I'm thinking we can take her out by the end of the summer."

"That's only two months away!" he cried, jumping up and down.

Back up on the bluff at Mr. and Mrs. Grapes's house, the rain continued hammering the ground. The fissures expanded rapidly, completely separating the house from the rest of the lot.

The house shuddered again, and the only miniature ship Harold had not packed, the replica of his own sailboat, crashed to the ground, covering the mason jar with a web of tiny cracks.

The shaking ceased, and the house settled down. The windows stopped rattling, and the lamps stopped swaying. The thunder outside faded, and the hail eased back to rain. But a moment later, just as Harold rolled over in bed, a new cracking sound shattered the calm. The growing fissures had reached down into the very core of the cliff, causing the whole foundation to break free.

The six steel cables strained with tension as the house pitched on an angle. Inside, the remaining pictures on the walls hung at severe angles. Moving boxes slid across the floor. The floor, ceiling, and walls creaked like dry branches about to snap.

The wind blowing in from the sea intensified, and one of the cables tethering the house snapped. It was a hurricane-force wind, identical to the one thirty-five years ago that brought the first storm clouds to darken the old shipyard where young Harold and Dylan kept working, oblivious to it all.

Harold had spent a couple of hours installing the railings on the deck while Dylan was busy polishing the rounded timber of the topmast that stood proudly in the center of the deck.

As twilight descended on them, Dylan saw a pale-yellow light blink by the stern and smiled. Silently, he went to the bag his mother had given him that still held the untouched supper and retrieved the empty jar.

A raindrop fell on Harold's arm. Surprised, he looked up through the holes in the shipyard's ramshackle roof.

"I think that's enough for today, Dylan," he said, dropping his hammer on a pile of timber.

"We're going already? But it's still early!"

"A storm is coming, son, and I don't want to get caught in it here."

"It's four raindrops, Dad. And, besides, I haven't caught any fireflies," he complained, pointing the empty jar in his hands toward the stern.

Harold watched the yellow glow of the fireflies flitting among the timber. He sighed and anxiously looked back at the sky.

"One more hour, and we're leaving!"

The severed cable whipped the wooden siding, and the ground beneath the house slipped, detaching from the rest of the yard and sinking several feet. The other cables strained.

Some hundred feet below the house, the waves crashed against the cliff's porous rocks. Two more cables snapped.

Rocks slid away from the enormous fracture below the cliff and were swallowed by the waves that furiously licked at its base.

In one of the wind's sudden attacks, the fourth and fifth cables were like giant slingshots and launched their anchors into the air. The sofa streaked across the living room floor as the house tipped at an uncomfortable angle. For a moment, time seemed to stop. There was only the sound of the rain falling on the wood house, as it had fallen on the old timber of the shipyard where Harold and his son worked all afternoon, when the black clouds of that earlier storm had covered the whole island under a gloomy blanket as thunder rolled closer and closer.

"Put this on," said Harold, handing Dylan an old yellow raincoat many sizes too big.

"What about you, Dad?"

"Don't worry about me. I'm used to getting wet."

They ran to the dock, guided by the glow of Dylan's firefly jar, as the rain fell hard on them. The wind slammed their rowboat against the wooden gangplank over and over. Harold helped his son, practically swallowed by the giant raincoat, into the boat. Then he untied the line, pushed away from the dock, and began rowing.

As the boat moved away from the cove, the rain and darkness seemed to devour them. As he strained at the oars, Harold's breathing accelerated. He wished he were stronger; he wished he could get them to land faster. He rowed without resting, cutting through the black surf that crashed into the boat on one side and then the other. Harold knew their destination wasn't far, yet the cove of the shipyard kept getting smaller and the port of San Remo farther away.

Then he realized his mistake. The current swirling around the island was too strong. It was pulling them out to the open sea. Harold's whole body tensed, and he looked at his son anxiously. But Dylan didn't appear afraid. It wasn't his first time on a choppy sea. Besides, he always felt safe with his father. Harold, however, was beginning to panic. He let go of one of the oars and grabbed the boat's line, throwing it at his son's feet.

"Hold on as tight as you can!" Harold shouted above the roar of the storm.

Dylan smiled at him, his face lit by the soft glow of the firefly jar. Just then, a wave slammed against the hull. The little boat flipped over, and darkness swallowed the light. It was precisely that moment when the pot of hydrangeas slipped from Mary Rose's hands and crashed to the floor in the little apartment, the moment she knew something terrible had happened.

If anyone in San Remo unable to sleep because of the storm had looked out their window toward the cliff, they would have seen something truly unbelievable. A three-story house tilted at a thirty-degree angle toward the sea, suspended as if by magic.

Or one last steel cable.

Inside the house, heaps of boxes, chairs, and furniture piled up against the walls, leaning toward the precipice. The only piece of furniture that remained in place was the heavy bed in which Harold and Mary Rose slept, submerged in a deep sleep by the powerful pills.

Thunder rolled over the island, and the earth shook again, shattering the precarious equilibrium. The last cable began to vibrate wildly, and the wind uprooted the utility pole in the yard. Then one of the strands of the thick steel braid split. More strands followed, unraveling, unable to support the titanic weight of the house.

If that hypothetical resident had indeed looked out the window a few minutes prior, surely they would have called the police, who might somehow have arrived in time to pull Mr. and Mrs. Grapes from their bed. Then Harold's and Mary Rose's lives might have continued as planned and what followed would never have come to pass. But that didn't happen.

The last section of earth supporting the house broke away from the rest of the cliff. The cable groaned and finally snapped. The yellow house, along with a section of garden attached to the foundation, began to free-fall toward the white-capped sea. The impact was brutal. Everything was cloaked under the dark of night. A darkness as deep as the one felt by the young Mr. Grapes as the rowboat capsized and he plunged into the water.

It took Harold mere seconds to resurface. Coughing up salt water, he tried to shout, frantically looking all around, but all he could see was blackness. He managed to grab a piece of lumber that had fallen out of the boat, but he didn't see any sign of the boat itself. Or of his son.

"Dylan!" Harold screamed. "Dylan!"

Harold let go of the board that was keeping him afloat and began to swim. His body rose and fell with the waves that hit him and dragged him under in a frozen embrace. He cried his son's name again, but he was alone. He dove under, waving his arms and legs wildly, in hopes of brushing against his son. But there was nothing. Only darkness.

Harold could hardly breathe. The waves beat against his face, and little by little, salt water filled his lungs. Harold was drowning. He closed his eyes and let himself be swallowed by the sea, his only wish to be with his son.

As his head slipped under, a yellow glow appeared. In front of him, he saw the mason jar filled with fireflies sputtering to their watery death. Harold grabbed it and bobbed back to the surface. Then the light became stronger, blinding. It was a spotlight from a fishing boat. Strong arms hauled him up and laid him on the deck. Harold began shouting his son's name again, still clutching the glass jar with its fading glow. He clambered to his feet, sobbing and striking out at the men who held him back from jumping into the water.

The fishermen made every effort to find the boy, but their search proved fruitless. They never found his body.

That day, the light that had guided the lives of Mr. and Mrs. Grapes went out. Nothing made sense anymore. The pain threatened to drown them. They buried their memories in the foundation of the house they built from their broken dreams and the wood of a ship that never set sail. From the only thing left of him.

Dawn

A faint ray of sunshine filtered through one of the broken shutters in the living room. Hundreds of dust motes swirled in the light, sailing over fragments of glass, china, and splintered wood partially submerged in pools of water on the floor. Pieces of paper slipped around like eels hiding between boxes and broken furniture, while water continued to drip from above, tapping on the dark reflective surface. Sunlight fell on the thick bottom of a broken drinking glass, passing through it like the glass was a prism, its light spraying into a fan of colors.

A speck of dust passed through the rainbow, carried by a breath of air that inched it toward gloomy darkness. The air swirled, lifting the mote that gently brushed past twisted metal and drifted up the stairs as if with a life of its own.

Its weightless form continued rising until it touched the ceiling. It bounced and rested on a cold metal chain that hung from the ceiling without its lamp, which lay broken on the floor. A gentle sway rocked the chain, and the speck of dust glided to the floor. A draft seized it again and swept it through the crack under the bedroom door to the darkness on the other side. Then the air current went slack, and the speck descended until it rested on the tip of something fleshy.

Mrs. Grapes sneezed.

She opened her eyes. The room was dark. She felt dizzy and disoriented. As she sighed, she heard a loud noise that startled her. Mary Rose felt for the lamp on her night table but found only emptiness. A moment later, she heard the noise again. She was sure it was knocking on the front door.

"Harold, wake up," Mrs. Grapes whispered.

Another bang echoed up the stairs. Mary Rose shook Harold harder.

"What?" said Mr. Grapes, waking with a start.

"We must have overslept! The movers are downstairs, pounding on the door."

"What? But the alarm didn't go off!"

"We must not have heard it. Those pills completely knocked me out!"

Harold felt clumsy, so clumsy he couldn't find the lamp on his night table either.

"I'm sure I left a flashlight here," he said, feeling around in the dark.

He reached down and felt the floor next to the bed. He was surprised to find it covered with clothing. Still half-asleep, he continued to feel around the floor and finally touched something hard.

"Here it is!" said Harold, sitting up in bed.

There was more loud knocking on the door.

"Coming!" Mrs. Grapes called out. "Let's go! Turn on the light, and let's get down there. At this rate, they'll tear the house down before we're dressed!"

Harold pushed the plastic button, and a beam of battery-powered light revealed what had been hiding under the veil of darkness.

Mary Rose tried to speak, but her words stuck in her throat. The bedroom was in complete shambles. The night tables, drawers, remaining contents of the dresser, lamps, mirror, moving boxes . . . everything was scattered, piled up, and half-buried under clothing. Only their bed and heavy wardrobe against the wall were as they should be.

"I don't understand," whispered Mary Rose.

Then something else caught Harold's attention. "What's that buzzing?" he asked. Harold got out of bed. Navigating around the jumble of clothing and other objects scattered on the floor, he walked toward the intermittent buzz.

"Well," said Harold, bending down to retrieve something out of the pile of clothes, "we didn't miss it. The alarm clock says seven. We still have two hours until the movers arrive."

"Then who's banging on the front door like that?"

"Stay here. I'll go see what's going on."

"Oh no! I'm going with you!"

Outside, the hallway hid under the same darkness as the bedroom. The flashlight revealed a path of destruction. Pieces of glass and splintered frames marked where pictures had crashed down against the floor. As they moved toward the soft light filtering up the stairwell, the banging on the door became more insistent.

Before reaching the bottom of the stairs, Harold stopped. Something wasn't right. No one was knocking. The front door hung ajar, banging open and closed.

He couldn't explain it. Disarray greeted them, just like in their bedroom. The small wooden console table in the entryway lay in a corner with some upturned boxes, clothing, and glass. But as they came to the bottom of the stairs, they saw something even more disturbing. The floor in the entryway was covered with large puddles of water.

A new noise caught their attention.

"I think someone's in the kitchen," whispered Mary Rose.

Harold peered over the banister, searching the dark hallway, but he couldn't see anything. Using the flashlight to check it out seemed too risky. He could think of only one thing to do.

"On three, we run out the door, OK? One . . ."

"Are you crazy? What if they see us?"

"Two . . ."

They heard pots and pans crashing in the kitchen.

"Three!"

Harold grabbed Mary Rose by the arm, dropped the flashlight, and ran. Without looking back, they dashed through the doorway and raced across the porch. An instant before barreling down the three steps to the yard, Mr. and Mrs. Grapes came to an abrupt halt—just before they would have plunged into the ocean.

Now What?

Gripping the porch railing and hardly daring to breathe, Harold and Mary Rose looked at the ocean spread out before them. Their yard full of hydrangeas, the gravel driveway, the cliff, San Remo . . . it had all disappeared. In front of them was only water. Miles and miles of ocean that ran like watercolors into the early morning sky.

"What . . . what is happening?" stammered Mary Rose.

Harold stared at her, not knowing what to say. His face was white; his eyes were bulging and full of terror and disbelief. Nothing made sense. His brain rejected what he was seeing, but everything felt real. He felt the ocean breeze filling his lungs, the warmth of the rising sun on his cheeks, and the rocking of the porch under his feet.

"This can't be real, Harold," said Mary Rose, stepping back. She could scarcely breathe, her whole body fighting the scene unfolding before her. "I must be sleeping. Or maybe I've finally lost it completely."

"We're not dreaming, Rose. And I don't think we're crazy either."

"So how do you explain this?" she said, pointing to the horizon. "How did we get here?"

Harold turned his attention to the splashing water that surrounded the porch. There was a rocky border no more than a couple of feet wide interspersed with puddles of water and patches of green grass.

"The cliff," said Harold.

"What?"

"The cliff broke off. The cliff broke, and we fell with it, Rose."

"There has to be another explanation, Harold. We couldn't survive something like that."

Harold looked at the three steps that used to connect the porch to the front yard. He stepped onto the top stair and heard the wood creak under his weight.

"What are you doing?" cried Mary Rose.

Harold went down another step and looked again at the portion of the yard. He shuddered as he considered the unfathomable depths just a few steps away. Part of him said to go back, go back on the porch with Mary Rose. He wasn't sure what he was doing, wasn't sure if the piece of rock would support him, but even still, he stepped onto the ground.

"Harold, please! It's not safe! You'll fall in!" Mary Rose shouted hysterically.

Harold looked at her. "Don't be scared."

"I'm not!"

"Yes, you are."

"Fine. I'm scared. Why wouldn't I be?" she said, throwing her arms up and looking around.

"If we want answers, we have to look for them," he said, holding his hand out to her.

Mary Rose grabbed Harold's arm and closed her eyes for an instant as her foot touched the scrap of earth. She was sure the ground would give way under their weight at any second, and they would plunge into the water.

Harold took short steps up and down the muddy bank and slippery rock. Mary Rose followed, taking care not to slip. She couldn't stop eyeing the dark blue a few inches from their feet.

At the first corner of the house, Harold peered around and was surprised to see the rock ledge was wider on that side. Mary Rose relaxed a little, and Harold's arm was grateful.

41

Yellow painted wood and pieces of slate roof tile were scattered around the edge of remaining yard. Harold looked up and saw a spliced steel cable hanging from the roof, blowing in the breeze. The hair on the back of his neck stood on end as he considered the enormous force the cable must have been under to fray like an ordinary rope. They continued carefully, ducking under another cable dangling uselessly from the roof and trailing into the water. Just in front of the back porch, the band of earth narrowed again. Like on the other sides, in front of them was only water and more water. There was no sign of the island or any coastline. Only the ocean.

As they rounded the last corner, Harold stopped short. On this side, the ledge was broader. It was the only area that still hinted at the splendor of their garden, with four barren vines and three withering hydrangeas huddled there.

Mary Rose released Harold's arm and went to the hydrangeas. She removed bits of slate that were crushing the flowers but knew she couldn't do much when the plants' roots were now surrounded by salt water.

"How could the house survive a fall of that magnitude?" asked Mary Rose, standing up. "And even more important, how could we?"

Harold went to the edge of the strip of land and peered into the depths where the rock entered the water.

"There's a question that concerns me more," Harold said quietly.

"What?"

"Isn't it obvious?" he said, crouching down to touch the rock. "How is the house floating?"

Just then, the water in front of them bubbled and foamed. The house rumbled, and Harold, still close to the water, lost his balance. He managed to grab onto a protruding rock just before falling in. The rock cut into his left hand, and sharp pain shot down his spine. Blood gushed from the cut, ran down the rock, and dripped, red, into the water.

Mary Rose leaped forward and pulled him back from the edge.

"You're hurt!" she cried.

"It's just a scrape."

"It's not just a scrape, Harold!" said Mary Rose, taking his arm to better examine the wound.

Harold felt his heart beating in the deep, raw gash in the palm of his hand. The blood ran down his wrist and onto Mary Rose's pajamas.

"Put pressure on it. We need to get inside and take care of you."

They returned to the front porch. Just as they started up the steps, the house shook again. More bubbles and foam swirled around the strip of land and looked like boiling water.

Harold had a bad feeling. "We've got to get to the basement!"

"First we have to stop the bleeding."

"There's no time for that, Rose!"

Harold threw open the door. With his uninjured hand, he grabbed the flashlight off the floor and made his way around the boxes, furniture, glass, and pools of water to the half-open door to the basement. Mary Rose took the flashlight from him and turned it on. Harold pushed open the door, and they started down.

The faint light coming from the open front door illuminated the first few steps. They were wet and slippery, and the smell of salt wafted up, as strong as if they were still standing in front of the ocean. As they approached the bottom of the stairs, they stopped. They shivered from the cold water covering their ankles. Beyond that point, the basement was completely flooded.

"Are we sinking?" asked Mary Rose.

"I think so."

Sinking

Books, appliances, scraps of wood, moving boxes . . . the hundreds of objects stored in the basement were now floating on the dark, greenish water that flooded the room.

"We have to find where the water is getting in," said Harold.

He took the flashlight from his wife's shaking hand and began searching the shadowy water for movement that could lead them to where the water was entering.

"There's too much floating around to see. We have to clear the surface."

Harold descended a few more steps into the water. A stab of pain shot through his palm when it contacted the salt water. He gasped, then clenched his teeth; there was no time to lose. He began grabbing whatever was closest. Boards, empty paint cans, sodden cardboard boxes, papers stained with runny ink . . . Harold pulled everything out and handed it to Mary Rose, who quickly ran them upstairs to the entryway.

As the area around the stairs cleared, Harold could go down the remaining steps to the basement floor. As the cold water hit his waist, it took his breath away. He paused before continuing through the cluttered lake of sunken objects that was their basement.

Finally, the water's surface was sufficiently cleared. Harold started back to the stairwell with the last object, a leather gardening glove.

But before he started up the stairs, another tremor shook the house. The water began circling around Harold as large air bubbles gurgled throughout the basement.

"Give me your hand, Harold!" Mary Rose said as she stepped in the water toward him.

The glove slipped from Harold's hand and was carried away in the bubbles and foam.

Harold and Mary Rose grabbed the wet banister and climbed up the steps that would get them out of the rising water. Finally, the vibrations and bubbles stopped, and with them, the rising water.

Mary Rose couldn't stop shivering, whether it was from her wet clothes or terror at the house sinking. Harold barely noticed the cold; he looked at his hand and saw it was still bleeding. With his other hand, he pressed on the wound and took deep breaths to focus on the immediate need: to stop the leak.

"We have to stop it before it's too late," said Harold, advancing down the steps again.

But then he was still. Harold grabbed the flashlight and shined it on the glove that now floated in the middle of the basement. The water was calm again; only a light ripple broke the smooth surface, a movement that pushed the glove forward by an invisible force.

"Look!" said Harold, pointing to the object floating toward them.

"What am I supposed to see?" asked Mary Rose, her eyes on the glove.

"There's a current pushing it this direction. That means the leak is on the far side." Harold shifted the light to follow the trajectory and added, "Just behind the washing machine."

They half waded, half paddled toward the washer and dryer. Harold went to one side of the stacked appliances, Mary Rose the other.

"We pull on three, OK?" said Harold.

Mary Rose nodded as she braced her freezing hands underwater against the back of the washer.

"One . . . two . . . three!"

They pulled as hard as they could, but it barely moved.

"Again!" said Harold.

They pulled again, and this time the tower inched away from the wall. Mary Rose's little-used muscles were burning; she no longer felt the cold water.

"More!"

Harold braced a foot against the wall and with the final tug, the appliance finally moved far enough to get behind. Without taking time to catch his breath, Harold squeezed into the space and bent down to feel the wall, keeping his head above the water. But no matter how much he searched, he couldn't find anything.

As she held the flashlight, Mary Rose couldn't help but notice that the splashing water was rising again, slowly but steadily.

"I'm going under," Harold said. He took a deep breath and disappeared.

Mary Rose moved closer, but the flashlight only penetrated the first inch or two under the surface.

Small air bubbles broke on the surface while Mary Rose anxiously watched Harold's blurry silhouette in the murky water.

Unable to see, Harold touched the debris-covered floor and began investigating the area around the wall. A current of cold water passed across his face. He stretched out his fingers and found an opening above the baseboard. A round hole, more than four fingers wide. When he touched it, bits of rubble broke off the rock wall and were pushed toward the surface.

Harold's lungs began to burn, so he came up for air.

"Did you find anything?" asked Mary Rose.

"I think so," he said, gasping. "There's a hole just above the baseboard. It's not very big, but I think it's getting bigger."

Mary Rose felt dizzy. "Harold, I don't want to rush you, but the water keeps climbing."

"We have to find a way to plug the hole."

The first thing they did was remove the boards serving as shutters over the portholes. Light filled the basement, and finally they saw the full extent of the destruction.

Without wasting any time, they began to search for Harold's toolbox. Mary Rose found it upside down under the workbench. Harold grabbed a handful of nails, stuck them in his pocket, and handed the hammer to Mary Rose. He gathered the boards they had taken down and went to the wall.

"Give me the hammer when I'm ready, OK?"

Mary Rose had no time to answer before Harold was underwater.

Harold felt around for the hole again. More bits of rock floated around his face. He placed a board over the hole, reached in his pocket, and took out a nail. Then he felt Mary Rose holding out the hammer. He grabbed it and began pounding the nail.

Harold had hammered thousands of boards in his life, but never underwater. The hammer moved clumsily, lacking any force. Each strike echoed in his head, and his lungs were crying for air. He had to come up. The board slipped off.

"How can I help?" asked Mary Rose.

"Try holding the board against the wall with your foot."

He went under again. This time he found the hole right away. Mary Rose's foot appeared next to him and pushed on the board he had just centered. He fished out another nail and began to hammer.

He felt the steel tip penetrate the wood. Then more resistance: he had hit the wall. He surfaced for a breath, then submerged again. He hammered as vigorously as he could; it was nearly secured when, from around the edges of the board, bubbles burst through like steam from a pressure cooker. The board was forcefully expelled and scraped against Harold's face with one of its sharp edges. He rose again to the surface.

"I tried holding it as tight as I could, Harold! But I couldn't," said Mary Rose.

Under their feet, the foundation rumbled. Water gushed in faster, striking them mercilessly with a whirlpool of debris. Then a small stream of water began falling on them. They looked up and saw water outside, halfway up the portholes.

"We're running out of time!" shouted Harold.

He dove in again, disappearing from sight.

Harold placed the board, but with the hammer in his other hand, he couldn't hold it in position. Hundreds of little rocks brushed his face while the incessant bubbling filled his ears. Suddenly, he felt movement next to him, and a moment later something held the board in place. Mary Rose was underwater with him, pushing the board against the wall with all her strength.

Harold felt for a nail in his pocket. He couldn't find one. Desperate, he felt the floor. He didn't even notice a piece of glass digging into his injured hand.

Mary Rose braced herself to keep pressure on the board, but she needed to breathe soon.

Harold was about to give up when he felt the misplaced nails. He grabbed them and positioned one on the board, pounding frantically. The thud of the blows underwater mixed with the bubbles thundering in his ears. More little rocks crumbled.

Harold managed to drive the nail home. He dropped the hammer and touched Mary Rose, telling her to surface.

They didn't emerge immediately. When they finally reached the air, they were frighteningly close to the ceiling.

They didn't need to say anything. Before diving again, Harold and Mary Rose looked at each other, knowing it might be the last time.

They took a deep breath and returned to the board. The bubbles and rocks continued to filter in along the unsecured edge. Mary Rose pushed again, and Harold hammered the four critical nails one by one.

With great effort, the nails were driven into the wall, and the bubbles stopped.

They reemerged and smiled at each other in relief, then swam toward the stairway, listening to the rafters creaking as if they were in pain. They made it to the top of the stairs and caught their breath on the few dry steps that remained.

The Other Voice

Harold and Mary Rose had been bailing out the basement for hours. It felt like trying to empty the ocean with a thimble. They didn't even speak until the water level started to decline, bit by bit, step by step. As the water decreased, so did the light; midday gave way to afternoon and then to night, and almost without their noticing, the darkness of the ocean enveloped them in its silence.

"I don't think there's any more we can do tonight," Harold said, out of breath.

With a bucket under her arm, Mary Rose stared at the remaining black water. Water still came halfway up the basement walls, but her distress had diminished some. She figured if they had stayed afloat with water almost up to the rafters, they were sure to stay afloat now.

Mary Rose looked at Harold, and they silently ascended the stairs. Every step, every movement of exhausted arms, legs, and back, was a reminder of the infinite trips they had made hauling water. Mary Rose barely had the strength to hold on to the bucket she was carrying. She had never felt such pain in her lower back. Harold's body ached too, but it was nothing compared to the pain in his hand. A burning pain throbbed in the whitish cut where the salt had crystalized around the blood.

In the entryway, they stopped, not knowing where to go or what to do. Nothing was intact or where it belonged.

With wet feet and guided by the flashlight, they moved on, hoping to find a place to rest. In the living room, they discovered a pile of broken chairs, cardboard boxes, books, and curtains torn by broken glass. Neither of them had enough energy to flip the damaged sofa back over.

The sight of the dining room was no more encouraging. The china cabinet was shattered. Chairs lay in a heap under the splinters and glass, not a single one with four legs intact. Silently, Harold and Mary Rose dragged themselves to the kitchen.

Amid the broken dishes, water, and piles of furniture and appliances, Mary Rose found a stepstool. She dropped the bucket and sank down onto it. Harold also put down his bucket and continued searching with the flashlight. He rummaged anxiously through the debris, looking for the water pitcher. He found it and, noting the water level, wished it were fuller. He took it to Mary Rose and noticed the old battery-operated console radio lying on its side next to her. Harold brushed off the rubble, sat on the radio, and set the flashlight on the floor. The shaft of light shone on the ceiling and dimly lit the room. Other than their measured breathing, the only sound was the clinking of some pans and the creaking of wood as the house rocked gently on the waves.

"Here," said Harold, offering the pitcher to his wife.

Exhausted, Mary Rose drank her share, then returned it to Harold, who finished the rest. "As soon as it's light tomorrow, I'll go back to the basement and refill it," said Harold.

Mary Rose nodded, unable to speak. Harold sighed, suddenly aware of the toll the destruction had taken on them. Mary Rose's hair had escaped the elastic band that held it back, and her pajamas were soaked and stained with his blood.

As Harold put down the empty pitcher, something caught his attention. Something was floating in the little bit of water left inside one of the buckets. Harold placed the pail on his knees, and despite his weariness, felt his heart begin to pound wildly.

"Impossible," he said.

"What is it?" asked Mary Rose, concerned.

"I think I know why we didn't sink," he answered.

Mary Rose looked at Harold and then into the bucket. All she saw was a bit of water and some little rocks that had come loose from the hole in the wall.

"I just see rocks and water, Harold."

"Yes," he said, staring at her. "Do you know how Brent Island was formed?"

Mary Rose didn't know how to answer her husband's cryptic question. She felt overwhelmed by fatigue. "What does that have to do with the house floating?" she said, somewhat irritably.

"Everything, I think." He paused, then continued. "Brent Island is volcanic in origin. The hill in the middle of the island is a dormant volcano. Our cliff is the result of layers and layers of sedimentary lava rock."

"Yes, I know. That's why San Remo's land is so fertile."

"But more than fertile," he said, fishing out the little rocks. "The volcanic rock is full of petrified air pockets, and that gives it a particular characteristic."

Then he tipped the bucket so all the water was on one side and tossed the rocks back in.

"They float!" she exclaimed.

"Exactly!"

"You think that the rock around the basement is supporting the house? It's why we're floating like a cork instead of sinking?"

Harold nodded, smiling.

"But the weight . . ." Mary Rose began.

"The extraordinary heatwave," a voice interrupted.

"What did you say?" asked Mary Rose.

Harold jumped up, knocking the bucket off his lap. He got down next to the radio he'd been sitting on and placed his ear next to the speaker. His heart skipped a beat when he clearly heard the crackling buzz.

"I thought it was broken," he whispered.

"Me too," Mary Rose stated.

There was a nervous fluttering in their stomachs as Harold turned the dial back and forth, trying to capture a signal.

"Following the storm, authorities in the area have affirmed... tfff... shsh...tfff..." The voice went quiet.

"Turn it again, Harold!" exclaimed Mary Rose as she bent down next to him, listening attentively to any change in the monotonous murmur.

"Shsh... two people are missing... tfff..."

"There, there!" Mary Rose shouted.

"Shsh... hopes of finding... tfff... are rather... shsh... tfff..."

Harold moved the dial again to recapture the signal but couldn't. Every part of the dial gave off the same meaningless buzz.

"I think they were talking about us," Harold said. "About a search for us!"

"Does that mean we'll get back to San Remo?" she exclaimed.

Harold smiled, and a second later, they caught something. This time it wasn't a voice, but music. At first it was faint, but little by little, as if coming closer, the signal got stronger until the sound of violins filled the kitchen.

"The Blue Danube," Harold said softly.

Mesmerized by the music, they looked at the radio as if it were a miracle, as if that day had never happened and they were still firmly attached to their safe and peaceful island. Finally, the song ended, and a woman's soft voice began to speak. The voice was clear, but this time they didn't understand.

"What language is that?" Mary Rose asked, surprised.

Harold listened to the words carefully, but nothing was familiar. His tired brain buzzed with new questions as the soft chords of the next song began to play.

"We can't be so far away, can we?" murmured Mary Rose.

Harold's smile had faded, turning into a look of disbelief and fear. "By this time, a ship could have gotten a good distance from the coast," mused Harold. "But this, well, we don't have a motor or sails or anything."

"What if we're so far away they've stopped searching for us?"

"They wouldn't have. The mayor must have initiated a rescue plan. It's just a question of time until a ship spots us."

"But, Harold," whispered Mary Rose, "do you think anyone will imagine we're still alive after falling from the cliff? Even if they did, who in their right mind would think to look for us floating aboard our own house?"

At that moment, static crackled from the old transistor, and the music went out. Harold desperately spun the dial; he pushed the buttons and even banged on it, trying to reestablish the signal but without any luck. The radio was mute and useless. Not even the gentle clanking of pots or creaking of wood, not even the soft sound of the ocean outside the windows, was enough to fill the emptiness that echoed off the walls of the house. It was a noise Mr. and Mrs. Grapes knew well and had lived with for years, softer with the passing of time but always present. A sound that echoed in their ears and through their bodies louder than any music or voice. The sound of loneliness.

"No one," whispered Harold.

Adrift

Despite their exhaustion, Mr. and Mrs. Grapes moved in and out of a strange dream in which they traveled aboard a house that could float, all alone and drifting aimlessly on the ocean. But every creak in the wood, sudden rocking motion, or rattle of the windows was enough to pull them from the fragile dreamland through which they wandered. When they opened their eyes in the dark room, they were caught in anguished doubt, unsure of what was real. Then their sore muscles, thirst, hunger, and a haunting melody in their heads affirmed the terrible truth that the dream was, indeed, reality.

When the first light of day tinged the bedroom red, they gave up the pretense of sleeping.

"I'll go get water," Harold said as he struggled to sit up.

When Mary Rose sat up, she saw dried blood on the sheet where her husband had been.

"Harold! Your hand!"

Harold had forgotten the injury; his whole body was so swollen with pain he could hardly distinguish the stabbing pain in his palm from everything else. Mary Rose slipped toward his side of the bed and gently took his hand.

"I don't like the color of your skin around the wound," she said, examining it.

"It's nothing. It'll heal."

"You don't have to act brave, Harold," she said, getting out of bed. "I'm going to see if I can find where I packed the first aid kit."

Mary Rose went into the bathroom, leaving Harold with a chance to escape.

He headed to the basement with the water pitcher and waded through the frigid water that remained. He turned the spigot on the front of the tank, and a stream of clean water began to flow into the container. But it had barely begun to fill when the tube began to gurgle, spitting out water in fits and starts. Alarmed, Harold looked in the cistern and saw it was almost empty. After a few seconds, the stream became a trickle, and then a final drop of drinkable water came out. That was it. The cistern was completely dry. Slowly, Harold closed the spigot and looked at the half-empty pitcher. Resigned, he returned upstairs.

Not finding the first aid kit in any of the boxes in the bathroom or bedroom, Mary Rose had gone down to the kitchen. The only items still in place were the cabinets and countertops. Everything else was lying on the floor in a mess of broken glassware and dishes, smashed jars of food, silverware, furniture, potting soil, and ocean water. The stool and radio were where they'd left them in the middle of the room the night before. She looked for the kit amid the rubble and half-open boxes but didn't find it.

Mary Rose went to the refrigerator, which was lying on its back atop withered hydrangea blooms, and opened the door. A foul odor assaulted her nostrils. Leftover fish soup had mixed with condiments and broken eggs, coating the inside of the appliance with an unappealing concoction seasoned with slivers of glass and other broken bits.

Mary Rose found a cracked but intact bowl amid the rubble and in it began to gather what little food she could salvage: a plastic jar of jelly, a couple cans of tomatoes, and an unopened package of preserved ham.

Harold returned with the water and stood beside her.

"Is that it?" he asked, noting the meager provisions.

Mary Rose checked the freezer drawer, hoping to find something else, but the half-thawed vegetables and mushy fish formed an inedible, revolting brown heap.

"That's it," she answered finally.

She grabbed a plastic trash bag at her feet, filled it with all the waste, and closed it tightly.

"There's more in the pantry, right?" her husband asked hopefully.

"Not much, Harold. Yesterday was supposed to be our last day." Then Mary Rose saw the pitcher. "Why didn't you fill it?"

"It's all there was."

"But the cistern was full!"

"I thought so too, but I guess some of the floodwater came from the cistern."

Mary Rose felt woozy. The nauseating smell of the food was overwhelming. Harold helped her out of the kitchen. On the porch, the clean air of the open sea washed away the stench from their nostrils.

Mary Rose still had the trash bag in her hand. Cautiously, she descended the porch steps and approached the edge of the narrow, rocky ledge. When she looked at the pink-tinged surface of the early morning water, she thought she saw something moving below, but it was too deep and dark to know for sure.

She opened the bag and, despite the stench, still felt hungry. Mary Rose felt awful throwing out the little food they had, even knowing it was inedible. She couldn't believe that after years of carefully stocking the pantry and storing water in the cistern, they now found themselves in this predicament. After looking at the contents of the bag one last time, she carefully emptied it into the water.

The gloppy mess quietly slid into the impervious darkness of the ocean and dispersed like the mist. As she shook out the last piece of fish, brown liquid dripped off the plastic bag and onto the tips of her shoes.

"What are we going to do, Harold?" asked Mary Rose, watching the rotten mess spread over the undulating water.

Harold joined her and looked toward the distant horizon that slowly was losing the reddish hues of dawn. "It's just a matter of time until a ship passes and sees us."

Mary Rose studied his face for a hint of confidence, but not even his voice matched his words. She took a deep breath. "Time?" Mary Rose repeated shakily. "We barely have water and food for a couple of days!"

Harold sighed. "At least we've got the ocean," he said.

"Are you suggesting we fish?" Mary Rose stared at him.

"What else can we do?"

"No offense, but you've never been much of a fisherman."

"Would you rather we die of hunger?" he retorted.

Indignantly, Mary Rose retreated to the porch and sat on the top step. She caught another whiff of the spoiled food and realized it was coming from her shoes.

"We have to try, Rose," said Harold, sitting down next to her.

"But even if we can catch something," said Mary Rose, "what about water? That's even more critical than food!"

Harold looked for some clouds that might bring rainwater but saw only clear blue sky. He looked to the spot where Mary Rose had dumped the spoiled food—all but a few small pieces of rotten fish had sunk. An entire ocean of water surrounded them, but not even a sip would help them survive. Years ago, in San Remo, he had built a system to have a reliable water supply. Now he felt the same helplessness he had before he solved that problem during those first besieged winters when frozen pipes couldn't carry water from town, when power lines downed by snow left them without electricity. It was like he was back there again, seated in the dark basement, a candle for light and blankets to keep him warm, searching for solutions.

He still remembered the moment it had occurred to him to install a water purifier for the cistern, the elation he felt plugging in the motor that pumped seawater to the house, and the sound of the first drops falling into the large plastic tank. Then the pleasure of drinking from their own supply as pure and clean as spring water. Since then, the desalinator had provided water even in the cruel winter months when the downspouts froze over and it was impossible to collect rainwater.

"If we want to survive, we have only one option," he said finally.

Mary Rose looked at him curiously, trying to read his pensive look.

"We need electricity."

Mary Rose was not ready for that answer. "And how do you propose we get that?" she asked, trying to remain calm.

"I don't know, but we have to find a way."

"That's crazy!"

As she shouted those words, she felt suffocated by the monstrous expanse of the ocean and trapped in a place with no escape. Wordlessly, she went into the house. Harold followed. A moment after the door closed behind them, something moved near the rocky ledge. A sudden splash and the last of the floating fish disappeared, swallowed by a mouth that rose from the hidden depths.

The Secret in the Water

It took Harold and Mary Rose one more day to bail all the water from the basement. During that time, they only stole away from the soggy mess in brief intervals, hoping to see a ship on the horizon. The thought of not being rescued was increasingly present as their meager supply of water and food diminished. Four cans of sausage, another four of tuna, three of fruit in heavy syrup, a couple bottles of grape liqueur, and a large container of nuts were all they'd been able to add to their stock of provisions. And as the basement was being emptied, so was the pitcher of water. With their sips rationed, Harold and Mary Rose were never able to quench their ever-present thirst.

On the second day, when the water level was less than a finger deep, Harold finally stopped the seepage of water by fully sealing the board holding back the ocean. After much searching, Mary Rose had located a can of resin. Now, the strong vapors emanating from the can filled the basement. Mary Rose stood on a wooden box and glanced outside as she opened one of the portholes for ventilation. There was nothing but an endless, barren landscape of water.

She got down from the box and returned to mopping up the remaining water. As she mopped, she attempted to bring some order back to the chaos, picking up books, tools, whatever she found. She stacked the sodden books along the staircase in an oozing, wet pile of black ink. The water-logged electronics and appliances that Harold had fixed over the years were piled next to the pantry. Then something caught her eye among the bolts and screws. Under a messy stack of wet papers was a fat, cracked jar. She bent down to pick it up and immediately recognized the small replica of the sailboat inside. Water dripped from her trembling hands like tears. Mary Rose felt a stab of pain as she held the fragile jar that was ready to shatter into a hundred pieces.

"I think I can fix it," Harold said behind her.

Mary Rose started. "I'm not sure it makes much sense to fix it now," she said, her face clouded with the weight of those memories.

Harold knew Mary Rose was right. He looked around and saw a piece of wet Bubble Wrap. He picked it up and gently wrapped the jar. Very carefully, they placed it in a damp, ripped box with the rest of the bottled ships.

Harold went back to the space behind the washer and dryer. "I'm done sealing up the hole in the wall," he said, trying to distract himself from the painful memories. "Once the resin dries, it will be nearly impossible for water to get in."

Deep in thought, Mary Rose only nodded.

"The cistern was cracked, which is why we lost all the water," he continued. "I fixed that too."

"And what good will that do if we can't fill it?" she said, returning to reality.

Harold winced, not from Mary Rose's sharp response, but because she was right. During the long hours he had been bailing water, he hadn't stopped thinking about how he might generate electricity. He knew it was crazy, given their situation. Yet every time he looked at the vast ocean, he knew their chances of survival were decreasing. If they had power, they could get the desalinator working, and that would give them as much drinking water as the ocean could provide. With electricity, they could cook whatever fish they caught and keep food fresh—assuming the refrigerator would still run. But he hadn't come up with a solution.

He had tried to generate their own electricity dozens of times over the years in San Remo. It had worked to a degree, but he had never gotten enough stable power to run the whole house.

"I didn't mean to be so short with you, Harold," Mary Rose said. "But this is all so hard. I'm tired of not knowing where we are or where the currents will take us."

Harold's head shot up, his eyes full of inspiration. "Of course! How did I not think of it before?" he exclaimed.

"What?"

Harold rushed to the pile of books Mary Rose had gathered and began looking through them. Mary Rose stood nearby as he rummaged through the books until he found what he was looking for.

"Rose, you're a genius!" said Harold. "I think you figured out a way for us to survive."

Mary Rose looked at the book curiously, trying to see the title.

"Come with me," he said.

Mary Rose followed him upstairs and out the front door. Harold, without speaking, carefully turned the soggy pages of the book.

"Here it is!" he said. Harold showed the book to his wife.

"Multiple Energy Forms," she read. *"How to Harness the Ocean.* What is this, Harold?"

"I think it's how we're going to generate electricity, Rose!"

Mary Rose looked again at the book but couldn't understand any of the blurred mathematical formulas or recognize any of the machinery in the bleeding black-and-white photos. Instead of being excited by the possibility of solving their problems, she was filled with the loneliness she always felt when Harold began one of his crazy inventions. It seemed to her that his constant tinkering and big ideas only served to keep them apart. She remembered the interminable snowbound winters spent in the kitchen, her own thoughts her only company. The long, lonely wait for Harold to finally emerge from the basement to eat or sleep. If he did talk to her, it was only about things like drain spouts for the water storage system or the number of cables needed to stabilize the house. At least those projects were successful. For the rest, Mary Rose only remembered the bitter taste of unhealthy obsession and frustration.

"I know we have a problem," said Mary Rose, still looking at the pages. "Well, a lot of problems, and some of them could be fixed with the flick of a switch. But, Harold, do you really think you can do something like this? It didn't work before."

"This is different, Rose. What I needed was access to the ocean currents. This book is about the stability of ocean energy. It's better than solar or wind power."

"That all sounds good, but how? Your workshop is in ruins!"

"I'll figure it out," said Harold, setting the book down in the sun, where it could dry.

Mary Rose wanted to beg him not to waste his energy on this wild new fancy, but a noise in the water interrupted her.

"What was that?" Mary Rose pointed to where water had splashed onto the porch.

"A piece of rock probably fell off," answered Harold.

Suddenly the water stirred, and from the foam appeared a dark, angular fin.

"Shark!" yelled Mary Rose.

The Man Who Could Fix Anything

Harold was restless. He'd been tossing and turning in bed for hours, obsessing over the thought of using ocean currents to build a generator that could keep them alive long enough to be rescued. His mind was a jumble of ideas that he couldn't untangle. He had to make it work this time.

He was sweating, and his mouth was dry. He wanted water but couldn't have even a sip until morning. Carefully, so as not to wake his wife, he got up and shined the flashlight toward the stairs. Down in the basement, he placed the flashlight on the floor, climbed on a beat-up wooden box, and looked through the porthole at the night sky. He could barely make out any stars. The ocean likewise was void of the unmistakable glimmer of a ship or the intermittent flash of a distant lighthouse. The loneliness he felt was matched only by the torture of thirst and hunger. But stronger than any other feeling was his will to survive.

Harold stepped down from the box, the ocean gently rocking the floor beneath him. The room was illuminated by the yellow glow of the flashlight, and he began to go over in his head everything he had read about generators and energy derived from ocean currents.

His thoughts were interrupted when the flashlight hit the floor, knocked over by the rocking of the waves. As Harold reached down to set it upright, he glanced over to where the light was shining. Seeing the clothes dryer illuminated by the beam gave him an idea.

Harold rushed up to the first floor; gathered all the candles he could; grabbed the book, *Multiple Energy Forms: How to Harness the Ocean*; and dashed back down to the basement. He arranged the candles around him on the floor and got his toolbox. A sharp stab of pain shot through his hand as he picked up the toolbox. He had forgotten about the injury again, but now saw the scab had torn. It was bleeding but not enough to slow him down. He felt a burst of confidence, convinced he finally had something he could work with. He grabbed a screwdriver and began to remove the back of the dryer while ignoring mental images of Mary Rose shaking her head.

An hour later, Harold had the machine in pieces. Controls, connectors, circuits, resistors, cables, a transformer, a motor, a belt, and a drum comprised the collection of electrical entrails. He carefully extracted some sketches of electric circuits he had drawn up years ago from the book. They hadn't worked for what he needed then, but he knew it had been a matter of resources, not a lack of understanding. There just wasn't enough sunshine on the island for his solar panels to provide reliable energy. His problem with wind energy was the opposite; the gusts on the cliff were too strong for the windmills he made to last more than a week without being knocked down. But this time, conditions were perfect.

He finally found the sheet of graph paper he was looking for. Despite the smeared ink on the damp pages, Harold was able to make out the sketches. He studied each one, taking inventory to be sure he had everything he needed to build a generator. He had to get it right; their lives depended on it. He took a cable connected to the transformer and began to attach the wires to the motor that turned the dryer drum. Electrical work was nothing new for Mr. Grapes. After leaving his job at the shipyard, he had made a career out of fixing, building, and selling household appliances, motors, and small electronics of all types. But tonight, despite repeating motions he had made hundreds of times, in addition to dealing with the pain in his hand, he felt as clumsy and sweaty as a new apprentice. His fingers trembled slightly, and his breathing accelerated. He paused, staring at the tangle of parts in front of him, at a loss. It was like reliving some of his first days working in San Remo de Mar's repair shop.

He felt like he was seated again in the workshop in the back of the dark and dusty store that was full of disemboweled gadgets. He recalled nodding mechanically as his new boss explained something that he just couldn't grasp, no matter how hard he tried. Far from the shipyard, boats, and the sea, he had never felt more out of place. He was away from everything he loved and everything he knew how to do. But it was precisely in the work of repairing domestic objects that Harold found solace for his pain. Little by little, his calloused hands forgot the rough feel of wood and chisel as he grew accustomed to the cold screwdriver and circuit boards.

Over the years, his time as a shipbuilder had faded from the collective memory of the town. He became the town handyman, the man who could fix anything. But Harold never liked that moniker. He knew that no matter how many appliances he repaired, there would always be things that couldn't be fixed. Returning to the present, he looked at the cable in his hands. Even though he still felt the throbbing pain, his hands had stopped shaking. His breathing had relaxed, and the jumble in front of him now made sense.

He glanced at the drawing and, without any more hesitation, attached the cable to the motor.

A small clock recovered from the rubble chimed four o'clock in the morning as Harold gave the final turn of the screwdriver, but he didn't notice. He opened one of the small portholes and slid the cable attached to the transformer through it. On the other side, he would attach the generator.

Harold wasn't completely sure if the invention would work. He had made the generator out of the dryer's drum, which was lined with metal blades screwed in around the perimeter. If everything worked as planned, the drum would rotate with the movement of the currents in the same way a waterfall drives a turbine. When the blades rotated, the motor connected to the drum would convert the motion into electricity, which would pass through the transformer he had just installed next to the porthole. The transformer would distribute energy throughout the house.

In theory. It was time to put his generator to the test.

He looked out through the opening, but under the dark of night, the ocean was invisible. He partially closed the porthole, got off the box, and went to the middle of the basement, where he'd left the generator.

Picking up the heavy contraption produced a new wave of pain in his hand, but he remained resolute. Step by step, he carried the enormous load up to the living room. He went back down for his toolbox, a rope, and a couple of candles he had left on the floor. He opened a living room window and shivered as the freezing night air poured into the room. The house rocked, knocking a leftover knickknack off a sagging shelf in the dining room and snuffing out one of his candles. The waves had kicked up, but they weren't strong enough to prevent Harold from going out and installing his generator. He needed to be quick and get it done before the weather got any worse.

Harold tied one end of the rope to the generator and the other to the upturned sofa. After double-checking the rope, he picked up the generator and slowly lowered it out the window. Toolbox in hand, he carefully climbed through the same opening to the rock ledge.

The first thing was to place the generator at the water's edge; then he only had to attach the mounting bracket to something sturdy and finally connect the wiring he had fed through the basement porthole. What made it difficult was the strip of land on the right side of the house. It was the best location for the generator but also the narrowest.

The ground under his feet was wet, and the wind was picking up. Slowly, he stepped sideways and placed the machine in the proper position. Submerging the drum under the water wasn't difficult. Now all he had to do was attach the machine's mounting bracket to the side of the house.

He set the toolbox next to him, carefully crouched down, and took out the screwdriver. Just as he closed the box, a wave broke over him, crashing against the side of the house. Harold managed to grab onto the bottom of the window ledge, but the toolbox was not so lucky. It was engulfed by the wave and dragged into the ocean.

Harold was soaked from head to foot. Blood flowed from his reopened wound. The rocking of the house got stronger, but he couldn't quit now. Tightening the bolts that anchored the generator to the side of the house was more difficult than he expected, but he finally managed. Last, he attached the cables that went from the generator to the transformer and called the installation complete. Now to go in and see if his invention worked. As he lifted his right foot to the windowsill, another wave assaulted the house. A torrent of water crashed over his back and threw him off balance, and this time he found nothing to grab onto. Harold plunged into the water.

The Iron Serpent

He was completely engulfed by the cold darkness. When he reemerged, everything was just as black as under the water. The fall had knocked off his glasses, and he'd lost his shoes. Disoriented and confused, he spun around, looking for the house, but all he could see were the black and gray waves that ceaselessly tossed him, pounded him, and pushed him under. Then, from out of the shadows, he saw a point of light, a beacon in the middle of the nothingness. It was the candle he had left in the dining room. Already exhausted, he began swimming toward the light, but the swells dragged him off course. He wasn't as agile or as strong as in his youth, and despite the herculean effort he put into every movement, he was desperately aware that the point of light was getting smaller and smaller. His muscles were stiffening under the weight of his wet pajamas. The beacon in the house had become nothing but a yellow pinprick in the distance, appearing and disappearing behind the crests of the waves. Harold had underestimated the sea, a deadly mistake he had made once before.

A wave struck him from the side and left him stunned for a few seconds. When he looked around again, the light had disappeared for good. He was reliving that fateful night when he lost his son, when he lost contact with what he loved most. The terror of seeing the light go out.

He began to yell, but like that other night, his cries were lost in the roar of the waves. Yelling only led to swallowing water and tiring himself out. At that moment, he realized this was the end. He would not reach the house. He would drown without saying good-bye to Mary Rose. Without telling her all the things he should have said throughout their lives together.

Another wave hit him full force from behind, swallowing him in a swarm of bubbles. His body twisted and turned like a rag doll under the water's attack and was dragged down into the depths. But as the burning spread through his oxygen-deprived lungs, his self-loathing faded away. Fate was finally forcing him to pay the price for his irresponsibility. He opened his eyes and saw in front of him a presence that was blacker and more solid even than the darkness. *Dylan?* he thought, closing his eyes. But just when he thought his lungs had used up the last bit of oxygen, something brushed against his arm. Fear shocked him into consciousness, and he began to fight to get away.

Air. Harold managed to get his head above water, and sweet air rushed into his lungs. Adrenaline had given him renewed strength, and he began to swim through the wet nothingness that surrounded him. He looked for the point of light, unable to process what had just happened underwater. Then a long, dark fin crossed in front of him. Harold had no time to react. A powerful tail struck him on his back, and he went under. He emerged, panicked. He kicked with everything he had, flailing, his only thought to get away from the triangular fin. Then he realized he had seen that fin before while standing on the porch with Mary Rose. Adrenaline mixed with unbridled fear; he knew the cut on his hand was bleeding, and if what was circling around him was a shark, he was a dead man.

Harold's arms were spent. All his effort to get away was futile against those merciless waves. He was propelled forward by another bump. The animal was stalking him. There was a sharp pain in his side, but he didn't give up; he kept fighting for his life. Then, over the crest of a wave, he saw it again: a blurry point of light. He was so exhausted, he could barely feel his body, but that yellow light filled him with the hope he needed to keep going.

Then rage too welled up inside him: against the ocean, against what it held, and against the fact it wanted to take him. The animal brushed against his belly, and, instinctively, he punched it.

"Get away!" he yelled as he went under, choking on the salt water.

And just as he emerged, what he most feared finally happened. The shark grabbed his arm and pulled. He felt his skin tear under the pressure.

Thrashing to strike at it only made its hold on his arm worse. But if he didn't fight, he would die there, drowned and mutilated by that creature. The animal spun next to him, bumping him so hard, Harold was pushed several feet forward and sucked under a thick wake of foam. Resurfacing, he noticed the pressure on his arm lessening. With his other arm, he worked to get himself free, feeling the strange snakelike form that had held him. It was thin and cold, but solid like—

His heart skipped a beat. It was not the shark that was dragging him by the arm, but one of the guy wires.

The steel cable loosened and released his arm, but Harold reacted quickly and grabbed it. He cried out in pain as he held on. His whole body lunged forward as he was again dragged by the cable. The swells continued to swirl around him, but he pulled himself forward, hand over hand, inching along the line.

Ever so slowly, the outline of the house took shape in front of him. Knowing he was connected to it gave him courage, but he knew he had to hurry. The shark was still lurking in the darkness, waiting to attack.

After several interminable minutes, Harold touched the rock supporting the house. Like any other ship he had built, the wood boards creaked as the waves rocked the land barrier that protected the house and kept it afloat. He struggled to climb up but slipped and fell back into the water.

Harold was beyond exhausted. He had almost no feeling in his body except for his injured hand. He stifled a cry of pain as he pulled on the cable to heave himself up onto the edge, but before he made it, a wave washed over the porch and a torrent of water pushed him down again.

Without losing his grip on the cable, he pulled his head out of the water and tried again. He couldn't give up now, not when he was inches from safety. He pulled on the cable again, but something wasn't right. The cable felt heavy and loose. Horrified, he realized the cable had just broken free, and once again, there was nothing connecting him to the house. A moment later, the rock was drifting away from him.

Harold didn't hesitate; he released the cable and started swimming. Adrenaline ran through his veins like fire, not allowing him to falter. The waves gave him no rest, but the ledge was getting closer. He was less than six feet away when the dark fin cut in front of him.

Harold wasted no time. He wouldn't let the animal beat him now that he was on the verge of safety. Fighting his way ahead with everything he had, he pushed past the dark shape, and his hands met rock. He began heaving himself up, his feet scrambling to find purchase, but his muscles were burning, failing at last. And then, just as he thought he was about to fall back in, he felt weightless.

A force from the sea pushed under his feet and propelled his whole body upward and out of the water. He tumbled onto the ground in front of the porch.

A Slippery Shadow

Harold felt as heavy as the rock he was lying on. For a long time, he didn't move, swaying gently with the house as the waves calmed down. Slowly, he opened his eyes and, with sloth-like movements, finally managed to sit up. He grabbed onto the handrail and staggered up the steps to the porch, his hand leaving a trail of blood. His right arm was also bleeding from where the steel cable had wrapped around it. He hardly felt any pain; his whole body was numb from the cold. His skin was purplish, and the only sign of life was the constant chattering of his teeth. Yet, when he made it to the porch and felt the wood boards under his bare feet, he couldn't have felt more fortunate.

Harold made it to the front door, then turned and looked again at the dark ocean, wondering what strange force had launched him onto the rock. He turned back to the entrance, but before he could reach for the doorknob, the door flew open. Mary Rose stood there in her flowered robe, holding a candle.

"What on earth are you doing?" she cried. In the darkness, Mary Rose could barely see her husband's silhouette. "You're soaked! And barefoot! Where are your glasses?"

"A wave got me on the porch. I guess they fell off," he said, so she wouldn't worry.

Mary Rose touched his arm, but Harold jerked away when her hand brushed against his injuries.

"And you're bleeding again!" said Mary Rose, her voice shaking.

He went into the kitchen, and Mary Rose closed the door after him. Quickly, she took off her robe and gently wrapped it around Harold, who was shivering uncontrollably.

"I'm fine," was all he could manage to say, his jaw stiff from the cold.

Mary Rose secured the robe around him and examined his sorry condition in the soft light of the candle.

"Come on. Let's go upstairs, and you can tell me what happened. You need to get out of those wet clothes."

Slowly, they crossed the kitchen and headed down the hallway. Mary Rose couldn't take her worried eyes off Harold's purple lips. As they passed the front door and started up the steps, Harold stopped abruptly.

"Are you all right?" Mary Rose asked.

But Harold didn't hear the question. He went to the front door and slowly turned the knob. Mary Rose appeared at his side, and when Harold opened the door, they were blinded by a brilliant light.

"It works," Harold said, almost to himself.

Mary Rose stared at the glowing porch light like she had never seen electricity before. She felt the same sense of disbelief as when she'd discovered their house was floating in the middle of the ocean. She stepped onto the porch with Harold and was bathed in the light spilling from the wrought iron fixture.

Harold looked just as stunned as Mary Rose. All the fatigue and pain he felt began to take on new meaning.

"Harold, you did it!" said Mary Rose, still incredulous.

Harold looked at his wife, her words bringing him back to reality. His whole body shook, not only from cold and exhaustion, but because he knew that little lightbulb could save their lives.

"We're going to make it!" cried Harold.

He felt the numbness and fatigue fading away. It felt like the electricity being distributed through the house also ran through his body and mind; he felt revived.

"I have to check the rest of the system to see if it's working correctly," he declared.

"Now?" Mary Rose was aghast. "You can barely stand up."

Harold knew Mary Rose was right, but he was desperate to make sure there weren't any problems. They couldn't risk wasting any time getting the water purifier working. Then a loud splash startled them. Harold and Mary Rose both turned to see where the sound had come from. A fin cut through the water.

"There it is!" cried Harold.

"What?"

"The shark that was stalking me—the one we saw the other day in front of the porch," he corrected himself.

Mary Rose looked at Harold skeptically, but then the water stirred again. Mary Rose left the porch and nervously approached the edge. "Harold, we have to get you inside," she said.

But even as she spoke, a long, dark form materialized in the water. Mary Rose took a step back. The shape moved closer to the surface and gradually became more defined. And then, when Mary Rose could just make out a large snout, the silhouette dissolved. Suddenly, a mass of bubbles and foam rose from the depths with the force of a geyser, and the animal leaped out of the water.

Mary Rose screamed.

She stumbled backward, her foot striking the riser on the step. She fell and landed on her backside on the wet stairs. When she looked up, she could see the slippery form emerge from the water again, arcing gracefully through the air.

"Rose! It's a dolphin!" cried Harold.

The animal dove into the water with the finesse of a mermaid, then jumped again—higher, stronger, reaching for the stars. And it was then that Harold realized this dolphin had rescued him and had pushed him back to the house. He knew it was crazy, but he wished there was a way to say thank you, because without the dolphin, that little lightbulb shining above him wouldn't mean a thing.

Lights in the Night

Mary Rose slowly got up and went to stand next to Harold. He was no longer shivering, and his heart rate was back to normal. His eyes were fixed on the marvelous creature that seemed to dance with the ocean itself. Its body slipped through the crest of a wave; it dove to gain momentum and jumped impossibly high. And as its outline was framed against the sky, Mary Rose's attention was caught by something even higher.

At first, she thought it was just an optical effect, the glare of the porch light, but when she looked more intently, she knew it was something else.

"What's wrong?" asked Harold.

Mary Rose gently placed her hand on his chin and guided him to look toward a pale, ghostly band of golden lights that appeared and disappeared in the starry sky.

"What is it?"

"I think it's the northern lights," whispered Mary Rose.

Harold was captivated, losing all sense of anything else. Even without his glasses, he found himself mesmerized by the otherworldly lights. He was hypnotized by the soft wave of colors undulating on the celestial dome. Then a different kind of light broke into his reverie.

As the porch light flickered behind him, the surging electricity made the aurora seem dim.

Mary Rose watched as he went to the porch. He stood next to the fixture and heard the unmistakable crackle of a loose bulb.

Harold reached up to tighten it, noticing a thin trail of blood coming from his hand. Suddenly, the bilious color of electric light fell like a heavy burden across his shoulders. When he lowered his shaking, bloodstained hand, wrinkled from age and water, he felt the scrapes on his arm against the bathrobe and the moisture of the boards on his bare feet. And despite the stunning lights dancing overhead, he felt like he was being swallowed again by the frozen darkness in which he had almost perished. He saw Dylan's diaphanous shadow coming toward him and relived the terror of losing him in the storm—the same terror he had felt less than an hour ago when he thought he would never see Mary Rose again. He turned to look at her, but the glare of the flickering light made him squint. He looked again at the incandescent bulb, then reached up and gently twisted it counterclockwise. The light he had worked so hard to illuminate, and that almost cost him his life, went dark.

When his eyes had adjusted to the darkness once again, he could see Mary Rose bathed by the glow of the northern lights.

"Why did you turn off the light?" asked Mary Rose.

"I didn't," Harold said, pointing to the sky. "I just turned them on."

Mary Rose turned toward the ocean and saw what Harold meant. Without the flickering lightbulb, the whole sky was illuminated with greater intensity. The diffuse yellow light, which until then had been a ghostly residue, filled the sky. The dolphin leaped from the water again, and for a moment, Mary Rose thought it had learned to fly. She saw in detail the powerful muscles in its tail, the water coursing over its curved back, and its smiling beak. Harold silently came down from the porch and stood at Mary Rose's side while the rippling waves of the aurora borealis changed colors.

As those strange lights bathed the sea and sky, the night caught fire. Harold and Mary Rose had never witnessed anything so beautiful. And despite their wet clothing and the ocean breeze, they didn't feel cold. Those rippling lights waving across the heavens seemed to wrap around them with a familiarity they couldn't explain. Harold and Mary Rose embraced each other, holding each other in a way they hadn't for years, intoxicated by a peace and happiness they barely remembered.

The Floating Island

Time passed almost imperceptibly, carrying Mr. and Mrs. Grapes along with it, much as the indomitable ocean currents carried them to an unknown destination. Those same inexhaustible currents turned the drum and generated electricity. Most of the household appliances, lights, and outlets were working again, as if they had never been torn from Death Cliff. But of all the improvements the generator had made, the most vital was potable water. After spending long hours drying out the motor and repairing the hose, Harold had finally managed to get the desalinator working again. Even before the cistern filled, Mr. and Mrs. Grapes drank glass after glass of sweet water until their thirst was quenched, and they felt a giddiness that not even the exquisite grape liqueur they jealously guarded had been able to produce. For the first time since the house had fallen, they could bathe. And even though the water wasn't as hot as they'd have liked, the feeling of clean water on their faces, of soap removing the salt, blood, and dirt, helped them feel at home.

Harold found an old pair of glasses. They weren't his current prescription, but they helped. His injuries healed almost without a trace. The only scar was on his hand, which he soon covered with a wool glove. The northern lights had been a portent of the cold that would soon penetrate the house. Harold and Mary Rose had no choice but to dig out their winter clothes from the moving boxes and add blankets to the quilt on the bed. But no matter how many layers they wore, their clothes hung dangerously loose. Mary Rose's cheekbones grew sharp, and Harold had to keep tightening his belt. The scant reserves of food were quickly depleted, and fish became their only source of nourishment.

With the help of a cut-off mop handle, they had built a pair of rudimentary fishing poles to which they tied the fishing line Mr. Grapes had used for his model boats. Bent needles served as hooks.

The first day, they managed to catch a couple of little silver sardine-like fish. The mouthful they provided for dinner wasn't much, and the couple went to bed that night with their stomachs still rumbling. The following days weren't any better; for several days, they barely ate, and Harold began to despair.

Mary Rose made a small net that they submerged with a rope and dragged behind the house for hours. When they brought the net up, they found only algae, a piece of plastic, and a medium-size red fish. But when they cooked the fish, a putrid smell befouled the kitchen, and they decided not to risk eating it.

It wasn't until a few days later that they managed their first decent catch: a large cod that emerged from the water like a shiny treasure. Harold and Mary Rose shouted with glee at this precious gift from the ocean, an ocean that seemed determined to keep them in a delicate balance between life and death. With careful rationing, that one fish fed them for several days.

Even during that time, they never stopped fishing. But the long hours sitting idle with a fishing pole got increasingly difficult to endure. The weather continued to worsen, and despite the layers, overcoats, and blankets, the cold air chilled them to the bone. As the temperature dropped, the sightings of the dolphin that had been following them were less frequent until, finally, they stopped seeing it altogether. On that day, the gusts of wind brought bothersome little drops of rain that turned to ice where they fell.

After that, Harold and Mary Rose took turns; while one fished, the other went inside to recover from the cold. Between shifts, they would work to put the house back in order. The cutlery, plates, and glasses that were miraculously intact had been returned to the kitchen cupboards. They cleaned the countertops and swept and mopped the floors. They unpacked all the tools and clothing they might need and repacked the boxes with anything broken and unusable. Little by little, they repaired chair legs and the kitchen table. And Mary Rose had transplanted the surviving three hydrangeas into chipped pots that she placed next to the window.

Mary Rose gently touched the damaged pompoms and momentarily took comfort. But when she looked out the window, she saw Harold on the porch. He was huddled up against the cold, thick blankets over his shoulders, holding a fishing pole and staring out at the water in front of him. Mary Rose was constantly amazed at the vast expanse of ocean. A part of her couldn't help marveling at its savage beauty, its imperturbable force. But the ache in her empty stomach and the creaking of the house around her made her feel small and defenseless. The miles of blue seemed to extend forever, devoid of ships and land, filled only with endless desolation.

Mary Rose looked to the sky, hoping for a patch of sunshine, but saw only the monotonous gray that had accompanied them for days. As she watched the horizon, it seemed to shift and move due to the winds that sometimes made the house slowly rotate.

Mary Rose went to the beat-up refrigerator and opened it. The florescent light illuminated her face, accentuating her gaunt features. Cold air poured out, as if trying to lower the temperature in the house even more. Mary Rose looked worriedly at the empty shelves. They held only a modest-size fish resting on a chipped plate. It was a small catch, barely sufficient to feed them for one more day. *One more day*, she thought as she brought the plate to her nose. The smell of ocean and salt water mingled with the faint acidic tang of food on the verge of spoiling. But not knowing when they would catch another one meant they couldn't afford to waste one bite. She placed their meal on the countertop.

Through the window, she watched for a moment as the horizon continued to rotate. Then, resigned, she began to carefully fillet the fish. Tiny water droplets began to spatter on the windowpane. Worried, Mary Rose looked at Harold, who had hunched down even further under the blankets. Just as she set the knife on the counter to go tell him to come in from the cold, something on the shifting horizon caught her attention. Her heart skipped a beat when she saw it cutting through the water.

"A ship!" she yelled, even though no one was inside to hear her.

A ship was coming straight at them. But as the house spun again, she realized that what she saw was too big, too irregular, and too uniformly white to be a ship. For a moment, she stood paralyzed with fear. Then a crash shook the house. The knife bounced off the counter and landed an inch from her foot. Mary Rose was thrown to the side, her ribs striking the edge of the counter. The blow knocked the wind out of her as pain seared her side. The meager contents of the shelves, tables, and cupboards fell as the house rocked violently. Mary Rose straightened up, reeling from pain and fear; opened the side door; and stepped out onto the porch.

Nothing Is What It Seems

Harold knew something wasn't right when the house began to spin. First he saw small fragments of ice floating in the water; then big, smooth ice floes; and finally the giant iceberg coming directly at them. He dropped the fishing pole and jumped up. Just as he started up the porch steps, a jagged ice floe crashed against the side of the house. He managed to grab onto a post, but his chair, blankets, and fishing pole disappeared into the water, immediately devoured by the ocean. Seconds later, as the house rose and fell in a constant state of instability, the door opened, and Mary Rose appeared.

"Stay inside!" Harold yelled when he saw Mary Rose coming unsteadily out to him.

Mary Rose seized Harold's gloved hand as the house was tossed from side to side. Harold held on tightly, fearing that at any moment another collision would knock them over, but the lurching began to subside. Although they relaxed slightly, the couple remained wrapped around the post with their eyes fixed on the scene in front of them. In every direction, the sea was jammed with ice. Harold and Mary Rose felt like they were trapped in one of those travel documentaries they used to watch on long Sunday afternoons. But this was completely real. Like giant rivers, the ice floes moved along invisible paths carved by the ocean currents. They cracked against each other, rose up, and sank as they crashed against the rock surrounding the house.

Harold felt like all the cold surrounding them was now concentrated in his chest, trying to freeze his wildly beating heart. Mary Rose felt his hand shaking in hers and squeezed it. Even though she wasn't wearing a coat to combat the icy gusts, sweat dripped down her back.

"How did I not notice it earlier?" exclaimed Harold, shakily. "I didn't see any ice until now."

Though the violent oscillations had stopped, every time an ice floe crashed against the rock that kept them afloat, the whole house vibrated like they were experiencing the tremors on the cliff again.

Harold let go of the post and drew Mary Rose toward the door, away from the water.

He looked again at the approaching iceberg and calculated that it easily rose three or four times higher than the house and was at least ten times wider. They had never seen anything so big or threatening. Unfortunately, this was not a documentary, and they couldn't change the channel. This was real. The unyielding giant iceberg was coming toward them.

"It must be half a mile away," murmured Harold.

Mary Rose was never very good at judging distances, but given the enormity of the iceberg, she would have said it was much closer.

"What should we do?" she asked.

Harold looked into her eyes and saw the same fear he felt, a fear as monumental as the iceberg. To his dismay, he had no answer to her question. Everything was happening too fast. There was no time to come up with a complex plan or design anything that would help them change course. They were sailing on a house that was at the mercy of unseen forces, a house made from parts of a ship, but not a ship at all. The sun shone through the gray clouds, then quickly was hidden behind the iceberg. The colossal white-blue shape was outlined against the sky and cast a long, wide shadow that darkened the surface of the sea remaining between them.

"We have to hope for a change in wind direction or currents," he said sullenly.

Mary Rose's hopeful expression darkened with terror. "That's it?"

"Rose, we don't have a rudder or sails. We can't steer. This is a house!"

"There must be something," she said, pressing him desperately. "I refuse to believe that standing by and hoping is our only option."

Harold let out a heavy sigh. He avoided looking at his wife, instead focusing on the iceberg. It advanced ruthlessly, without any consideration as to what might be in its way, even the house of a terrified retired couple lost at sea. It was like seeing their own death silently coming for them, with no chance of hiding. He knew that even if they survived the crash, if they fell into the ice-cold waters, they would soon freeze to death. He felt sick.

Another ice floe collided with the rock around the house, and the impact threw them against the siding. Mary Rose felt her head hit wood and heard a sharp crack. The sheet of ice splintered, sounding like dry branches cracking, and threw up a wave of frigid water mixed with ice fragments that littered the porch like megalithic marbles.

Just as the house began to stabilize, it was hit by another floe, and Harold and Mary Rose were ruthlessly catapulted over the railing. A piece of wood broke against Mary Rose's right knee, the splinters slicing through her pant leg and embedding in her skin. Mary Rose cried out in pain as the house pitched and turned on its axis. Harold dove toward his wife and pulled her to him. They clung to the post and waited for the house to stop spinning. After a few minutes, the house settled, and when it did, they were completely blinded by the sun.

"We have to go inside!" said Harold, looking worriedly at the blood flowing from Mary Rose's knee.

"Why?" she exclaimed furiously. "I don't want to die hiding in a corner like some scared old woman."

Mary Rose wiped her tears and looked back at the enormous mountain of ice. The imposing iceberg kept coming. But Mary Rose noticed that, now, something looked different.

"You're injured!" Harold exclaimed, indicating her bloody knee.

Mary Rose wasn't listening; she didn't even feel the pain throbbing through her kneecap. Something didn't add up. The sun's rays were shining through the iceberg. Mary Rose couldn't believe what she was seeing.

"There's a hole!" she exclaimed.

Harold looked at her questioningly, then understood.

"It's not possible," he whispered.

As the iceberg got closer, more light shone on them through a huge passageway.

"Do you think we can go through it?" asked Mary Rose with renewed hope.

Harold studied the tunnel. He was sure the house would fit, but the opening did not line up with the house's current path.

Another fragment of ice hit the rock. Harold and Mary Rose stayed firmly anchored to the post while the house seesawed and gusts of icy air burned their skin.

"Our alignment is off," said Harold, still studying the iceberg.

"And there's no way we can change course?"

Harold knew if they were going to make it, they had to act quickly. If they wasted effort on anything that didn't make a difference, they would pay for the error with their lives. He could only come up with one possibility, but he hated to say it aloud.

"Our only option is to leave the house."

"What!" shouted Mary Rose.

"The more time we waste here, the worse it will be, Rose."

"And where do you think we should go?" she shouted, pointing at the ocean. "We'll freeze to death, Harold!"

A gust of wind carrying a cloud of icy pellets took her breath away. She could barely feel her trembling, purplish hands as she gripped the sturdy wooden post with all her might. The shadow of the iceberg finally reached the house and, in a stealthy death march, began to ascend the porch steps, advancing toward their feet.

"No!" Mary Rose exclaimed, and Harold looked at her in surprise. "We've made it this far for a reason," she continued firmly. "And I don't think the reason was to freeze to death in the middle of the ocean. There has to be something we can do." Mary Rose took his hand and calmly looked him in the eye, adding, "I believe in you, Harold."

A vivid memory overcame Harold. He saw the light of fireflies fighting the darkness. He felt the rowboat being tossed and buffeted by the waves, the hindering rain, the anguish of not knowing how to get out of the storm, and the regret at not having listened to his instincts. From the corner of his eye, he saw the wave that would crash against the side of the boat and knock them into the water. He couldn't do anything to stop it, but just before the impact, Dylan had looked at Harold, a look of extreme peace illuminated by the fireflies. Then everything was obscured in a whirlpool of black bubbles.

Now the cold, blue shadow of the iceberg finally enveloped the whole house.

"Quick! Come inside with me! I need your help," shouted Harold.

Inside the house, everything was rattling. Harold stopped at the bottom of the stairs. "We have to open the windows—but only the ones on this side! You get this floor, and I'll get upstairs, OK?"

Harold didn't wait for an answer; he was already halfway up the stairs. Mary Rose didn't stop to think either. Adrenaline pumping, she didn't notice the pain in her knee. She ran, stumbling, to the living room and began opening windows. The ice-cold wind whipped into the room like a raging spirit and filled the air with frozen droplets that swirled around her. She returned to the entryway and headed down the short hallway to open the one kitchen window on that side. Before she got there, the whole house heaved, and Mary Rose was thrown backward onto the floor. The house groaned as if about to split in two; furniture and objects crashed to the floor. Harold didn't take long to reappear, reeling and with blood running down his forehead.

"Don't worry. I'm OK," he said.

Harold helped his wife up. They opened the last window, then returned to the porch. Crushed ice covered a large part of the deck, and two of the steps had been lifted out of place. The titanic frozen mountain was now a mere quarter mile from the house. From that distance, its behemoth size seemed even more exaggerated. A glacial cold enveloped them. It felt like the life-sucking breath of death itself, a breath emerging from the ravenous maw of an icy Jurassic beast. And there was nothing more they could do.

The wind blew hard, but it didn't seem to be steering the house as Harold had hoped. The iceberg was nearly upon them, and the opening was still misaligned.

"Do you think we'll make it?" murmured Mary Rose.

"The tunnel is big enough. We just need a little more time to get lined up," Harold said quietly as he circled his arm around his wife's waist.

Around them, fragments of ice were breaking violently against the rock as whirlpools and waves increased in intensity due to the propulsion of the iceberg. Harold knew that if they hit another floe, there would be no possibility of passing through the tunnel. There was no plan B.

They were a hundred yards from the inevitable encounter, eighty . . . fifty . . . almost imperceptibly, Harold sensed the house change course. They needed to shift only a few more degrees to be perfectly lined up, but it seemed impossible given the short distance. Forty . . . thirty-five . . . thirty . . . suddenly, what he had feared came to pass. An ice floe collided with the rock and abruptly changed their direction. Harold grabbed Mary Rose and rushed inside. While they clung to the banister with all their might, the house struck the iceberg.

Through the Mirror

The left side of the house smashed against the wall at the entrance of the tunnel, causing the windowpanes to shatter as if from a bomb blast. The whole house shook, and the ice that formed the roof of the passageway cracked and formed hundreds of blue fissures. Pieces of ice came loose from the side of the iceberg and fell like a meteorite shower. Some fell inches from the house, and freezing water shot up like geysers all around it. Others fell directly on the roof, the impact snapping off the tip of the central pole. The house was now dragged along by the tremendous thrust of the iceberg. A wave formed in front of the rock ledge, splashing the side of the house and coming in through the broken windows. Then a loud cracking sound resounded through the tunnel, and the iceberg wall crumbled. An enormous hole opened, and the house clumsily slipped through into the depths of the giant ice gorge, just as Harold had hoped.

The light, filtered through the layer of ice, tinged everything a pearly blue. The roar of water was reduced to an endless, resounding echo. The polished, jagged walls inside momentarily reflected the image of the house like an enormous deformed mirror. Then the right side collided with the other wall. The surrounding rock there was wider and buffered some of the impact, but a sharp projection from the sapphire-blue ice sliced along the side of the house. The wooden structure shook as the icy dagger ripped apart the yellow slats, forming an ever-deepening scar. Finally, the pressure of the house broke off the ice, and the house surged forward.

The giant jagged ice blocks that filled the cavern were tinkling, cracking, and showering down a thin layer of frost that froze the air. The light waned further, leaving them in bluish twilight. The cold was powerful, penetrating every crack in the house and freezing the water that had splashed into the dining room, living room, and hallways.

The house again collided with the wall of the passageway, and a chunk of ice fell, causing an enormous wave that rocked the structure mercilessly. The path through which they navigated had turned into rapids, whirling and seething with turbulence. The whole passage was breaking apart, and chunks of ice hanging from the tunnel's dome began to break and fall like deadly spears into the water and onto the slate roof.

Finally, the other end of the tunnel appeared, and the light once again grew brighter. It bounced over the walls, creating sinuous, glimmering flashes on the water. The house was about to emerge again into the open sea when it hit a protrusion, breaking it off and creating a wave that pushed the house back inside the tunnel. The fissure expanded, snaking toward the sides until it connected with deeper cracks that had appeared all over the ice. Then a deafening grinding sound filled the whole passage.

The fissures began to split, and sections of ice as large as the house came loose. The tunnel canopy began to cave in. A sheet of ice fell onto the roof, shattering the chimney, sending bricks sliding down the slate roof and into the water. The impact of ice against the water reverberated throughout the ice cathedral as it collapsed in on itself. The exit again appeared in front of the house, but then a fragment of ice twice as big as the house broke loose and sank as if in slow motion; it sucked the house toward the whirlpool that formed around it.

Inside, Harold and Mary Rose tenaciously gripped the spindles of the banister but felt themselves weaken as hundreds of fragments of glass and ice bounced down the hallway and hit their feet. They were oblivious to the blows, the pain, the cold, and the pieces of glass piercing their skin. The front door blew open violently, and a frigid breath of air and snow burst into the house like a hurricane. There was nothing they could do. They held each other and closed their eyes for the final assault.

Water began to wash over the porch and into the vestibule where they were standing. But just as the house was on the verge of being sucked under, the massive block of ice stopped sinking and began to bob back up to the surface with the same force as it had gone down, creating a powerful rush of water that violently catapulted the house free of the ice tunnel.

Harold and Mary Rose felt the full force of energy as they were propelled out into the sea. Mary Rose felt her hands slipping on the spindles, but Harold held her and the baluster. He was determined to hold on to the end.

A second later, the ice corridor they had just left behind finished collapsing, sending up a high cloud of water and pulverized ice that descended on the house, pushing them farther away. The water around the house swirled furiously, but the remains of the iceberg steadily drifted into the distance and faded away. A thick mist slipped over the surface of the icy sea, eventually enveloping the house completely.

Starting Over

Harold's stiff hands slowly let go of the baluster, and he embraced Mary Rose, pressing his body against hers to hold in the tears. Mary Rose buried her face in Harold's chest, feeling the trembling in their bodies, and the runaway beating of their hearts combined in synchronized, booming percussion. She inhaled his scent as if it were the perfume of the first bloom after a hard winter.

"We're alive?" she finally whispered.

Harold opened his eyes and, through the open door, saw the sea veiled by mist and snow. They no longer heard the thunderous sound of ice breaking or the impact of it hitting water. The movement of the house had returned to a gentle rocking. Harold filled his lungs with air and let out a long sigh as a faint smile appeared on his frozen face. And, finally letting it all out, he wept. Fat tears flowed freely, spilling down his cheeks as his relieved smile turned into boisterous laughter.

Mary Rose looked up with concern. Then she too began to laugh from pure joy.

"We're alive, Rosy!" shouted Harold.

And then, despite the pain and fatigue, he lifted Mary Rose by the waist and spun her around.

"Harold, put me down!" she said, laughing.

Harold gently placed her on the ground, and before she could protest further, he kissed her. Mary Rose felt a tingle run through her body, and the pain in her knee and the cold of the room eased. It had been years since they had kissed with such passion.

The snowflakes coming through the front door, the water soaking their feet, and even the fact they were each bleeding—none of it mattered. Leisurely, their lips finally separated and, smiling, they looked at each other like young lovers with their whole lives in front of them.

Then a gust of wind blew the front door closed with a bang that froze their smiles; the house was covered in a tense silence once again.

As the door swung open, Harold propped it ajar before it could slam shut again. Under his feet crunched fragments of ice, glass, and other broken pieces that intermingled with puddles of water. Mary Rose looked at the trail of puddles with resignation and followed them to the kitchen.

Plates, glasses, silverware, furniture . . . everything was once again on the floor like after the fall from the cliff. Mary Rose felt a stab of grief that surpassed the physical pain in her knee. She saw the fish she had begun to prepare that morning lying mutilated on the floor. She bent down and gently picked off the bigger pieces of glass, in hopes of salvaging a few bites. But it was dirty and inedible, the tender meat full of shards.

"Don't worry about that now, Rose."

Mary Rose nodded weakly and got up, now noticing the intense pain in her knee. She felt worn out, so exhausted she couldn't speak.

Harold held her and found her whole body was shaking uncontrollably.

"You're frozen through," he said, squeezing her arm. "Let's go upstairs and rest."

Things didn't look much better upstairs. Mary Rose sat on the bed, and Harold got a couple of thick blankets from the wardrobe and wrapped them around his wife's shoulders. He ripped an old T-shirt into strips and used it as a bandage to staunch the bleeding from her knee. As in the kitchen, most of the windowpanes in the bedroom had broken and were letting in a constant swirl of snowflakes. Harold covered the windows with blankets. Now the room was illuminated only by the light that filtered in around the edges of the blankets and under the door.

Harold flicked the light switch, but everything remained dark. Carefully, he made his way around the broken glass on the floor and tried the other switch, with the same result.

"Power's out," he said, looking at the unresponsive light fixture swinging above their heads.

"Leave it be, Harold," Mary Rose whispered as she sat on the bed.

Harold looked at her knee again and suddenly felt the weight of responsibility fall heavily on his shoulders. Without saying a word, he snuggled up next to his wife on the bed. But despite the proximity of their bodies and the thickness of the blankets, the cold in the bedroom was unbearable. A frigid draft blew through the gaps under the door and fluttered the blankets. The only sounds were the brittle shattering of ice against rock and the creaking of the house. Like the increasing cold, the hunger and pain they felt grew more pronounced, but complete exhaustion began to take over.

"We're alive," repeated Mary Rose, feebly.

Harold realized she was talking in her sleep and gently laid her head on the pillow. He leaned back next to her and watched over Mary Rose as he futilely fought the heavy weight of his eyelids. In the dim lighting, her face seemed more gaunt and pale than ever, and he was afraid.

Hidden in the Brume

Deep in the thick brume, Mr. and Mrs. Grapes's house continued its relentless journey through the frozen waters. It seemed only the house knew where it was going. Night fell, and the cold intensified; a delicate veil of frozen mist began to stick to the roof and rock surrounding the house. Sheets of ice packed together and thickened, piling up around the rock, until it finally happened. Little by little, an amazing change occurred, unbeknownst to the sleeping Mr. and Mrs. Grapes.

Mary Rose was awakened by pain in her neck. The image of the ship on which she had been sailing in her dream faded away. Groggily, she opened her eyes to find Harold's elbow poking into the back of her neck. Moving Harold's arm alleviated that discomfort, but a much more intense pain began to awaken. Every muscle in her body screamed in agony, and her face felt like it was on fire. Torpidly, she managed to extricate herself from the heap of blankets tangled around her, and the intense cold of the room assaulted her body. As she attempted to stand, a stabbing pain in her right knee forced her to sit again. Carefully, she raised her pant leg and removed the bloodstained bandage. The wound was no longer bleeding, but Mary Rose was alarmed to see her knee had doubled in size. She had expected everything to be better in the morning, but now she felt even weaker and more fatigued. She sighed and lowered her pant leg. Fighting back tears of pain and frustration, she struggled to her feet. Harold shifted under the heavy blankets.

"How are you feeling?" he murmured as he opened his eyes.

Mary Rose reached down for a pile of clothes on the floor and had to pause before she was able to respond.

"My knee stopped bleeding, and it doesn't hurt much," she lied.

Harold got up and helped Mary Rose pick up the pile of clothes and placed it on the bed. They got dressed in thick pants, wool sweaters, gloves, and jackets, putting on as many layers as possible to fend off the cold. But when they opened the door, it all seemed in vain.

Harold and Mary Rose stood frozen in place, assailed by the cold and the view in front of them. The walls, floor, banister, stairs, and even the lights still hanging from the ceiling were all covered by a white layer of frost. The interior of the house looked like the work of a giant ice sculptor.

Mary Rose felt dizzy, bewildered by what she was seeing. She hardly recognized their home.

Harold stepped forward and slipped. "Be very, very careful."

Mary Rose looked at the sparkling floor with misgiving. Her knee throbbed just with her body weight. She didn't want to imagine what would happen if she made a misstep.

Harold and Mary Rose moved cautiously to the top of the stairs. Clenching the banister, they slowly descended the glassy steps until they reached the bottom. There, the situation was even worse. The frost was thicker, and piles of snow were heaped against the walls underneath the open windows. Harold tried the light switches along the way, but none of them had the desired effect. Each time, he felt more disheartened, certain his generator had been destroyed by the iceberg.

They went to the kitchen, where everything seemed strangely calm. They could hardly hear the wind through the broken windows or feel the soft rocking of the house.

Harold went to the kitchen door and opened it, the snow tumbling in and covering his shoes. But instead of moving out of the way, he headed straight through it.

"Where are you going?"

"I need to see if the generator is still there."

Mary Rose studied the pristine layer of snow that covered the porch. It melded seamlessly into the thick fog still surrounding them. It was difficult to see where the stairs began.

"Harold, it's too dangerous! You could slip and fall into the water." She looked again at the opaque fog.

Harold knew she was right. But what could he do?

"We need power now more than ever, Rose. I'll be as quick as I can. I promise."

And in front of the speechless Mary Rose, Harold turned and walked slowly over the soft snow. When he reached the railing, he shortened his steps, searching for the stairs hidden in the huge drift of snow. Harold proceeded along the narrow strip of rock, holding tightly to the porch railing to keep from slipping and falling into the ice-filled sea. Cold water had soaked through his shoes, and his feet were already tingling. He knew it was risky but forced himself to move faster. He made it to the corner of the house and began to walk along the ledge, having nothing to hold on to. Boards stuck out from the house like porcupine spines. Careful not to lose his balance, he gingerly moved past them.

When Mary Rose lost sight of him, she closed the kitchen door and, as quickly as her knee and the slippery surface allowed, moved to the living room. There were two windows in that room, but only one was still intact. As she went over to it, she realized the pane was full of cracks, so she didn't dare open it. She went to the other window and, careful not to cut herself on the sharp pieces of glass still embedded in the frame, stuck her head out the opening to find Harold.

Harold stopped. If he remembered correctly, the drum should be right about there. He crouched down and urgently began to dig in the snow. The top layer was soft, but as he got deeper, the snow hardened, and his gloved fingers were soon numb. He had no choice but to stop and blow on them to warm them up. The woolen gloves weren't meant for this, and his hands were already wet. He had to hurry.

He sank his hands back in the hole and kept digging. His fingers scraped firmly against the compacted layer of snow, and it didn't take long to hit rock. Nothing. Not a trace of the wiring or mounting plate. He moved forward and started digging again. No sign of the drum.

"Can you see anything?" asked Mary Rose impatiently.

Harold's teeth were chattering so hard it was impossible for him to answer his wife. He moved forward a little more, not knowing where the snow stopped and the water began. His hands were stiff claws as he scraped back and forth; he couldn't move his fingers. The falling snow was slowly accumulating on his shoulders and back. The cold seemed to cut through his nasal passages with every breath. Even so, he kept digging. Then he felt something colder and harder. He took his paralyzed hands out of the hole, peered in, and saw a piece of plated metal. Elated, he threw himself back into digging. Like a fossil being uncovered, the big silver drum appeared outlined in the snow. With every handful of snow that he removed, Harold's hope grew. Finally, the drum, motor, wiring, and mounting bracket that connected it to the house were exposed. He couldn't believe the drum was still firmly attached after all the blows the house had sustained. But it wasn't turning.

Harold went closer to the edge, Mary Rose watching his every step. He reached toward the water and found that ice surrounded the part of the drum that was underwater. Harold knew it would be impossible to break the thick ice without tools, so he got up to get what he needed.

As he did, he slipped and disappeared in the brume.

"Harold!" screamed Mary Rose.

Suddenly, she didn't feel cold or pain or fear falling. She stumbled out to the porch. Without thinking, she staggered through the snow, down the steps, and around the loose boards sticking out from the house until she reached where Harold had fallen.

"Harold!" she yelled again, desperately. The freezing air blew hard, flooding her lungs as her body shook with panic. Slowly, the wind blew away the thick layer of snow, but her tear-filled eyes couldn't see beyond the rock. "Harold! Please! Say something!"

Mary Rose squatted down and felt with her bare hands the edge of the rock that marked the break between the house and the water. She reached out her arm, but with the fog and snow, she couldn't see anything. She didn't know what to do—jump in the water? Then she heard a voice in the distance.

"Rose?"

Mary Rose felt a surge of joy upon hearing Harold's voice. "Harold? Harold, I'm here!" Mary Rose stretched out her arm as far as she could into the brume and then saw something coming toward her slowly and taking shape in the thick fog.

"Harold! Here! Follow my voice!" But suddenly, Mary Rose feared the shape coming toward her. It was too tall, too big to be Harold. Fear and confusion overwhelmed her. What was it? Where was Harold? "Harold! Say something!"

The shape was getting denser and more defined, zigzagging from one side to the other as it approached the house. She squinted and strained to see what it was.

"Rose?" Harold called from somewhere in the distance.

"Harold, hurry, please! Something's coming!" The shape was no longer as blurry. This didn't make Mary Rose feel any better. She thought what she was seeing must be a hallucination brought on by exhaustion. It looked like a human shape, but they were in the middle of the ocean!

"Rose?"

Harold's figure materialized. The fog enveloping the house continued its retreat. Before her eyes appeared a field of blue ice that seemed to go on forever. How hadn't she felt the collision? Out on the ice, Harold was slowly making his way toward her, concentrating on his steps to stay upright. However, when he was a few feet from the rock, he slipped and tumbled forward, flat on his face. The sheet of ice groaned under Harold's weight, but didn't break.

"Harold!"

Mary Rose stepped onto the ice and carefully made her way to him. She gave him her hand to help him up, but then she slipped and fell too. The pain from her knee was excruciating, but it didn't matter now that she knew Harold was alive. Lying on the ice, the two hugged each other as the breeze dispelled the last fog banks. Now gray clouds quickly began to break up, and a momentary ray of sunshine broke through a crack of blue sky. At that moment, the last veil of mist lifted, and Harold and Mary Rose saw a sparkling black mountain peak.

In the Shadow of the Mountain

Harold and Mary Rose had to get inside. They were numb and shaking from the cold and from what they had just seen.

They went to the living room and covered the open window with a blanket. Then they stared at the dark mountain range through the cracked window, transfixed, with hopeful conjectures flying through their heads. Finally, after so many weeks of wandering aimlessly upon the vast ocean: land. Harold and Mary Rose had never seen such a high mountain range.

"It feels so strange," said Mary Rose, gazing wide-eyed, "to see the horizon so firm and close. I've never seen such big mountains!" She laughed.

Harold smiled when he saw hope glimmering in her green eyes.

"I really thought we'd never see land again, Harold."

Vapor from their breath formed ice crystals on the window in front of them. Harold felt a sense of relief when he saw the shape of the mountain through the frost. He felt sheltered by the grandiose shadow and the knowledge their floating home was firmly moored at last.

His eyes ran over the deep layer of snow that covered the dark side of the mountain. Then he slowly turned his gaze to the opposite side, where long tongues of ice descended between heavy fallen rocks. He began to search each nook and cranny, hunting for a path, a lamppost, ·

or a structure of any kind. His heart beat faster as his eyes ascended the steep, frozen slopes. But the landscape revealed only ice, snow, and rocks.

Hours passed. Harold and Mary Rose huddled under blankets, trying to bring life back into their extremities while they continued studying the mountains in search of some sign of life. Not hunger, thirst, not even cold or fatigue could force them away from that frozen window for fear of missing something. The sunlight started to fade, then was quickly hidden behind a thick buildup of clouds spilling across the sky. As snow began to fall harder, their view of the mountain was obscured, but still neither moved from their position. Harold followed the descent of the shadow down the side of the hill, despairing as a mantle of darkness slipped over the mountain. Then, just before the shadow covered it completely, something moved.

Harold jumped up and pressed his nose against the cracked glass.

"What is it? Did you see something?"

"I'm not sure," he answered, squinting.

Mary Rose looked in the same direction. They stared silently for a few more minutes until darkness hid the mountains completely.

"Probably just a snow slide," murmured Harold.

The snow came down harder, and darkness began to advance over the barren plain. And then a shriek pierced the silence.

"What was that?" cried Mary Rose.

"It could have been the wind whistling."

They heard the shriek again, much louder this time. Harold and Mary Rose looked at each other, not knowing what to think.

"Let's go upstairs and see if there's a better view," said Harold.

As quickly as the slippery surface allowed, Harold and Mary Rose climbed the two flights of stairs to the attic. They were so focused on the shriek that they didn't register the snow falling through an enormous hole in the roof left by the iceberg. Harold and Mary Rose went swiftly to the large circular window.

Although the light continued to fade, from their elevated position they had a much better view of the frozen landscape. For a moment, they were transfixed by the enormity of the vast plateau of ice and snow, as impressive as the seemingly endless ocean they had crossed. For a few minutes, they just listened to the gusts of wind that blew snow around the attic. Then they heard a second voice, more distressing than the first.

Mr. and Mrs. Grapes moved closer to the window. Thick snowflakes lashed their faces. Mary Rose felt the frost sticking to her eyelashes as she squinted to see through the dark and snow.

Then, out on the plain, she spotted two shadows. "Harold! There!"

Harold looked in the direction Mary Rose was indicating, and his heart pounded furiously.

"We're saved!" cried Mary Rose. "Come on!"

Mary Rose turned toward the stairs, but Harold remained in front of the window, studying the two shapes. Something about the scene didn't feel right, and his elation turned to dismay.

"Seals," he whispered.

"What?" asked Mary Rose as she returned to the window.

Through the window, she saw two figures swiftly gliding across the snow. Not people, but seals: an adult and a pup. They were both pearly gray, with the same patch of black over the right eye. Mary Rose had never seen a real live seal, but her disappointment outweighed her curiosity.

She leaned against the wall and looked dejectedly at the tall post standing in the middle of the room. Despite the burn marks running up and down it, Mary Rose felt like it was the only solid thing left in the house. She wanted to be as strong as that post, but she felt her hope cave in like the roof of that old attic.

"This isn't the end," said Harold, moving next to her and tenderly wiping a tear from her cheek. "When it stops snowing and visibility improves, someone will find us. You'll see."

Mary Rose nodded sorrowfully. Then another, more dreadful cry rang out. Harold and Mary Rose looked out the window again, and something else appeared in the snow: a large, white bear.

There was no mistaking the polar bear. The animal roared, and the rumble of his voice resounded over the plain, making their hair stand on end. Mary Rose gripped the window frame with trembling hands, terrified at their weakness against this wild and ferocious landscape where they didn't belong and at hearing the roar of a beast appearing out of nowhere. The bear ran toward the seals with surprising agility, bellowing and kicking up a white cloud under a powerful stride that thundered hollowly on the ice.

Before they knew what was happening, the bear threw himself on the fat seals in a mortal embrace. Mary Rose screamed and looked away just as the bear lashed out with a final swipe, spilling its victims' blood on the white canvas. Harold couldn't move; he was holding his breath and shaking. The little seal slipped through the claws that held it down and fled as quickly as its chubby body allowed. The bear snarled furiously, raising the hairs on Harold's neck again. But instead of chasing its prey, the bear remained to finish off the bigger kill. Then it carried the limp carcass away in its razor-sharp maw, leaving a red trail on the pristine snow until it disappeared in the fog.

Mary Rose couldn't stop shaking. Finally, turning to look at Harold, she asked, "Where are we, Harold?"

He didn't dare look at Mary Rose. He couldn't take his eyes off the red stain quickly being erased under a fine dusting of snow. And then he had a terrifying thought. A thought that turned his stomach, and he dared not voice it aloud. Harold realized that, after weeks of floating aimlessly on the formidable ocean, they had landed in a place even more savage and solitary.

The Signal

The snow stopped falling, and visibility was so clear that, through the cracked glass in the living room, Harold and Mary Rose were getting to know every nook and cranny of the mountain by heart. Despite the long hours in front of the window, they had not seen any more seals or polar bears, nor had they seen any sign of people. The evidence that they were alone was increasingly alarming. The food reserves were almost depleted. They had a handful of nuts, one can of fruit, and the water in the cistern, but that was frozen and hard as a rock. Fishing was their only source of hope, but even with a new improvised pole, all their attempts had failed. Everywhere they tried, the ice was too thick to cut through with the limited tools still at their disposal.

Harold gave up the idea of repairing the generator; the cold outside was unbearable, and without the ocean currents, it would have been wasted effort. To combat the cold, they covered all the broken windows with boards and blankets and used broken furniture to build a fire in the dining room fireplace. But a few minutes after they lit the fire, black smoke filled the room. Harold and Mary Rose had to put the fire out quickly and uncover the windows to let out the toxic cloud. When Harold inspected the chimney, he found it was completely blocked by damage from the iceberg. After that, they improvised with a more modest hearth in the living room. They placed the metal carcass of the dryer Harold had gutted next to a broken window. Harold fitted it with a homemade tube to vent the smoke outside and keep them safe from asphyxiation. The small fire they built wasn't enough to warm the house, so they rarely left the room. They no longer slept in their bed, and they curled up next to each other on the tattered sofa, a pile of blankets covering their languishing bodies. They slept in a state of semiconsciousness, just alert enough to maintain the critical fire that was keeping them alive.

"The fire is almost out," said Mary Rose.

"That was the last broken piece," answered Harold. "We'll have to start burning the good furniture."

Mary Rose sighed bitterly and stared at the dark mountain through the cracked window. "Do you think they had a nice funeral for us?" she asked, lost in thought.

"I don't think there's any such thing as a nice funeral."

"I suppose not," she said, dark memories coming to mind.

"Besides, as far as I know, we haven't died yet."

The flames went out, and the warmth that had bathed their faces was gone. Mary Rose struggled to her feet and stirred the embers with the fire shovel. "But do you think it will be long before we do?"

"Not if we stay here, waiting for a miracle."

Mary Rose stared at her husband. "It would be insane to leave."

"You're probably right. But it's crazy to stay too."

Mary Rose sighed and saw the sun move behind the formidable mountain. "You don't think we'll just freeze out there?"

"At least out there we might have a shot, Rose," said Harold, motioning to the window. "Maybe there's a town on the other side of the mountain."

"And if there isn't? What if there's only more ice, wild animals, and death?"

The embers crackled, and some angry ashes leaped out near Harold's feet. Mary Rose broke into tears, letting go of the shovel, which clattered to the floor.

"I wish we'd died when the house fell from the cliff," she sobbed.

Harold went and sat on the floor next to her. "Don't say that, Rose," he said, embracing her.

But in the same way the cold was penetrating the room, Harold felt despair seeping into his soul. Mary Rose rested her head on Harold's bony shoulder, and her sobs turned to ragged breaths. Harold kissed her forehead and looked again at the mountain, which from his angle on the floor seemed higher and more jagged. The sun slipped back behind the ghostly brume scattered around the peak, spilling down its sides in long, thin tentacles. Harold noticed that, behind one of those fog banks, something was ascending to the sky. He squinted through his old glasses, focusing on that spot.

Mary Rose looked up and dried her cheeks with the sleeve of her sweater. She had seen the strange movement on the mountain too. Hesitantly, she proceeded to the window with Harold following her and tenderly putting his arm around her waist. Mary Rose looked at him and saw a spark in his eye. Then she hugged him. They jumped up and down, amid tears and laughter. A wispy gray line climbed in the afternoon sky and dissipated among the clouds in a hope-inducing trace of smoke.

The Yellow Dot

The frigid air woke Harold and Mary Rose. The fire had gone out sometime during the night without either of them noticing. Numb with cold, they struggled to extricate themselves from the pile of heavy blankets on the sofa. With a certain amount of dread, they made their way to the window. Fog from their breath clung to the glass as dawn's pink beams peeked over the top of the mountain. But they weren't looking for the sun. After several anxious minutes, the lower levels of mist slipped down one side of the ridge, and Mary Rose smiled when she saw the smoke.

"We can't waste any time," said Harold calmly.

Mary Rose's smile faded, and her muscles tensed. Her eyes roamed over the jagged peaks, the frozen range, and the cold fog that still jealously protected the mountain. Eventually, her gaze came to rest again on the gray smoke winding its way to the heavens.

"How far away do you think it is?"

"Maybe five miles—"

"Five miles!" exclaimed Mary Rose. Even though her knee felt better than the previous day, she couldn't even imagine how difficult the journey would be.

"It's not that far, Rose."

"It's not just the distance, Harold. What might we find on the way?" She paused. "What if we don't make it?"

Harold glanced at the backpack they had prepared the night before that was leaning against the sofa. There was no survival gear, supplies, or equipment inside that would help them trek through the snow and ice. The beat-up bag held only a couple of blankets, a change of dry clothes, a flashlight, a handful of nuts, and a canteen of water.

"We've made it so far, haven't we?" he said, trying to sound confident.

But deep down, he wasn't sure about the expedition either. He didn't know what was behind the mountains—he didn't even know if they would make it to the mountains. But what other choice did they have?

When they opened the front door, a gust of arctic air swept snow in from the porch. Mr. and Mrs. Grapes stepped out of the house, and Mary Rose closed the door slowly, as if she hadn't quite made up her mind to do so. The familiar sound of the latch clicking made her pause. Then she filled her lungs with air and followed the tracks Harold left in the virgin snow on the porch. Mary Rose felt a stab in her right knee as she was going down the stairs. The swelling was mostly gone, and she had told Harold the pain was too. But it wasn't.

"Ready?" Harold's voice was muffled by the scarf covering his face.

Mary Rose simply nodded, attempting to mask the pain and fear she felt upon seeing the barren, icy plateau in front of them. Her first step sank her old fishing boots more than a foot into the fluffy snow. With difficulty, they started across the expanse that lay between them and the base of the mountain. Each step forward, the snow got deeper. They were soon breathing heavily, and the cold penetrated their woolen scarves.

Mary Rose's foot got stuck; she lost her balance and fell, facedown. The jolt that shot through her knee was so painful she hardly noticed she was in the snow. Harold hurried to help her but also lost his balance, and he went down too. It didn't take long for the moisture to find its way through the gaps in their clothes. Standing clumsily while bracing his feet in the snow, Harold helped Mary Rose up.

She managed to get to her feet, but her knee throbbed angrily. As his wife fought back tears, Harold looked at her with concern. He brushed the snow off her coat, pants, and hat.

"We can go back."

Mary Rose turned toward the house and saw they hadn't covered much more than a quarter of a mile. She couldn't believe it had taken so much effort to go such a short distance. She felt exhausted and uncoordinated. What she really wanted was to turn around. But she knew they couldn't. If they were going to survive, they needed to act, to follow the dancing wisp of smoke to its origin and seek help.

"I'm fine. Let's keep going."

They resumed their trek, slowly making headway across the soft snow. Harold stayed close to Mary Rose, attentive to her progress and the look of pain on her face with each step she took.

As they approached the base of the mountain, the wind threw up a sharp spray of frost that stuck to their clothing.

The snow became more compacted, and the terrain began to ascend. At first, Harold was happy he no longer sank into the snow, but then the snow changed to ice, and it was difficult to gain any traction.

Mary Rose grew more anxious with each step, constantly fearful of slipping on the treacherous, icy incline. The pain in her knee now was just one of many. But she pressed on.

After several hours, the slope got steeper still, requiring them to lean forward and slow their pace. Harold looked up and saw the distant wisp of smoke appear and disappear behind the rugged crags above them. He was worried. They had covered a lot of ground, but it felt like the swirling gray line was just as far away as when they had started.

They reached the top of a large crag and stopped to rest. Sitting on some rocks to stay off the snow, they ate a few nuts and drank water that was beginning to solidify from the canteen. Below them, the plain fanned out to the sea. Through the heavy banks of fog, they saw a smudge of yellow. A yellow house that stood out against the whiteness.

Harold and Mary Rose were weak and sore, and they were amazed to see the distance they'd covered.

"It seems so small from up here," said Harold.

Mary Rose had never seen her house from above. It looked out of place—seeming to cry out in the middle of the nothingness. A tiny yellow dot testifying to its own smallness and that of a world it had miraculously escaped, brazenly contrasting with the immensity of the current setting. She felt more vulnerable than ever. She couldn't fathom how they had left their peaceful life in San Remo to find themselves in such circumstances. Had it not been for the biting wind lashing her face or the pain in her knee, she would have thought she was asleep having a terrible nightmare. She turned to look for the smoke, straining to see the gray smudge through the snow. At that moment, she realized there was no turning back. If they didn't find the source of the fire before their strength was exhausted, and before nightfall, they would perish. Going back to the house was no longer an option.

Harold got up from the rock, and they continued walking in silence. His eyes were two slits of frost, and a thick layer of snow and ice covered his shoulders and backpack. He was aware that Mary Rose had slowed down and was increasingly hunched over. He too moved more clumsily with every step. His legs felt like tree trunks, and a harsh cough tore at his lungs. Although the smoke seemed to be dissipating, it also seemed closer. The thought gave him strength. They couldn't waver; they must go on.

His eyes glued to the ground, he didn't notice a rock jutting out into the narrow pass and was violently yanked to a stop.

"Are you OK?" exclaimed Mary Rose.

A swift and penetrating cold pierced his side. He saw a long gash in his coat. "Just snagged my coat," Harold said between coughs.

Mary Rose looked concerned. His cough didn't sound good. She inhaled deeply and with torpid hands, pulled the blankets out of their bag.

"Here," she said, offering one to Harold. "Put this on."

They wrapped the blankets around themselves like capes and, holding tightly to the ends so the wind wouldn't snatch them away, set out once more.

The snow was getting deeper again, and their steps became slower and heavier.

Mary Rose didn't know how long they'd been walking, but it was clear they couldn't go much farther.

After a while, they needed to rest. The wind was getting stronger by the minute, and even seeking shelter behind a small crag did not protect them from the blowing snow. They took out the remaining nuts and decided to eat half. They opened the canteen, and the icy water froze their throats. Harold and Mary Rose looked at each other, worn out. They couldn't give up.

Harold searched for the wisp of smoke, but the snow made it difficult to see anything. Daylight was fading, but after a few seconds of panic when they thought they had lost the trail, the signal reappeared so close it took their breath away.

No Return

Euphoria spread through his body like fire, reviving his stiff muscles and infusing his weakened spirits with hope. Mary Rose ignored the constant throbbing that hammered her right knee, focusing instead on moving as quickly as possible through the snowstorm that was unleashing its fury against the mountain. A blast of wind ripped off Harold's blanket, but he didn't stop; his long strides carried him in a straight line toward the smoke.

Around them, the rocks rose higher, and the dissipating trace of smoke was lost. Harold couldn't make out anything through the thick snow that pummeled him, but he was certain they were skirting the final rocks that were concealing the smoke.

And then they saw it. The thin line of gray smoke they had been following for hours appeared some hundred yards in front of them, swirling weakly in the unrelenting wind and snow.

Harold took Mary Rose by the arm, and they broke into something like a run. They could see almost nothing in the swirling snow and fading light. They called out to announce their presence, but the icy wind drowned them out.

Harold's foot struck the circle of rocks that ringed the campfire. Inside were the dying embers of a fire about to burn out. Harold and Mary Rose anxiously scanned the area, but now snow was falling so hard, all they saw was white on white. Harold felt his initial surprise turn to panic. He didn't understand. Where were the people who had built the fire?

"Hello?" shouted Harold. "Is anyone here?"

A blast of wind swept through the empty expanse, extinguishing the last embers crackling in the snow.

Mary Rose walked a few feet from the campfire to a rock overhang, hoping to catch sight of someone, but under the shelter of the rock she found only a tattered blanket half-buried in the snow. She felt dizzy, confused by the white darkness closing in on them. Her legs began to buckle, no longer able to bear her weight.

"We're too late," she said before collapsing.

Her hands and knees drove into the snow, an unbearable, raging pain emanating from her knee until her whole body was convulsing. She screamed in agony and despair as Harold ran to her, tripping over mounds of snow. He knelt and pulled her to him, wrapping her tightly in his arms while tears streamed from her eyes and froze on her cheeks.

"Please! We need help!" But Harold was racked by coughs that cut him off. His chest was seized with pain, a burning pain that scraped through his lungs. "I was so wrong," he murmured to himself. "Why did I insist we leave?"

Harold tried to help Mary Rose up, but neither of them could stay on their feet. Clumsily, he helped her get closer to the cold walls of the rock shelter, where they could huddle together. Harold dropped down next to Mary Rose. He was too exhausted to bear the weight of regret growing inside him. The black guilt that had festered all these years spread like poison through his system. He had sworn never again to put another's life in danger because of his irresponsibility. Now, it seemed, he had made the same mistake.

A whirlwind of snow stirred the ashes in the campfire and scattered them across the pristine canvas. The ashes landed near them. It didn't matter. Harold shouted again, but his voice only echoed against the rock walls that surrounded them. He struggled to open the backpack, managing to retrieve the canteen, but the remaining water was frozen solid. The expedition was a failure. They had traversed miles of snow and ice only to find a deserted camp. Now they were defenseless and too exhausted to return home. He looked at the sky and was gripped with terror when he saw that night was closing in on them.

Then Harold's eyes fell on the tattered blanket. When he pulled on it, a squeal came from inside the folds. Mary Rose opened her dull eyes. Harold tugged harder on the blanket, freeing the fabric. He found a little seal curled up inside. The animal clumsily righted itself and began to cry. A black spot covered one eye, and its belly was red from a deep wound. It was the seal pup that had escaped the polar bear attack. Mary Rose showed no response as the seal slipped over the snow and hid under the blanket on Harold's lap.

"Get off me!" Harold yelped, pushing it away.

But the seal worked its way back under the blanket. Harold felt its little body trembling, and the blood from its wound stained his coat. He couldn't bring himself to push it away again. Mary Rose looked at him as if she hadn't registered the presence of the seal. With an exhausted smile, she closed her heavy eyelids. Her pale face and purplish lips scared Harold. He removed the extra clothing from the backpack and awkwardly spread it over her, then pressed against her. Mary Rose's body felt like dead weight, and he was terrified. He shook her to wake her, but she didn't move. She didn't open her eyes. Harold tried to yell, but he couldn't. His body was gripped by a heavy, painful sleepiness, forcing his eyes to shut against his will. He felt defeated, drowning in the certainty that he would die attended by pain and regret, without having told Mary Rose all he longed to say.

Finally, the cold ceased to bother him, and Harold felt a warm yellow light caress his face. With Mary Rose and Dylan by his side, he stood on the recently varnished deck of the ship he'd built, watching in silence as the sun sank forever into the unfathomable sea.

The Ship Without a Name

No matter how hard Harold tried, he couldn't open his eyes, move his extremities, or emit a sound. He sensed only a cold sweat rolling down his temple and a cacophony of noises blending with the roar of the waves and thunder. His body floated; then suddenly he felt dry. A weak light filtered through his eyelids.

"Dylan?" he whispered.

As he said the name, he felt the wave slam the side of the boat. He felt the inertia of his body as he plunged into the water and saw his son's face, illuminated by the yellow glow and looking at him serenely a second before his whole world was submerged in icy blackness.

In front of him materialized a head of tangled brown hair and bloodshot green eyes that seemed to look right through him. Harold knew it was his wife, but there was nothing of her left in those eyes. This was the shell of an empty, lifeless woman drowning in infinite suffering. And kneeling next to her, he felt the pain ensnaring him too. He started to weep.

The image blurred, but the pain in his chest was sharp. He noticed the gentle swing of his arms and wet grass under his feet. As he walked, his fingers brushed against the brown leaves on the withering grapevines around him, knocking them to the ground. The ocean breeze carried icy raindrops that fell on him, but he didn't care. The cold was the only sensation that assured him he was still alive.

His feet paused just at the bottom of the slope. In a few more steps, the green grass abruptly stopped. It was the border between land and sea, the cliff of life as well as the cliff of death. Apprehensively, he looked up. He saw the indifferent sea stretching from infinity up to the craggy rock of the cliff.

"I hate you!" he shouted wildly.

He glanced over at the old shipyard. A tall mast towered above the dilapidated structure, the mast of the ship that needed only a name to be ready to set sail. He felt sick and had to sit down on the moldy ground that was overrun by grapevines. He lay back and closed his eyes, allowing himself to be swallowed by the twisted branches, wishing he could bury all his pain in this putrefying land.

The warmth of the sun woke him. When he opened his eyes, he saw the sunlight filtering through the rotting timber in the shipyard. Before him rose a ship under construction, and the pain grew. The hammer and nails were right where he had left them, as were the bundles of boards and buckets of tar. Everything was covered by a thin layer of dust, the place frozen in time, an embalmed, hollow, artificial version of what it had been. The joy, motivation, and aspiration to fulfill a dream had vanished without a trace. These timbers only tortured him with reminders of what he had lost.

Something creaked. Turning, he realized he wasn't in the shipyard anymore, but in their small San Remo apartment. Coming through the door was a man with greasy black hair and bleak eyes like a crow, looking at him smugly.

"This can't go on," said the man with an irritating voice. "If you don't pay your rent, I'll have to throw you out."

"You can't do that to us," whispered Harold.

"The apartment is mine, and I can do whatever I want," he spat through his rodent-like teeth.

"We just need a little more time."

"Don't get me wrong. I know what you're going through, but people in town are starting to talk. This crazy idea of building a boat, leaving the island, and sailing around the world! Nothing good can come of it. People like us weren't made for that kind of life. So put the rumors to rest and get back to work. Pay your rent already. And forget about these ridiculous fantasies!"

Harold sighed. He closed the door and went to the tiny window in the dining room. He looked up at Death Cliff, high and defiant and withstanding the powerful ocean's constant aggression. That precipitous strip of land was the only thing he had inherited from his family. He knew the plot, overgrown with unattended vines, was too far from town for anyone to want to purchase it. His eyes misted over, and he knew what they had to do.

His tears turned to sweat. Sweat that ran down his bare back. He looked up; the midday sun shone on the skeleton of a house under construction. The thick rafters that at one time had supported the frame of their ship now supported the roof. Boards from the extensive deck were now floors. The gunwale railing had been converted to the stairway banister. And the mainmast, the great spar that had soared high over the sailboat, was now the central support beam that ran through the house, holding it together.

Harold left his hammer on a pile of wood and walked toward the cliff. The house was surrounded by a carpet of new mauve-and-fuchsia hydrangeas that Mary Rose had planted. Gradually, they were overtaking the twisted, dying grapevines. Harold reached the edge of the rock and felt the soft breeze blowing in from the ocean, drying his sweat. He looked with some bitterness at the cluster of houses in San Remo. He avoided looking at the old shipyard and rested his eyes on the vast sea in front of him. A white patch captured his attention. It was a sailboat slowly raising its sails to harness the winds and travel far from the island. A small dot floating on the broad expanse. He imagined the three of them on the deck, looking back fondly at the island as they gradually slipped away, off to live their dream and embrace the freedom that unfolded before them. Harold felt his insignificance, the insignificance of humanity. Turning back to the house, he wondered if the price they had paid for renouncing their dreams hadn't been too high. Then a dazzling white light flooded everything around him.

The Encounter

As Harold's eyes adjusted to the light, he made out a whitish patch moving near him. He didn't know where he was; his brain was still on the cliff, but his body told him otherwise. A stabbing pain was boring into his temples. His breathing was shallow, and he scarcely had the strength to blink. Bit by bit, he began to remember the cold, snow, and wind, and he truly thought he was dead.

Slowly, he turned his head to the side. It took a few seconds to focus on what he saw. Mary Rose was lying next to him. Her cheekbones stuck out prominently, as did her narrow, sharp nose. Her cracked lips were as white as her skin, and there was dried blood in the corners of her mouth. Harold couldn't hear her breathing, and fear produced enough energy for him to shake his wife.

"Rose."

He was overcome by a coughing fit, and an intense burning sensation spread through his chest. Mary Rose opened her eyes and sat up with a start. Her accelerated breathing and bulging eyes gave her the look of one who had just fled the gates of death. She looked around in distress, not knowing if what she was seeing was real or part of a dream. But physical pain convinced her she was no longer sleeping.

Harold managed to stifle his coughing and moved closer to his wife. Mary Rose looked at him as if she were seeing a ghost. His skin was nearly transparent and purplish smudges outlined eyes sunken from hunger. If she'd had the strength, she would have cried.

"Where are we?" she asked, looking around in confusion.

They began to examine their surroundings. A dirty, heavily patched white tarp was shaking in the wind only inches above their heads. Attached to its corners were four thick, rough wooden poles. These were buried in what looked to be a wall of ice and snow, no more than two feet high, that surrounded the area on three of its four sides. The ground was cold, but rough boards served as a floor to keep them off the snow. A strong animal scent permeated the space; it was coming from the thick hides piled underneath them like a mattress. Harold looked around for the backpack but found nothing hiding among the blankets. All they had were their coats and boots.

Despite their extreme weakness, they were relieved to be out of the wind and snow. And even though they didn't know where they were or who had brought them there, Mr. and Mrs. Grapes stared at each other in amazement: they had been saved.

"I thought it was the end." Mary Rose's voice trembled.

"Oh, Rose," whispered Harold weakly.

Mary Rose tried to smile but only managed a strange grimace. Harold wrapped his trembling arms around his wife in a loving embrace. They remained that way for a long time, too tired to do anything but hold each other and keep breathing. Then they heard the crunch of snow.

"What was that?" whispered Mary Rose.

Mr. and Mrs. Grapes shifted nervously on the hides and stared at the tattered material shaking around them. Then the crunching stopped.

Harold was about to speak when the noise resumed. Mary Rose looked worriedly at him, but Harold's attention was focused on the tarp. The sound was just outside, and Mary Rose squeezed Harold's arm with what little strength she had left when she saw a shadow projected on the mended covering.

Then the semitransparent sheet was pulled aside.

Mary Rose gasped, and her nails dug into Harold's skin like claws. Neither of them moved.

A man appeared before them. Harold and Mary Rose could hardly remember the last person they'd seen before their house plunged from the cliff and they began their voyage across the ocean. They suddenly felt like they had spent their entire lives adrift.

Yet seeing this man's face imbued them with a strange sense of intimacy and familiarity. It was like hearing the melody of an old song they hadn't heard for years and thought they'd forgotten. Harold and Mary Rose couldn't stop looking at the man's weather-beaten brown face. Mary Rose took a gulp of air and slowly exhaled, as if she could finally breathe after having been underwater a long time. She slowly relaxed her grip on Harold, and her heart rate returned to normal.

"Who . . . who are you?" Harold stammered.

The man removed the hood of his fur parka, further revealing dark eyes and severe features. He looked at them with an expression as cold as ice. He didn't answer.

"Where are we?" Mary Rose's voice was soft.

A gust of wind blew through the opening, and snowflakes swirled furiously inside the tiny tent. Harold began to cough violently, but the man wasn't moved. He impassively observed them from the entrance while Mary Rose rubbed Harold's back. Finally, the fit subsided.

"You're the one who rescued us?" Harold's voice was hoarse.

The man remained silent.

"You don't know how grateful we are." Harold hoped to soften the man's expression. "We've been lost at sea for a long time, and we need help to return—" He was interrupted by another coughing fit.

Mary Rose pleaded with the man. "Could you help us get home?" she whispered, holding the man's gaze.

"I don't think"—Harold attempted between coughs—"he understands us."

There was something in the man's icy expression that Mary Rose couldn't put her finger on. Suddenly, he made a move for something behind him. Harold and Mary Rose instinctively recoiled. The man didn't like their reaction. His thick black brows bunched together even tighter, and he began to speak sharply to them. Mr. and Mrs. Grapes didn't understand anything he was saying. Despite their efforts, they couldn't make out a single word. Mary Rose felt her heart begin to race, and all the relief she had felt turned to fear.

Finally, the man quieted down, giving them a final look of scorn. He brought forth what he had behind his back, grudgingly leaving it at Harold's feet. It was a plate of food and a bowl of water. Mr. and Mrs. Grapes had no time to react. The man had already turned and yanked the plastic covering closed. A moment later, his footsteps were lost in the snow, and silence filled the tent. Mary Rose burst into tears.

Harold locked his sore arms around Mary Rose and held her until her trembling eventually subsided.

A putrid smell filled the claustrophobic space that confined them. Harold looked at the grayish concoction the man had left and found it was the source of the stench. He picked it up and felt even more dejected when he saw the moldy, shapeless mass in the dish.

Their stomachs were so empty they didn't dare waste the opportunity to eat. Attempting to ignore the repulsive flavor, they slowly consumed the strange food, cleaning the plate. The water helped wash it down, but the bad taste in their mouths stemmed from more than just the food.

Harold felt his chest burning like hot coals and suppressed the urge to cough. But the cough came over him again. It was several minutes before he recovered, and then a residual pain remained lodged in his chest. Harold tried to conceal his discomfort, lying back on the rough hides to catch his breath. He was exhausted, and his eyes were burning under his eyelids; he could hardly keep them open.

Mary Rose looked at him with concern and lay down next to him. She slipped her arm around him the best she could and concentrated on ignoring the piercing pain in her knee. The rotten smell of food mixed with that of the animal skins, and the wind continued to buffet the stiff plastic over their heads.

In spite of everything, they both fell asleep.

The Middle of Nowhere

The plastic tarp rattling in the wind woke Harold. He didn't know how long he'd been asleep, but the light bathing the interior of the tent was a pale purple. Sitting up, he found the burning sensation in his chest had diminished. Suddenly, he felt an overwhelming urge to urinate. He needed to get out of the tent but at the same time questioned if he should. The frigid wind never stopped shaking the shelter. Raging snow smacked the tarp, at times blowing in. Harold noticed one of the support poles was wobbling wildly. How was the haphazard structure still standing? Careful not to wake Mary Rose, he slid over the fur skins and moved to where the man had opened the tarp. His legs were so numb, all he could do was drag them behind him. When he arrived at the opening, he was already tired, as if he had gone on a long hike.

He felt pressure and knew he couldn't wait much longer, so he moved closer to the exit, then paused. Quietly, he listened for any sound that would let him know if someone was lurking nearby. He couldn't hold it any longer—he had to go.

He began to push aside the tattered tarp, trying not to make any noise, but every movement in the folds of the stiff plastic rustled loudly. Harold turned his head to see that Mary Rose was stirring, but her breathing remained deep and heavy. He pushed the sheet farther to the side and snowflakes swirled in. The air temperature dropped, and Mary Rose woke up.

"Harold?" she murmured with her eyes still half-closed, not fully comprehending where she was.

Harold sighed deeply and closed the plastic sheet. "I have to go out for a moment. I need to go to the bathroom."

Mary Rose struggled to a seated position. Her hair looked like a rat's nest, partially tumbling down the back of her neck. Her eyes were so swollen, Harold could just make out a hint of green iris.

"It's too cold to go out." Her voice was thick and heavy.

"I'll only be a moment." Harold began to open the tarp.

Mary Rose grabbed his arm. "What about the man?"

Harold stopped. It was a question he had been asking himself since he'd woken up.

"Rose, if he wanted to harm us, do you think he would have bothered saving us?"

Mary Rose looked at him apprehensively. Harold turned back and opened the flap all the way. As he stuck his head out, a blast of wind threw razor-sharp frost at him and blew through the gaps in his coat, transporting him back to the snowy hell they had walked through almost to their deaths. All the hair on his body stood on end, and his vision blurred briefly.

"Do you see anything?"

Harold didn't respond. He was confused. It looked like they were alone in the middle of that inhospitable wilderness. He felt the pressure on his bladder getting worse; he couldn't wait another second. Gathering courage, he got up. He stood for a moment, but the wind swept across the plain, and he fell to his knees.

"Harold!"

Mary Rose struggled to get up; the sharp pain in her knee made her collapse along with Harold. She breathed deeply and clenched her teeth to keep from crying out in pain. Looking up, she saw the harsh plain.

Nothing but miles and miles of compacted snow and ice that spread out in front of them like a frozen sea. Like the sea that had carried them here, full of the same solitude and despair.

Harold's head spun; he couldn't understand.

"Where'd the man go?" asked Mary Rose, staring into the empty distance.

Harold looked at her anxiously. Confused by the question and terrified by the answer. "I think he left us."

Dying Winds

Like two battered marionettes, Harold and Mary Rose struggled against the layer of snow that covered them to return to a standing position. The wind slithered like tongues of white fire across the smooth surface of the barren and desolate landscape in front of them. They fought to stay on their feet and keep their eyes open. The piercing cold penetrated deep inside them all over again, freezing even their thoughts and words. The pressure on his bladder brought Harold back to the present, but he couldn't move. His feet felt welded to the crust of ice and snow. He raked his gaze over the plain, hoping to see something that broke the monotony. But there was nothing. Only white.

Mary Rose grabbed Harold's arm and stepped forward. As they turned to study the landscape behind them, frost flew at them as if trying to tear them apart. The ratty shelter continued to rustle and shake. Mary Rose closed her eyes to protect them from the razor-sharp needles of ice. The icy wind ran through her hair, whipping it like it was a tattered flag.

"Why did he rescue us?" Mary Rose wondered aloud.

Harold looked with concern at his wife's purple lips, her papery skin, and the bones protruding from her face. He held on to her, not knowing what to say. He was desperately confused and dispirited.

"Let's go back in." Harold supported Mary Rose so she wouldn't lose her balance and fall on the tent.

Harold bent down and pushed aside the opening. Mary Rose looked around her one last time, and something caught her eye.

"Harold! I saw something!"

Harold immediately returned to her side. Minutes passed, but they saw nothing.

"I'm sure something was there." Mary Rose's eyes remained fixed on a bank of snow that kept changing shape in the wind.

"Maybe it was . . ."

Harold couldn't finish his thought; he was seized by violent coughs. Mary Rose pulled him against her. Then the wind subsided.

Harold regained control over his coughing fit and eventually looked up. A comforting ray of morning sun filtered through the dissipating clouds, tinging the expanse of snow with a warm pink patina. The sun shone in the distance, a perfect circle of light. Harold and Mary Rose could feel the delicate rays warming them, easing the ice, desperation, and loneliness. Finally seeing the sun again momentarily made them feel like they were safely back home, like it was the reassuring beacon of a lighthouse after long, desperate nights lost in a storm. The brume continued to disperse. In front of them, illuminated by the intense red hue of dawn, they saw a large grouping of mounds rising out of the snow.

Isolation

"Where are we?"

Harold didn't know how many times they had asked that question since being torn from San Remo, but every time the question was posed, the answer was different and always strange.

What they did know was that they weren't alone. In fact, their shelter, although it was located a good distance from the others, was one of many in this inhospitable wilderness. The structures looked like rounded shells, crowded together as if protecting each other from the cold, practically camouflaged by the snow accumulated on top. Sunlight blinded them, and Harold shielded his eyes with his hand. At that moment, he was reminded again he had yet to empty his bladder.

"I really need to go." Harold walked away from Mary Rose.

A faint smile came to Mary Rose's lips as she contemplated the impossible task of finding privacy in the middle of the empty landscape and from relief in knowing they were no longer alone. Even though they knew nothing about the people living here, returning to San Remo felt like a real possibility.

A few minutes later, Harold staggered back to her side, coughing.

"Let's go back in," said Mary Rose.

"What? We need to find out who lives there."

As she looked at the settlement, Mary Rose didn't see any sign of movement; everything seemed hidden under the vast layer of snow. The harsh tone of the man who had come to their tent came to mind, and she shivered. "I don't think that's a good idea. We should wait for someone to come to us."

Harold shook his head. "I don't want to wait. We've got to know if they can help us get back home, Rose."

"But we don't know what we'll find. It would be better to rest a little longer."

Harold furrowed his brow. "If you don't want to go, you can wait here. But the only way to know if we can get back to San Remo is to talk to them."

Mary Rose continued studying the camouflaged homes but couldn't see anything. She sighed and looked nervously at Harold. He was right, of course.

"Fine," she said. "But let's just keep to the outside and observe first, before asking for help. Let's see if we can get an idea about who lives here."

They began walking toward the encampment. Mary Rose's heart rate quickened with each step. She didn't know where in the world they were or who inhabited the area. She hadn't determined if what she had seen in the man's eyes was hospitality or hostility. She tried to stop thinking and concentrated on each step so she wouldn't lose her balance. They were a little over halfway across the open area separating them from the camp when she had to stop and catch her breath. Her knee still wasn't strong enough to be walking.

Harold moved to her side and helped her keep going. They inched forward one step at a time. Mary Rose's knee was aching, but she concealed her condition and concentrated on the huts that were getting closer.

Finally, the first of the many shelters was in front of them. It was one of the smallest. A dark spot of brown hide sticking out of a mound of snow. It looked like it would be a tight fit for one person lying down. As they moved on, the huts increased in size, some even big enough to stand and walk around in. Some shelters were as small and low as theirs, built with three long poles that joined in the center; others were circular. A couple stood above the rest. They had several long poles that supported a roof in the form of a canopy about ten feet high and wide enough to shelter a whole family.

A plastic tarp covered their tent, but these sturdy wooden frames were covered with animal skins of different textures and colors: long, stiff brown fur; gray with black patches; short, dirty white fur . . . all the tents had been repeatedly patched and mended, some with hides worn smooth. Taut guy wires were attached to the tops of the larger tents and anchored in the snow. They reminded Harold of the metal cables he had installed to stabilize their house.

But as they circled the settlement, Harold and Mary Rose detected no sign of life. They didn't hear any voices or footsteps; they didn't even see any sign of a fire. All they heard was the creaking of their own boots, their own agitated breathing, and the howling wind blowing over the tents.

"This silence makes me nervous," whispered Mary Rose.

As Harold started to answer, a tickle rose in his throat that felt like an army of tiny ants stirring, and he began to cough violently. Mary Rose drew him close.

"I told you this wasn't a good idea; we're not strong enough yet," she murmured as she looked around anxiously.

Harold had to hold on to Mary Rose to keep from collapsing as his coughing continued unabated.

"We should go back," she said quietly, placing Harold's arm over her shoulders.

They began to retrace their steps, when suddenly, Harold's coughing fit was interrupted by a shriek.

They stopped dead in their tracks.

"What was that?" whispered a terrified Mary Rose.

A pearl-gray shape zipped around a hut and came barreling right toward them. Startled, Mary Rose stepped back, tripping on one of the cords attached to a tent. Harold tried to catch her but also lost his balance, and they both fell into deep snow.

The fall sent a sharp pain through Mary Rose's knee, and for a moment, she didn't know what was happening. Harold was looking at her anxiously when a ball of gray fur pounced.

"Get it off, Harold!"

Harold flailed, trying to get up. His coughing stopped him, but then he had to resist the urge to laugh at the sight of his wife's panicked face.

"It's just a seal, Rose."

Mary Rose got up with Harold's help, clenching her jaw tightly to fight the pain in her leg. She looked down and saw a little seal yipping shrilly at their feet.

"Shhh," Harold said.

But the pup refused to quiet down. On the contrary, it seemed more distressed, and its barks got increasingly loud and shrill.

"Let's go, Harold. With all this commotion, someone will be here any minute."

But Harold didn't move. He was staring at the animal wriggling around them. "It's the same seal."

Uneasy, Mary Rose ignored the pup, looking instead for someone to appear. When she finally looked down at the animal, she saw it had a black spot over its right eye and a fresh pink scar running across its ribs.

"It's the baby seal that escaped from the polar bear," she murmured in disbelief.

"And that huddled in our laps before we lost consciousness."

Mary Rose remembered when they had fallen in the snow, all alone, completely sapped of energy. She had been sure it was the end. She had noticed the ball of fur next to her, but she had been too exhausted to be afraid. After that, everything went dark.

Mary Rose looked again at the small animal as it wiggled around her feet like a cat looking for attention. Suddenly, the crunch of footsteps put her on guard.

Harold and Mary Rose turned and were surprised to see a little girl. She stood frozen in her tracks, her dark eyes looking at them in fear. Her face was framed by a white fur hood that contrasted with her dark complexion. Her clothing was bulky, made of the same type of hides used for the shelters, and she held a small wicker basket. Mary Rose guessed she couldn't be more than six years old.

Mr. and Mrs. Grapes looked at each other without moving, not knowing what to do.

"Hello," said Mary Rose, trying to appear calm.

The little girl's eyes widened. She retreated, dropping the basket. Two small silvery fish and a rudimentary, child-size fishing pole tumbled onto the soft snow. The seal pup pounced on the fish and devoured them. Mary Rose stepped forward and, being careful of her knee, picked up the basket and fishing pole and held them out.

"We won't hurt you," Mary Rose said soothingly.

The girl screamed and ran back the way she'd come. Mary Rose glanced at Harold, not knowing what to do; then she followed the girl, Harold trailing behind her.

"Wait!" she called breathlessly.

Mary Rose moved through the snow, following the girl's tracks around some low shelters and emerging at the edge of a clearing in front of the two largest ones. Carefully avoiding the guy wires, Harold and Mary Rose went around the tent, following the girl's terrified cries. Then they stopped in astonishment.

Behind the tent was a sled with several dogs milling around. They began to bark, startling the people around them. The little girl ran to a middle-aged woman cloaked in light-colored hides. Her long black hair flowed out from either side of her hood like two symmetrical waterfalls. An adolescent with the beginning of a beard stood next to the heavy dogsled and held tightly to the reins. Eyeing them harshly from his position on the sled was the man who had brought them food the night before.

The dogs' loud barking and growling intermingled with the high-pitched yipping of the seal as it came toward them across the clearing. The little girl called the animal to her, but instead it rushed to Harold's and Mary Rose's feet. At a stern look from the man, the teenager quieted the dogs, and moments later, a tense silence reigned. More people emerged from surrounding tents. Adults, young and old, and children slowly crowded around them. Some appeared curious, others suspicious. Harold calculated about twenty people in all. Mary Rose realized she still held the little basket and tiny fishing pole. Her body was on the verge of collapse, but she made her way toward the little girl, with Harold anxiously observing her painful advance. The man scowled at Mary Rose.

"We didn't mean to frighten her," she said, looking for an understanding face. "We just wanted to find out where we are."

Mary Rose stopped a couple feet away and held out the pole for the little girl to take. Uncertain of what to do, the child looked at the woman she was holding on to. Mary Rose guessed it was her mother. Then the woman said something, and the little girl took a hesitant step forward and quickly took the fishing pole from Mary Rose. With all eyes on her, Mary Rose stepped back and bent down to leave the basket on the ground. When she stood up again, her knee gave way with an audible crunch, and she collapsed, landing facedown in the snow.

"Rose!" Harold ran to her.

The woman made a move to help, but the man shouted something that made her stop. With what little strength he had left, Harold bent down to help his wife up. The seal slid over to them and resumed its shrill barking, wriggling around them nervously.

"What's wrong?"

"It's nothing." Mary Rose tried not to grimace. "I just didn't have the strength."

"Let me see."

"Really, it's nothing."

Harold helped his wife sit and gently rolled up her pant leg. He was shocked to see her knee so red and swollen. Mary Rose quickly covered it up and avoided her husband's eyes. Harold looked up at the woman who had wanted to help. In her face, he thought he saw understanding and concern.

"Please, could you help us?" His voice shook.

The woman looked uneasy. She turned and, after whispering something, entered the large structure. The others also retreated as swiftly as they had appeared. Only the little girl, the adolescent boy, and the man remained. Harold looked at him, hoping for some compassion, but found only indifference. Frustration rose in Harold and boiled over.

"We just want to go home!" he shouted.

The strain of yelling caused more painful coughing to rip through his chest. The man said something, and the girl sat down in the sled next to him. He gave them one more look of contempt and then, without a word, whistled loudly. The dogs began to pull, and the long blades scraped against the snow as the sled started sluggishly. The boy pushed from behind, running faster as the sled gained speed. Finally, he jumped gracefully onto the sled and sat with the man and little girl as the dogs sped them across the plain.

Harold and Mary Rose were alone again, silently watching as the sled got smaller and smaller, until it disappeared in the thick fog rising to cover the golden rays of the sun. For a second, the little girl turned to look at them curiously. Harold's coughing ceased, and Mary Rose helped him up. The barking of the seal brought them out of their reverie. With slow, exhausted steps, they began the trek back to their tiny refuge, not having learned anything about where they were or who had rescued them. They felt as alone and isolated as they had on the open sea. Loneliness was a feeling they knew all too well from living on Brent Island.

An Unexpected Visit

"You're injured." Harold stared at Mary Rose's swollen knee. Her red skin looked taut and shiny, like plastic, and purplish bruising covered the area like an inky stain. Harold tore a strip of blanket and gently tied it around Mary Rose's knee to stabilize it.

Rarely had Mary Rose seen Harold so worried. "I don't think it's serious. I just need to rest. I'll be fine in a few days."

Harold looked around the tiny tent and was filled with despair.

"How? We're not going to get any help!"

Mary Rose was at a loss. She sat up next to him, trying not to move her leg. In doing so, she felt another wave of pain, and her already pale face blanched.

"We just have to trust and be patient."

Harold sighed and tried to calm down. He thought about what Mary Rose said but then remembered the man's cold, impassive face. His anger flared again.

"They hate us," he spat.

"They saved our lives, Harold," Mary Rose replied gently, caressing his face.

"What for? To just abandon us like a couple of stray dogs?"

Mary Rose exhaled loudly, trying to control her own emotions.

"We're still condemned, Rose! In these conditions, we'll die in a matter of days!"

"And what do you think would have happened if we'd stayed in the house? By this time, we would have died from thirst or hunger. Or both. Are you now saying you'd have preferred that?" she exclaimed.

Harold clenched his jaw angrily and looked at the clumsy bandage around Mary Rose's knee. "Maybe it would have been better than this!" he bellowed, his eyes bloodshot.

Mary Rose felt as if she'd been punched. A pressure in her chest began to grow, and before it could explode, she drew Harold's head to her and held him tenderly. "Don't ever say that again," she said, repeating Harold's earlier words to her. "If we hadn't taken this chance, we never would have survived."

As she moved, pain radiated from her knee. She squeezed her eyes shut to keep the tears from spilling out, and the pair remained that way, in a silent embrace. The diffuse sunlight weakened, and the snow continued to blow up and down the sides of the tent like sand rippling on the desert. The sound transported Mary Rose back to the beach in San Remo, back before their lives had been turned upside down. She realized just how many years it had been since she'd gone to the beach. She could hardly remember the sense of freedom she used to feel swimming in the cold water. How she used to love to swim! Tears welled up as she thought of that time, so long ago. The pain in her knee seemed insignificant compared to the much deeper pain that occasionally still caught her like a sudden undertow.

Harold sighed, defeated.

He carefully helped Mary Rose lie back, and kissed her. Then he lay down too. Despite his exhaustion, he felt too anxious to sleep.

The tent seemed smaller now, more suffocating. They could hardly move without brushing their heads against the walls or their feet on the sleeping seal. The wind whistled past like a mischievous spirit. The rattling of plastic was increasingly irritating. Harold couldn't stop star-ing at the four swaying poles that held the whole thing up, fearing it would all come crashing down on them at any moment.

Then a flickering circle of amber-colored light shone on the plastic. Harold wiped his tears and sat up, his vision blurry. His movement bumped the seal. Startled, it began to yelp. Harold had completely forgotten it was there. After the animal had followed them to the tent, they'd had no choice but to give it shelter.

"What's going on?" Mary Rose sat up.

Before Harold could answer, the light caught her attention. Despite the din caused by the seal, they heard the unmistakable crunch of boots on snow. The circle of light got bigger until it illuminated the whole front of the tarp, and a second later, a thick mitten appeared and moved the flap aside.

They were momentarily blinded by the light shining in their eyes, but soon they could make out a shape holding a torch. It was the little girl's mother. The woman crouched down, stuck the handle of the torch in the snow, and placed a basket in front of the opening. Another gust of wind swept across the plain, and the flame guttered, sounding like a flag flapping in the gale. The icy air made Harold cough, but the attack only lasted a few seconds. The woman took out two steaming wooden bowls of thick, gray soup; a container of water; and a third bowl with pieces of raw fish that immediately quieted the pup. Harold and Mary Rose accepted the bowls as if they were priceless treasures. The heat from the wood transferred quickly to their icy hands, sending a tremor of pleasure through them.

"Thank you so much," said Mary Rose as she raised her eyes to meet the woman's.

The woman looked away and glanced nervously behind her. She reached again into the basket and took out a small clay pot and a thick bundle of bandages, which she held out to Mary Rose. Mary Rose took them and looked at the thick brown paste in the pot, not knowing what it was for. The woman pointed to her knee. Then swiftly gathering the basket and pulling the torch out of the snow, she disappeared again into the silence of the night.

With the tarp closed again, the tight space filled with the warm, foul-smelling steam emanating from the bowls. Harold turned to look at his wife, and he saw the corner of her cracked lips curl in a faint smile of victory. Seeing the small clay pot and the food the woman had left made him feel terribly ashamed about what he'd said.

Mary Rose raised the bowl of soup to her lips and slowly began to sip the thick liquid. Harold did the same, trying to drown out the echo of his accusations with the pleasant warmth of the soup that ran through his frozen body. When they finished, they were still hungry, but the soup and water put a little something in their bellies and provided comfort.

Then Mary Rose removed the strip of cloth from her knee and held the small pot out to Harold. He scooped out some muddy salve with his fingers and spread it on her red, swollen knee. A fresh, almost minty smell immediately began to combat the stench left by the soup, and Harold hoped that the mysterious substance would heal her knee. Taking care not to rub the ointment off her skin, he wrapped his wife's knee with the bandages. Then both lay down in the narrow space.

Mary Rose fell right to sleep. Harold turned over and gazed at his wife, her long hair covering part of her uncharacteristically haggard face. He snuggled a little closer and held her to share his warmth. He thought back to those last days they'd spent in the house before leaving to follow the trail of smoke. They were lying together on the sofa, bodies pressed close to combat the cold, just as they were now. Harold heard Mary Rose's words ringing in his ears: "And what do you think would have happened if we'd stayed in the house? By this time, we would have died from thirst or hunger. Or both." He was an idiot, ashamed of everything he had said when blinded by anger and despair. His eyes began to flood with tears, imagining what would have happened to them. They would have felt the same glittery frost that covered the walls, floors, furniture, and even their memories begin to cover them too. Life would have ebbed slowly, submerging them in a deep lethargy as they were frozen forever in death's eternal embrace.

Far from Home

A high-pitched squeal woke Harold and Mary Rose. For a moment, they were disoriented, but the seal wiggling at their feet reminded them where they were. Harold sat up sleepily and opened the front of the tent, letting the animal out. The biting cold of dawn slapped him awake. It had stopped snowing, and a layer of white stretched out infinitely before them. Mary Rose sat up next to him.

"You keep lying down." Harold carefully checked the bandage. "It's still quite swollen."

"But it doesn't hurt as much," she said with a weak smile.

Harold smiled back in relief.

After a few minutes, the pup rushed back in and hid under the blankets. Harold stuck his head through the opening to see what was happening outside.

At first, he didn't see anything unusual. But as he continued to stare through the bank of fog, a ghostlike shape emerged. Harold tensed as he saw it speeding toward them, finally emerging from the mist as a sled being pulled by a large team of dogs. Their barking reverberated over the plain, and a piercing whistle slowed them down. Mary Rose joined Harold at the opening and poked her head out.

The dogsled stopped near the settlement, and three figures hopped down. Harold and Mary Rose recognized the man, the teenager, and the little girl. The man unharnessed the dogs, shouted something, then disappeared into the frozen mist, followed by the pack. The boy unloaded some bags and crates from the sled, then followed the man's trail. The girl waited a few moments by the sled.

When the boy disappeared in the mist, the little girl jumped onto the sled and moved back and forth, unloading a couple of crates. The two boxes were bigger than she was, and she could hardly see around them. She started in the direction the men had taken. After a few steps, she stumbled and fell, spilling the contents of the boxes all over the snow.

Harold and Mary Rose flinched when they saw her go down.

"I think she's hurt," said Mary Rose, watching the girl's movements.

"Stay here. I'll go see if she's all right."

"What if the man comes back?"

"It's the least we can do," he said, looking at Mary Rose's bandaged knee.

Mary Rose began to reply, but Harold had already started across the plain. The little girl looked upset as she put things back in order. She didn't notice Harold coming toward her.

When Harold got closer, he saw the boxes contained fish. Dozens of fish were scattered across the snow like brilliant blue and silver gemstones. The crunch of snow finally alerted the girl, and when she saw Harold so close, she leaped away from the boxes and looked around, not knowing what to do.

"I just want to help," said Harold, knowing she wouldn't understand his words.

Then he bent down next to one of the boxes and began gathering the fish and putting them back in. After a few seconds of doubt, the girl came closer and, keeping an eye on him, began to fill the other box.

From inside the tent, Mary Rose watched the scene nervously, knowing the man could return at any moment.

The girl finished filling her box but dropped it again when she tried picking it up. Harold saw that her hand was bleeding. He looked around for the man or boy but didn't see them anywhere. So he stacked the two crates and picked them up himself. His muscles threatened to give out, but he forced himself not to think about it. He smiled at the girl, and, wordlessly, they began to walk together in the direction the footprints led. Mary Rose lost sight of them in the fog.

Harold felt a painful burning sensation in his emaciated muscles and slowly advanced across the snow to enter the camp. Sunshine poked through the thick layer of clouds and reflected brightly on the clearing in front of the big tent. Harold didn't see any sign of the men—or anyone else. The footprints ended in front of a small round tent. They headed there, stumbling on the loose snow, and then Harold set down the heavy load. He felt like his arms had been ripped off. When he stood up, he detected something moving behind him out of the corner of his eye. He turned and saw the man and teenager. They glowered at him.

"She hurt herself," he said, pointing to the little girl's hand and trying to explain what had happened. "I was just helping her carry the boxes."

Harold glanced at the girl, hoping for assistance, but she'd lowered her head, fixing her eyes on the snow. The man looked at her bloody hand and scowled deeper. He seemed to have gotten it all wrong. Harold didn't know what to do or say and was overwhelmed by frustration at not being able to communicate.

The man spoke to the girl in his deep voice. She slowly raised her head and, after a few moments of silence, began speaking rapidly. Harold didn't understand the words, but he guessed she was explaining what had happened. When she finished, the man turned to Mr. Grapes, but then something strange happened. His face paled and his harsh expression turned to panic as his eyes focused on something behind Harold. Harold turned slowly, confused and afraid of what he might find.

But there was nothing. Just the open plain surrounding the camp that was now outlined against an incredibly blue sky. As the clouds and heavy fog lifted, the black mountain range they had first seen from the icebound house reappeared. A long, dark-blue edge delineated the point where the ice field met the sea. Thousands of floes and icebergs leisurely floated away from the colossal glacial sheet and entered the open sea.

Anxiously, Harold scoured the barren land, not understanding what had disturbed the man so. Then he saw it. He felt his chest tighten when he spotted the yellow dot standing out from the palette of blues and whites. A yellow dot that glowed in the sunlight like a lighthouse in the dead of night. Their house.

It felt like an enormous hand was crushing his lungs as he began to cough. His face went as white as the landscape around him. He knew it hadn't been very long since they'd left, but seeing the house again in the middle of that glacial landscape made it seem like an eternity had passed. It felt like nothing he was seeing could be real. The crunch of snow behind him interrupted his thoughts. Harold controlled his coughing and turned to see more people had gathered. They were all murmuring and pointing with fear and suspicion at the faraway house stranded in the ice. He turned to the man again and saw his surprised expression had disappeared. Now his sharp eyes were filled with an anger that chilled Harold more than the icy wind. The threatening silence was palpable. He didn't know what to think, and a deep fear gripped his heart. He felt like prey surrounded by a pack of hungry wolves. Before he could move, two men had seized him by his arms.

No Words

Mary Rose was lying restlessly among the blankets in the tent, waiting for Harold's return, when the entrance of the tiny shelter was jerked open so hard part of the plastic sheet ripped along a seam. She sat up at once in alarm. She hardly felt the stab in her knee or heard the hysterical squeals of the seal. Harold burst in, scattering the snow that was stuck to his pants and boots all over the blankets.

"What took you so long? I was getting worried!"

Harold looked at the bandage protecting her knee. His forehead was lined with deep wrinkles as he looked his wife in the eye. Mary Rose trembled at the strange expression on his pale face. His eyes were bulging and jumping around like he was searching for something. His breathing was agitated, and there was a thin sheen of sweat on his forehead. Then she heard the crunch of snow outside and saw three large men bundled in hides standing in front of the tent. Mary Rose spotted the angry man and was gripped by fear. His expression was as cold as a block of ice and sharp as the frost.

"What's happening, Harold?"

"He saw the house. They've all seen it."

"The house?"

"But before I could say anything, it all went awry. They started looking at me like I was a danger to them, Rose. They grabbed me by the arms and dragged me here. I think they want us to go with them to the camp."

The man raised his deep voice and brusquely gestured for them to get out. Harold and Mary Rose glanced at each other briefly, not wanting to take their eyes off the men. They stumbled out, knowing they had no alternative. They couldn't run away, they couldn't explain anything—all they could do was follow.

Harold tried to hide his growing fear as he supported Mary Rose to keep weight off her injured knee.

"It'll be all right," he whispered.

Mary Rose heard the slight tremor in his voice. She looked at him, but he avoided her eyes.

With every step, Harold felt more tense and frustrated. They had spent so much time alone, and now that they were finally with a community of people, they felt more isolated than ever. It was a little like their self-imposed isolation on the cliff. They had always told themselves that they'd left the apartment in town to escape the pain. That financially, their only option was to dismantle the ship and build a house on the land he owned. But deep down, they knew that wasn't the case. The truth was, they could have left and gone somewhere else. Instead, they had chosen to remain on the island they so detested. Close enough to town, but far enough not to have to listen to the talk. With views of the infinite horizon they so wanted to reach, but rooted in the solid rock that kept them firmly in place. Harold now wondered if distancing themselves from the looks of reproach had served to protect them from pain or if it had only deepened it.

"What do . . . do you think they want with us?" stammered Mary Rose, trying to quiet her chattering teeth.

Mary Rose's voice brought Harold out of his musings, and he noticed they were winding their way between shelters in the settlement. Harold looked sideways at her and shrugged helplessly. He scanned each one of the huts, searching for movement.

The people who had just recently crowded around him had disappeared, and Harold wondered if perhaps they were inside, quietly awaiting a signal.

The three men directed them to one of the largest structures. Thick smoke rose from the roof and was silhouetted against the now-cloudy sky. Snowflakes began to fall on their bare heads.

The man they already knew stopped in front of the structure, and the other two walked away. Grabbing a handle, he moved a flap aside, revealing a dark interior. The man gestured with his head for them to enter. Mary Rose looked sad and a little sick as she glanced at Harold. He squeezed her hand in an effort to calm her. With all the courage he could muster, Harold faced the man and defiantly returned the same severe, glacial stare with which he had been observing them. The man was unfazed. Harold peered through the dark opening and, after a moment's hesitation, stepped through with Mary Rose.

When the man followed, the crack of light closed behind them, and for a few moments, they couldn't make out anything in the darkness. Then the man's voice broke the tense silence, clearly urging them on. Mary Rose squeezed Harold's arm.

As they stepped forward, a dense, acrid smell lodged in their frozen nostrils as their faces brushed against hanging fabric. The floor was soft, but they couldn't see what was beneath their feet.

More cloth and hides hung in front of them, blocking their path and dividing the tent into smaller rooms. Gradually, a dim reddish light emerged from the back. The room was spare, empty of furniture and objects.

The man paused in front of a thick curtain of rough fur. His figure was silhouetted by the red glow that emanated through the opening in the curtain. Trembling, Harold and Mary Rose clutched each other, their breathing ragged. The man pulled aside the curtain and passed through. Mary Rose instinctively took a step back, and it occurred to Harold they could use this split second to run. But even if they managed to get out of the tent, there would be no chance of escaping the settlement. They each took a deep breath, glanced at each other in the warm red glow, and passed through the thick curtain to the other side.

Again, it took a moment for their eyes to adjust to the change in light. Little by little, they could distinguish the intense tongues of fire that burned in the middle of a large circular room. Here, the high ceiling was reminiscent of a circus tent. The floor was covered with plush hides, like in their tiny shelter, but these hides were thicker and softer. The strong smell of smoke blended with a putrid stench coming from a black pot over a fire. Only the crackling of the flames and the undulation of the walls in the wind could be heard. Despite the welcome heat of the fire, Harold and Mary Rose were shivering. They quickly took in the fishing nets hanging from the support poles and the long knives flashing in the fire's glow. Then their eyes locked on the three people sitting by the fire. They were observing Mr. and Mrs. Grapes, their faces full of questions and suspicion. Standing together at the entrance, Harold and Mary Rose returned the look, not daring to move a muscle.

The angry man silently crossed the room and sat next to the boy they had seen unloading fish from the sled. In front of him was the woman who had brought them salve and bandages. Next to her was the girl, looking at them wide-eyed. Now inside, they were no longer wearing their voluminous hooded fur coats. They had changed into lighter, more form-fitting pieces made of fur and leather covered with bits of white fabric in geometric shapes. None seemed to be wearing adornments or other ornamentation.

The man indicated with a brusque gesture for them to sit next to the fire. They cautiously moved across the bulky collage of hides scattered on the floor. The heat of the flames reddened their cheeks, and they felt strangely feverish. Despite the sour smell of the thick, gray substance bubbling in the pot, their stomachs rumbled, tortured by hunger.

They sat hesitantly in the ample space next to the girl and stared uneasily into the fire, no longer daring to look at anyone. They could not risk offending these people. However, the family did not seem to have any qualms about studying them as if they were exotic wild animals. The man stirred on the blankets, and Harold and Mary Rose tensed, feeling like prey caught in a trap. He cleared his throat, paused, and addressed them: "Who are you?"

A Long Story

Harold and Mary Rose were floored by the revelation that the man spoke their language. Mary Rose could hear the pounding of her heart. The man's sharp eyes seemed to slice right through them as he scrutinized their reaction.

"Who are you?" he repeated with hostility.

"My name"—Harold stammered—"is Harold Grapes. This is my wife, Mary Rose."

The man narrowed his eyes and looked them over slowly, as if weighing the truth of their names. He saw the poorly concealed trembling of Mary Rose's hands and furrowed his brow angrily.

"Why are you here? What do you want with our land?"

Harold tried to remain calm. "We drifted here." Harold's answer was too vague. He felt dense, his senses muddled by the unexpected heat and extreme tension of their situation. Just as he was about to clarify, the man spoke again.

"And the house you built on the ice field?" he growled, as if trying to control the rage that was brimming over.

"What? No! We didn't build anything," Harold burst out, flustered. "The house is how we got here."

The man scowled, and Harold realized his mistake in letting his nerves get the better of him.

"That's not a ship—it's a house!" the man stated, leaning toward them. His face was red from heat and rage.

Harold was about to respond but thought better of it. He needed to pull it together and consider his answers carefully. He didn't want to sound like they were lying.

"Yes, it is a house," Mary Rose intervened shakily. "It's been our home for more than thirty-five years. Not as a ship, of course, but as a house. It was on a cliff on a remote island." She paused to collect her thoughts. "There was a terrible storm, and the edge of the cliff broke off. When we woke up, we found ourselves floating in the middle of the ocean, and since then—"

"They're lying!" the boy interrupted hotly.

The man turned his head and grunted to silence the boy, who then stared stonily into the fire. The atmosphere in the tent became even more oppressive. Then the man gestured with his chin for Mrs. Grapes to continue.

"We know it sounds crazy," she said cautiously. "But it's true."

"That's ridiculous. A house couldn't fall from a cliff and remain intact," the man interrupted.

Mary Rose didn't dare look at Harold; it would seem like she was getting help with her story. Ignoring the man's threatening gaze, she took a deep breath and continued. "Please, just listen."

But the precarious floodgates holding back the man's fury broke. He snarled at her. "I will not allow strangers to disrespect me or my family with such lies!"

As he got up, the flickering flames accentuated his threatening presence. Harold knew they had to prevent the situation from getting out of control. The man and his family would never believe them if they told the story in bits and pieces or omitted personal details and experiences. If he and Mary Rose wanted to get out of there safe and sound, the family needed to hear everything that had happened.

"If, after you've heard everything, you still don't believe us," Harold said, trying to sound as reasonable as possible, "then we'll accept whatever you want to do with us. But please, just listen."

Before the man could respond, the woman spoke for the first time. "We will listen," she said calmly, with authority.

The man gave her a ferocious look, but the woman did not back down. Her expression was not angry or sympathetic, but firm and unyielding.

"Continue," the woman prompted.

Harold and Mary Rose looked at each other and, for the first time, they realized how truly unbelievable their story was. They didn't know where to start without it all sounding like a fairy tale. This whole time, they hadn't had contact with anyone. They'd been so focused on staying alive, they'd hardly had time to reflect on what had happened to them. And now they felt adrift again, disoriented in a sea of confusing thoughts. Uncertainty and fear gripped them, and suddenly they weren't even sure if what they'd experienced was real.

"As I thought. Tall tales to make us think they mean us no harm," the man said scornfully.

Then Mary Rose's mind cleared. Her confusing thoughts fell into place, and the puzzle pieces now formed a complete picture of their story. She took a deep breath as she closed her eyes to concentrate. For a split second, she smelled the salty air that blew around their home. She began with newfound confidence. "We are Mr. and Mrs. Grapes."

Mary Rose paused. She could hear the low roar of the waves breaking against the porous rock at the base of the cliff and the raucous shrieks of the seagulls flying over the house. As she slowly opened her eyes, she met the man's questioning gaze.

"Our house, unlike the houses and shops huddled together down on the beach," she continued, "was outside of town, at the highest point on Brent Island. It was perched right on the edge of Death Cliff."

Harold took her hand gently when she arrived at the part of the story when they received the eviction notice. At that moment, the woman's impassive face cracked, revealing doubt. Mary Rose noticed and realized she probably didn't understand the concept of eviction. Mary Rose explained it the best she could and, upon seeing the woman's stoic demeanor return, continued. When she got to the night the house fell, Mary Rose felt the clarity of the story break down, and her heart raced. She explained the moment the lightning struck the house, the smoke they found coming from enormous holes in the yard, the heavy rain, and the gusting wind that buffeted them. She finally got to the moment in the story she had wanted to avoid, the part where they really couldn't explain what happened.

"We can only guess what happened then." Her tone was serious. "We think the lightning cracked the rock the house was anchored to, and the wind and rain helped loosen it from the rest of the cliff until it fell."

The man, still standing next to the fire, crossed his arms. His face, which had seemed to soften as he listened, hardened again. "Impossible!" he snorted.

"We know that nothing should have withstood that kind of fall," Mary Rose quickly acknowledged. "Yet our house did."

The man uncrossed his arms and leaned toward Mr. and Mrs. Grapes. "Even if the house did fall off the cliff," he growled, "even if it survived the impact, why didn't it sink?"

Harold saw the woman's countenance also begin to darken, and the boy knitted his brows. Mary Rose stammered something but couldn't answer. Harold decided to intervene.

"Because of the rock the house was anchored to," he said firmly.

The man's face was a mask of fury. But before he could say anything, Harold hurried on with his explanation, telling them about the volcanic composition of the island and the flotation properties of volcanic rock. He knew it was just a theory, his own understanding, but his conviction left no room for doubt. Still, Harold could see in their eyes that they didn't accept the story of a house falling off a cliff and floating aimlessly across the ocean—except for the little girl, who listened with great fascination, like she was hearing a fantastical story in which anything was possible. Harold wondered if that wasn't exactly what it was. But before he lost his train of thought, he continued. He told about the moment they opened the front door to the porch and discovered they were surrounded by ocean. He described in detail all the damage the house had suffered and about how he cut his hand on one of the rocks, showing them his scar. Although the man's face remained stoic, Harold was sure he'd seen a hint of surprise in his skeptical eyes.

After explaining the disastrous moment when they went down to the basement and discovered water leaking in through a hole in the wall, he talked about the agonizing fight to patch the hole before the whole house sank. The countless hours bailing out the basement. The desperation upon finding the cistern cracked and realizing they had no drinking water. And he recounted how he had successfully found a solution to get the desalinator working.

"Desali—what?" interrupted the teenager.

"Desalinator," Harold repeated slower.

But the boy looked unsatisfied.

"It's a water purifying machine that runs on electricity. It removes salt from the seawater to make it drinkable."

Then the boy looked at him incredulously. "And how did you get electricity in the middle of the ocean?"

Seeing a hint of curiosity in the boy's face, Harold relaxed a little. He explained in detail how he'd turned the motor and drum of the dryer into a generator. How he went through the window to install the invention and a treacherous wave knocked him into the water. The anguish at seeing the house floating farther and farther away as he was tossed by waves that repeatedly pushed him under. How he was able to survive, thanks to one of the loose cables trailing behind the house and the help of the dolphin. As he described the feeling of immense relief when he was back safe and sound on the porch deck, Mary Rose let out a gasp. Turning to her, he realized his grave mistake. His wife's face was a mask of hurt and restrained anger.

"You told me it was a wave," murmured Mary Rose.

"I didn't want to worry you, Rose."

Mary Rose turned away, then saw the looks of bewilderment from their listeners. Before Harold could continue the account, she took up the story. She told them of the majesty of the otherworldly northern lights that flashed across the sky and how the intense cold had begun to penetrate every corner of the house. She recounted the distress they felt at seeing the giant iceberg on the horizon. The horror when they realized they would be crushed by it. And the destruction it caused to their home as they somehow managed to pass through.

Then Mary Rose noticed, out of the corner of her eye, that the man, who until then had been standing, had discreetly sat down in front of the fire. Looking around at the other faces, she smiled when she saw the wide eyes of the little girl as she listened raptly to every word. When she returned to the story, Mary Rose's expression became more somber. She spoke of the hunger, thirst, and constant fear of freezing to death. When she got to the part about the house getting stranded on the ice field, she skimmed quickly over the polar bear attack on the seals and described the elation they felt upon seeing the smoke in the mountains. She concluded with the difficult decision to leave the house to search for the source of the smoke.

"What you saw was smoke from the campfire my children and I made," the man interrupted, his expression easing. "You were lucky we were hunting in the southern mountains and found you. Or rather, that my daughter, Kirima, found you."

Harold and Mary Rose diverted their gaze to the little girl, who blushed and looked down. They smiled at her.

"Thank you so much," said Mary Rose. "We owe you our lives."

The girl looked at her and shyly returned the smile. "It wasn't hard to find you," she spoke up in a melodious voice. "We could hear the *nattiq* from a long way away."

"Nattiq?"

"Nattiq means 'seal,'" the boy explained.

"When we found you, the nattiq was lying on your legs," the man continued. "I don't know how it got there, but I'm sure it bought you a few minutes, thanks to the extra warmth."

Harold remembered the seal emerging from the blanket in the snow and felt guilty for trying to chase it away. If not for that seal, he now realized, they would be dead. With the account of their ordeal concluded, neither the crackling of the embers nor the bubbling in the pot could fill the silence. But this was a different kind of silence. It was the silence of an audience taking in an incredible story and wondering if what they had heard could possibly be true.

Harold and Mary Rose knew there was nothing else they could say to prove the veracity of their story.

After a few seconds, the man looked at the woman and raised his voice again. The woman responded in their language. Harold and Mary Rose were anxious. Harold squeezed his wife's hand when he felt her trembling and turned his head to look into her eyes. Mary Rose desperately wanted to speak with Harold, but knew she had to wait. Harold and Mary Rose looked at the boy and little girl, but the children didn't meet their gaze. Mr. and Mrs. Grapes started to feel dizzy. Harold squeezed his wife's hand harder, but she didn't even notice. She longed for an answer, a sign of approval or rejection.

Then the woman came forward abruptly. Harold and Mary Rose jumped back. She offered them two wooden bowls of the thick concoction boiling in the pot. This small gesture released the tension in the room. They had accepted Mr. and Mrs. Grapes's story.

A Veil of Darkness

That night, Harold and Mary Rose barely slept. They were cold, and despite the relief of knowing the family believed them, they still didn't know what was going to happen. In the morning, snow crunched outside the tent. They saw the face of little Kirima peeking through the opening. She looked at them with a mixture of shyness and curiosity and asked them to follow her.

Walking toward the camp, Harold and Mary Rose felt knots in their stomachs again. Smoke rose from the highest roofs in the settlement, and far away, they heard the muffled bark of a dog. They were surprised when Kirima did not lead them to the big tent. She strode confidently around the perimeter of the camp while Harold and Mary Rose struggled to keep up. Mary Rose was unable to walk very fast, but the pangs in her knee were less intense than before.

The sound of barking dogs got louder, and Harold and Mary Rose nervously peered between tents, looking for movement. They had no idea where the girl was taking them. When they asked, they received no reply.

They had crossed the entire camp and passed by the outermost shelters when Kirima stopped in front of a round tent covered by a thick blanket of snow that gave it the appearance of meringue. Kirima went to the entrance and whispered something they couldn't hear. Harold and Mary Rose looked around for other people, but the two tall tents behind them blocked the view of the rest of the camp.

The slit between the hides moved, and two figures dressed in thick fur parkas emerged. It was Kirima's parents.

Harold and Mary Rose looked at them in surprise.

"This is your new tent," the man said, pointing with his mittened hand.

Harold and Mary Rose looked again at the tent. Unlike the precarious shelter they had been sleeping in, this was made of thick, dark hides. It was a sturdy structure, tall enough to stand in without touching the top and wide enough to sleep in without brushing against the walls.

"Inside, you'll find more appropriate clothing," the woman added, eying their stained, torn coats.

Before Harold and Mary Rose could say anything, the couple gestured to their daughter, and the three of them disappeared behind the big tents. Mr. and Mrs. Grapes turned and went into their tent.

Inside, they smelled the same acrid odor that had permeated the big tent, but it no longer bothered them. A candle burning on a cracked plate cast a soft glow, making the interior less gloomy. Thick skins and a couple of soft cushions covered the floor. The heat in the room flushed their hollow cheeks, and the cold that had settled in Mary Rose's injured knee overnight was disappearing. The room made them feel comfortable and safe.

They went over to the only piece of furniture in the room. It was a rough leather chest, so dark it looked black. They opened it and found clothing inside. Two thick fur parkas with hoods lined in a soft gray fur, two pairs of pants made of the same fur as the coat, two pairs of sturdy fur-lined boots, two pairs of mittens, and their backpack. They had forgotten about their backpack. They opened it and found it still contained the two pairs of socks, a change of underwear each, two light sweaters, the worn blanket, the flashlight, and the canteen. The flashlight no longer worked, and the canteen was empty, but none of that mattered now.

Until then, they hadn't thought about how many days they had been wearing the same clothes. Slowly and stiffly, they got undressed. What they saw was shocking. For the first time after so many days of hunger and trauma, they had a full view of their injured, emaciated bodies. Their collarbones and ribs protruded painfully. Their muscles were weak, and bruises and scratches covered their translucent skin. Sorrowfully, Mary Rose touched a large yellowing bruise that spread over Harold's shoulder like an oil spill. Slowly, as if she had magical healing powers, she delicately placed her lips on the bruise and kissed it. Harold felt the tingle of his hairs standing on end and lovingly pulled Mary Rose to him, tenderly embracing her. They held each other, naked, feeling each other's heartbeat and the warmth of their breath. Silently, they looked at each other under the soft flicker of the candle, marveling that, despite the stories their bodies told, they were alive.

Silence

For the first time in a long while, Harold and Mary Rose didn't wake up in the middle of the night, startled by strange noises, hunger pangs, or the breath of an icy breeze slipping inside. For the first time in months, they felt the hard layer of anxiety and tension that had kept them alive crack like a dry, brittle crust. For the first time, they felt safe, protected by the warm shell of the tent and the peaceful silence inside.

Ice Nomads

The days passed lazily. With sleep, a warm tent, and fatty foods, their frail bodies slowly recuperated, bulking up, just like the landscape outside under layers of snow. Their gaunt faces softened, their arms and legs got stronger, and only scars remained of their wounds. Harold's harsh cough had disappeared almost completely, and Mary Rose began to walk in the snow without fearing her knee would fail her.

Harold and Mary Rose became more comfortable as people in the camp began to accept them. It was clear everyone had heard Mr. and Mrs. Grapes's story. Even though few dared speak to them, people stopped avoiding them when they walked by, and their eyes no longer showed fear or suspicion.

Kirima was in charge of escorting them around the camp. At first, Harold and Mary Rose thought she had been assigned the chore, but as the days passed, they realized it was something she wanted to do. Each morning, her timid face would appear in the opening of their tent to tell them good morning. She always brought a bowl of water and one of the little silver fish. The fish was for the seal, or Nattiq, as Harold and Mary Rose also learned to call their furry companion. Upon the little girl's arrival, the seal would uncurl from where it was sleeping and bolt outside like a clumsy missile. As they listened to the little girl's soft laughter blending with the sharp barks of the seal, Harold and Mary Rose would get dressed in their heavy coats and head outside.

It wasn't far from Mr. and Mrs. Grapes's tent to the family's home, but as the days passed, Harold and Mary Rose noticed that Kirima started walking slower, wanting to prolong the time with them to ask more questions. This morning ritual was Harold and Mary Rose's favorite time of day. The little girl wanted to know what it was like where they lived, if everyone looked like them, what the food tasted like, and what the land was like. Life in San Remo was anything but exciting, but for Kirima, each of their answers was fascinating.

"But you don't have any ice fields for fishing?" she asked, her brow furrowed in thought.

When they saw the little girl's confusion, Harold and Mary Rose couldn't help but laugh, which left her even more bewildered. As she got to know Mr. and Mrs. Grapes, Kirima's shyness melted away. She had many questions, but the topic that seemed to interest her most was the time they had spent drifting across the ocean in their house. With each new story, new anecdote, new detail they told her, her questions multiplied exponentially. Her curiosity was insatiable, but Harold and Mary Rose didn't mind. They loved to see her little eyes widen as if it helped her take in more information. Her expression was so innocent, so full of life, it looked like she could unravel all the mysteries of the universe. It was the same look Dylan had. Thinking of Dylan, their hearts felt squeezed by an ancient pain hidden deep in the shadows and only visible as a brief flicker in their eyes. By the time Harold and Mary Rose entered Kirima's family tent, they had reburied the glimmer of pain.

Like Kirima's shyness, the tension they felt when they passed through the wall of skins into her family's home diminished a little more each time. Before they knew it, the heat from the flames no longer was scorching and oppressive, and although they still weren't used to the strong flavor of the food, they could eat it without feeling nauseated. More importantly, much of the change taking place in that tent was due to her father's attitude. Amak's icy stare and irritated tone were slowly softening. His expression relaxed, and without the vertical lines creasing his brow, Harold and Mary Rose realized he was much younger than they had first thought.

One day, sitting in front of the fire, Kirima asked them a question that caught them off guard.

"Will you go back to your island someday?"

Harold and Mary Rose looked at each other, not knowing how to respond. They had been asking themselves the same question since the moment they woke up floating aboard their house, adrift on the sea. They'd thought that, with their rescue, they would finally have an answer. But they didn't. Even after many days of living in the camp, they still didn't know how far they were from San Remo or if there was the slightest chance of returning. Harold and Mary Rose had learned that these people spoke English because of trade relationships, but since they'd arrived, there had been no contact with the outside world.

Amak saw their concern, and before Harold or Mary Rose could respond, he interjected, "I should have spoken with you about this before." He paused and looked at them, observing them closely.

Harold and Mary Rose felt their unease grow, and for a second, it felt like they were reliving the first time they entered this tent.

"I know it worries you to not know if you will be able to return to your island, but it's too early to know. First, you must regain your strength while we wait for the weather to change."

Harold and Mary Rose felt strangely relieved, and a pressure that had been accumulating for months was released. They didn't know how long it would take to get the answer, but now they were able to entertain the possibility of returning. For the first time, they fully trusted this man's judgment and the honesty and goodness of the people. So they gave themselves time for their wounds to heal and for the relationships they were forming to strengthen.

As the days passed, Harold and Mary Rose discovered Amak was the leader of the remote community that made its home in this barren, icy land. He was very restrained, but Harold and Mary Rose came to realize that his tough demeanor was due to the heavy responsibility he bore to keep his people and his family safe. Almost daily, he went out to fish or hunt, sometimes not returning for two or three days. But he never went alone. He explained to them that ice fishing was his people's primary source of food, but it was also terribly dangerous. Two were needed in case the ice cracked and someone fell in. If you weren't pulled out immediately, death was certain. Amak was almost always accompanied by Ukluk, his adolescent son. Kirima wanted to go with them every time they set out, but she didn't always get to. The girl was much more interested in fishing than in playing with the other children. And she was just as obstinate as her father, who never came back empty-handed. No matter how long it took, he would return with crates filled with dozens of shiny codfish and sometimes even caribou that Harold and the rest of the men would help unload.

The first time Harold and Mary Rose saw a caribou, it was a cold, windy morning. Their island didn't have much wildlife, and the closest thing to caribou they'd seen there were the deer that sometimes ventured from the protection of the forest to root around in San Remo's garbage. Caribou were much larger and hairier than deer, with thicker, heavier antlers. It took several men to unload the animal from the sled's trailer. One caribou provided enough meat to feed the community for days.

A few nights later, Amak returned with an even more surprising load. Harold and Mary Rose were nestled in their tent when they heard shouting. At first, they were frightened, but when they stepped outside, they saw everyone in camp circling around Amak's sled, holding torches and lanterns and cheering exuberantly. When Harold and Mary Rose managed to make their way to the gathering, they were amazed. There was a gigantic tail lying on the ice. Apparently, the men had found a dead whale trapped in the ice field. The body had been mostly devoured by predators, and the tail was the only thing they could salvage. But for this community, the tail was as valuable as gold. It was divided among the joyful residents, and that night, Harold and Mary Rose sat among the blankets, watching Amak's wife, Aga, cook the fatty whale loins. The meat produced heavy vapors, which soon filled the tent. The blubber was as yellow as butter and gave off such an acrid smell, it made them woozy. They hesitated when Aga offered it to them, but didn't want to offend her by rejecting the delicacy. Much to their surprise, when they tried it, they liked it. A lot.

Aga was not only a good cook but also the community's healer. One night after supper, when Mary Rose got up to return to their tent, she tripped on one of the skins, twisting her injured knee. She let out a moan and sat back down. Aga examined her knee, gently palpating the kneecap and watching for her reaction.

"Are you still using the ointment I gave you?"

"I finished it up a few days ago. But it had already stopped hurting by then."

Aga pursed her lips to the side, thinking. The next morning, when they returned to the main tent with Kirima, Aga was seated in a corner, leaning over a long board and mixing various ingredients in a mortar. Since they had been in this barren land, Harold and Mary Rose had not seen a single plant, but the wooden box next to Aga held small bottles of all kinds of dried leaves, pieces of curled horns, and gelatinous cartilage. Soon, Aga offered her a new pot of ointment, and a few days later, Mary Rose's knee finally stopped bothering her for good.

During this time, Kirima began teaching them some words.

"*Irniq* is 'son,' and *panik* is 'daughter,'" she said, pointing to two puppies as examples.

Harold and Mary Rose repeated each one of the words, trying to get the correct pronunciation. But each time they attempted to use what they were learning in front of the family, it caused everyone to burst out laughing, making them blush.

The days went by quickly and easily. Yet as time passed, Harold and Mary Rose felt increasingly guilty for not being able to repay their friends for their hospitality. This community that had almost nothing never hesitated to share with them. In comparison to this challenging existence, their life in San Remo was lavish and frivolous. The homes in the settlement were not crammed with heavy furniture impossible to transport, walls weren't decorated with idyllic landscapes, and everything they possessed served some function essential to survival. There was no hot water or electricity. The water needed for drinking, cooking, and bathing was melted from snow, and light was provided by the fire in the hearth, candles, and oil lanterns. Nestled in the darkness of the tent, Harold recalled his own unexpected reaction to the lightbulb that miraculously shone from their porch in the middle of nowhere. The lightbulb that blinded them in the darkness. He remembered how, as soon as he had unscrewed the flickering bulb, the most marvelous golden lights they'd ever seen appeared in the night sky.

A timid voice came through the tent opening. It was morning and Kirima had come to wake them.

The Great Breach

Harold and Mary Rose followed Kirima into the family's tent. The little girl scampered around on the blankets and skins that covered the floor, then hopped to her seat. Around the fire were Amak, Aga, and Ukluk.

Harold and Mary Rose made their way to the fire and greeted everyone as they sat down in the space between Kirima and Amak. The smell of boiled cod made their stomachs growl with hunger. Aga offered them each a bowl with a piece of fish, and they began to eat in silence, the only sound being the flames crackling under the pot. At this hour, no one ever talked much, but the silence this morning was longer than usual; they seemed to be considering something.

Harold glanced sideways at Amak and saw he wasn't eating. His eyes were fixed on the flames, and long, deep wrinkles cut across his windburned forehead. Amak sighed, and Harold quickly looked away.

"Tonight, my son and I will go fishing," he said slowly.

Hearing this, Kirima squirmed on her cushion. "Can I go too?" she begged, her mouth still full.

Amak sighed and weighed his response.

"You only get in the way!" Ukluk muttered.

Kirima quickly swallowed and frowned at her brother. "Only because you never let me do anything!" She shifted her eyes to her father. "Please! You haven't taken me with you for a long time!"

The girl's eyes shone with emotion and jumped quickly from her father to her mother in search of an answer. Her lively face stirred up painful memories in Harold and Mary Rose, but neither Amak nor Aga noticed anything amiss. They seemed to be communicating with each other without words.

"You know fishing on the ice field is dangerous, Kirima," Aga said calmly. "I don't think it's a job for such a little girl."

Kirima rolled her eyes and threw her head back. "I'm almost seven! At my age, Ukluk was already helping you break the ice!"

"But I was twice as strong as you are!"

Harold and Mary Rose couldn't help smiling at seeing the girl's face turn the same shade of red as her father's had the day they'd met him. There was no doubt Kirima had inherited her father's temperament. But she also seemed to have her mother's ability to keep it under control. She took a deep breath and ignored her brother.

"It's not right to treat me different because I'm a girl. You said so yourselves." She tried to control the shaking in her voice.

Amak sighed and looked at his daughter with concern, but her smile and the spark in her eyes seemed to soften him, bringing a smile to his own face. "You never give up, do you?"

The little girl smiled even wider and shook her head energetically. Amak looked at Aga out of the corner of his eye and, finally, he reluctantly agreed. "OK, you can go with us. But on the condition that you help your mother pack for the move when we get back."

At once, Harold and Mary Rose looked at each other.

"It's time," Amak explained to them. "In a couple of days, we will break camp and move north."

Mary Rose suddenly found it hard to breathe.

"North?" murmured Harold.

"At this time of year, the ice field begins to melt. In a few months, all of this will be water," he said, motioning to the ground around him.

"We have to head north, where the ice is solid, and the camp will be safe."

Amak turned to Aga, his expression asking for help. But she didn't respond, so he continued. "There are two routes to the north. The first one crosses the mountains, which is where we usually spend these months. The second takes us to the Great Breach."

Harold and Mary Rose each saw the stunned look on the other's face. It was the same look Kirima had when she didn't understand what they were saying.

"During the months of the thaw, the Great Breach forms north of here. It's a water passage several miles wide that is only open a few months of the year. It connects the two seas that otherwise are closed off from each other by an ice barrier." He stopped and looked at the fire. "For those few months, it is traveled by thousands of ships. Every day, ships pass through, traveling to various cities."

Harold and Mary Rose finally understood. Their hearts began pumping wildly, but their thoughts remained slow.

"Both are long, difficult journeys, and that's why I need to ask you"—he inhaled and then looked them in the eye—"do you want to stay with us in the mountains, or do you want to go to the Great Breach so you can return home?"

Silence fell heavy over the room. They had spent months staring at the ocean, studying the sky, and crossing miles of water, snow, and ice. Now, after all the suffering they had endured, Amak was offering them the chance to return to the island, to San Remo—surely the only chance to return home for a long time. The silence didn't last long.

"But their house is here, Papa! We saw it on the ice field!" Kirima said angrily, as if trying to make sense of her father's words.

They all looked at her for a second, without registering her words. Tears of happiness ran down Mary Rose's flushed cheeks. Harold threw himself at his wife and hugged her so tightly she couldn't breathe. Their bodies trembled together, this time not from cold or fear. After so many months fighting, surviving, and hoping, the moment to return home had finally come. Then Kirima got up, laughing and jumping around, filled with a contagious happiness she didn't understand. Without thinking, she jumped on Mr. and Mrs. Grapes, squeezing them from behind. Harold and Mary Rose missed the family already.

Night was falling when Harold and Mary Rose left Amak and Aga's tent. A soft curtain of snow covered the hide huts. For the first time, Harold and Mary Rose didn't mind the cold snowflakes on their smiling faces. The snow crunched under their boots as the breath from their reddened noses hung in the air. Everyone in this nomadic community was sheltered inside their homes. Smoke rose lazily from one of the shelters that marked the outside of the camp, while in another the glow of a candle flickered weakly against the worn skin wall. It didn't take long to return to their tent, the warm shelter that had provided a peace and comfort they hadn't felt in a long time.

Then, just before arriving at the entrance of their tent, Harold slowed down and stopped. The remaining sunlight was hidden behind thick snow clouds, but even in the twilight, there was enough light to see by. The brume was clearing from the horizon, pushed away by a strong wind. Mary Rose grabbed Harold's hand and rested her head on his shoulder, imagining his warmth through their fur coats.

Before them was a sea of ice sheets and floes that piled up along the edge of the field. Harold squeezed Mary Rose's hand, silently studying the ice moving into the sea. What captured their attention was not the ice or the sea, but a distant spot that had appeared on the edge of the thawing ice field. A dot of yellow, so pale it was easy to miss in all the white. A house anchored between tons of snow and ice, facing a sea of possibilities that seemed to stretch out endlessly before it.

Harold and Mary Rose held each other as the last light of day faded away, swallowing the house under the veil of night. They knew the moment had come to say good-bye to it and everything it represented. They thought of the day they had moved in. They heard the echo of their steps resonating through the empty rooms and felt overwhelmed by nostalgia. It was the same feeling they'd had when they recognized parts of their ship in the sweet little house they had built on top of the cliff. A gust of wind froze their faces, and Harold knew that, no matter how difficult it was to acknowledge, that house was no longer a home. It was an empty shell, frozen and lifeless. He didn't even think it would remain standing much longer. He imagined the hard ice slowly pressing against the structure, closing in around it, crushing it like a gigantic fist. He imagined the rocky base creaking under pressure, crumbling like sugar cubes, the timbers ceding to the weight of the snow and splintering like dry old branches. Eventually, the house would sink like the ship it once was.

The Departure

For the first time, Harold and Mary Rose woke without the cheer-ful voice of Kirima on the other side of the tent. Feeling around in the dark, Harold located a match and lit the candle. Its weak orange light illuminated their sleepy faces, revealing their lack of rest due to the constant lashing of the wind against the tent. They stretched and dressed quietly, trying not to wake the seal. When they pushed aside the opening, a gust of icy wind roared inside and blew out the flame. A chill ran through Mary Rose.

They went outside and habitually looked in the direction they had last seen the house, but snow was falling heavily, concealing the entire field under a flurry of blowing ice. They began to walk slowly through the thick layer of new snow, hunching over to protect themselves from the sharp pellets the wind was lashing against their bare faces. It seemed strange to walk through the snow in silence, without Kirima's lilting voice peppering them with questions: *What kind of fish do you eat? What are the houses like where you're from?* Harold and Mary Rose were sad, knowing that soon they would no longer see the little girl at all. They would miss the thrill in her eyes and her innocent laughter. Soon, they would no longer walk along this interminable white plain or feel the intense cold pounding in their ears. Nor would they feel the comforting warmth of the shelters, eat the strange food, or hear the incomprehensible language.

As they left their tent behind and entered the camp, their wandering thoughts were cut short. The camp bustled with activity, unusual for this hour and in this inclement weather. Dozens of men and women were moving swiftly between shelters while dogs barked and ran around. A group of boys passed them carrying long poles and carefully folded skins that they loaded onto a huge sled. Some of the smaller tents had already been removed. The camp was being disassembled faster than they had imagined possible. Harold and Mary Rose had an uncomfortable feeling in the pit of their stomachs, a combination of happiness to be going home and sadness for leaving a community they had connected with more deeply than the one they left in San Remo. Seeing the boxes and crates piled on the sleds and the skeletons of tents partially disassembled made them think about the moving preparations they had gone through. They thought about all the weeks that they had spent packing their own things. The boxes filled with kitchen items, summer clothing, and horticulture books. The many rolls of Bubble Wrap they had used to protect the fragile bottled ships. The distinctive sound of the packing tape as it was rolled across box after box.

Their lives felt heavy and stationary compared to the lives of these people, who changed locations as lightly as a feather blown in the wind. In a few hours, the oasis of warmth these gracious people had created would return to an icy, uninhabited wilderness. What's more, all this was accomplished without the trauma or reproof Mr. and Mrs. Grapes had felt during their eviction. In this community, finding a new place to call home was an exciting prospect. The only thing that would be left to mark Harold and Mary Grapes's presence was a wooden house with no connection to anything around it. A house full of sorrowful memories that would sink like an old galley ship in the sea of ice.

They kept walking, their bodies stiff from more than just the cold, and arrived at the clearing where the larger tents were still standing.

Wisps of smoke rose above the blanket of white, dancing and circling in the wind. The sight comforted them, and they went to Amak and Aga's shelter. Once there, they hesitated. Kirima had always been there to lead them inside; they had never entered alone.

To their surprise, the space was empty, devoid of even the few objects normally stored in the spare room. The thick skins that covered the floor had disappeared, revealing a thin, patched ground cover. Also gone were the two large trunks and the board on which Aga prepared her medicinal remedies. The long poles supporting the tent swayed with the strong winds and were bare of their fishing nets, knives, and leather thongs. Next to the cooking pot, which bubbled silently over the flames, were a few cooking utensils, creating the illusion that all was as it should be. But Harold and Mary Rose knew things were different. Their time here was coming to an end, and the emptiness in the room flooded them with the same loneliness they felt in the cobblestone streets of San Remo.

The residents on the island were nothing like the people here. In San Remo, everyone shut themselves up in their own homes, cut off from their neighbors, only interested in gossip and judging those around them. Harold and Mary Rose had come to realize that not even the mayor could be considered a true friend. He had always treated them with respect, but from a distance; he showed compassion, but not understanding or genuine comfort. The community here was different, not needing to hide behind a wall of convention or a false "how are you?" Their relationships were real and authentic. None of them had hidden their initial distrust, but neither did they hide the mutual esteem and affection that had been building daily. Suddenly, Aga burst into the tent, covered in snow and carrying a large empty box.

"Oh! I didn't expect you up so early," she said.

"We apologize; we didn't know if we should come in or not," said Mary Rose, a little embarrassed.

Aga set the box down and removed her hood, careful to keep the snow off her long hair.

"Of course. This is your home," she said, smiling. "Come. Come closer to the fire; it's going to be cold today."

Aga moved to the fire and took off her thick coat. Lacking the normal layer of blankets and cushions, she spread it out and sat on it. Harold and Mary Rose did the same, and soon the heat of the flames caressed their faces, and the comforting smell of mush wafted over them. They would miss this.

"We've already cleared out most of the tents," Aga said as she filled their bowls. "Now we're just waiting for Amak and the children to return tonight so tomorrow morning we can take down the rest of the tents and start north."

Hearing this, Mary Rose felt her stomach tighten. In a few weeks, perhaps, or months, she would be seated at a table with a tablecloth and chairs, in front of food served on ceramic plates and with glasses and shiny forks, knives, and spoons of varying sizes. Mary Rose took the rough, rudimentary bowl from Aga's capable hands and, in that moment, knew she didn't need anything more. The soft warmth of the wood, worn by years of use, spread through her hands and arms. Mary Rose looked at Aga's serene eyes and, without thinking, hugged her.

"Thank you," she whispered.

Aga was surprised but immediately returned the hug. Mary Rose knew she still had time with her friend as they traveled together to the Great Breach, but this moment felt like a good-bye.

A strong gust of wind whipped the tent, and a few flurries made their way into the room. Aga and Mary Rose slowly released each other, and the three enjoyed their breakfast and talked about the preparations for the journey.

"Have you packed all your things?"

Harold and Mary Rose looked at each other, wondering how the question applied to them. In the tent, they had only the old backpack with the canteen, the flashlight with dead batteries, and the tattered clothes they had been wearing when they were found.

"Everything we have is in the house or gone," Harold said with a sad smile. "We have nothing to pack."

Aga nodded sorrowfully. She picked up a long iron rod and stoked the fire.

"We've had this tent just over a year," she said as she set down the stick. "The cold, the wind, and moving the camp every few months wears on them. We frequently need to repair the tents or make new ones. It's difficult and tedious work." She looked at Mr. and Mrs. Grapes. "But we don't mind."

Harold set down his empty bowl and looked around at the austere room that was completely free of clutter, totally different from the countless appliances, furniture, and stuff that filled the homes where they were from. "The lifestyle of a nomad," he affirmed.

Aga looked at Harold and smiled softly. "We're all nomads, Mr. Grapes."

They were struck by her statement.

"A home isn't built with walls or determined by where we are," Aga said. "A home is built from our experiences, from the people we meet along the way, and, more than anything, from how we decide to journey through life. Life is movement. A precarious equilibrium that can change in an instant."

Her final words chilled the room. Mr. and Mrs. Grapes knew how life could change in an instant, and how dreams could be destroyed in a second.

"Sometimes things happen that keep you from your journey," murmured Mary Rose, her gaze drifting to the fire.

She thought of her son and couldn't breathe as she remembered his big blue eyes, so full of life, just like Kirima's. Tears flooded her eyes, and Mary Rose knew she had to share Dylan's story with Aga. She needed to tell her the reason for the pain that stained her soul.

Aga looked at them, not understanding the reaction. Then, as Mary Rose began to speak, a violent gust of frigid air penetrated the opening, shaking the structure and blowing out the fire. The room was left bathed in an eerie reddish glow, the color of blood. Immediately, they heard a commotion of barking, howling, and shouting. Aga jumped up and raced out of the tent without her coat. Mary Rose felt the same chill run through her as when the pot of hydrangeas shattered on the floor in their little San Remo apartment. The night Dylan died.

White Darkness

They followed her out of the tent and were battered by the vicious snow swirling around them. Harold took Mary Rose by the hand. They could barely see, and the shouts and barking carried on the wind seemed to come from all directions. Harold saw a dark smudge moving between the tents. It was Aga, running through the snow toward the voices. They stumbled after her. Then a high-pitched wail pierced the air, and their bodies vibrated like fine crystal. The howling of the dogs got louder, and three figures appeared before them. Harold and Mary Rose were terrified as they ran toward them. Then their world plunged into devastating darkness as they saw Amak cradling little Kirima's pale, lifeless body in his arms.

The Coldest Cold

Harold and Mary Rose were hit by an unbearable wave of pain, one that drowned out the dogs' howls and the roar of the wind. The only thing penetrating Harold's consciousness was the sound of Aga's desperate wails, combined with those of Mary Rose and his own. He was drowning, drowning again like he did that night. The water covered him completely, penetrating his very soul, his thoughts rotting away, trapped in a sticky spiderweb. The present cold, wind, and snow were nothing compared to the pain that was deeper and more real. Harold felt the anguish, heard the roar of the waves as they crashed against his defenseless body, experienced the impenetrable darkness that covered everything. He fell to his knees in the snow, defeated, as tears froze in long tracks on his cheeks. Under his bare hands he felt the deck of the fishing vessel that had pulled him out of the sea and the sailors fighting to keep him from throwing himself back in after his son. But this time it was Mary Rose who held him in her arms. Nevertheless, the sobs that came from Harold and Mary Rose were only an echo of the desperation and pain of Aga and her family. An echo that had never stopped for Harold and Mary Rose over the last thirty-five years, eating away at them like the waves eroding Death Cliff. Time and again, wave after wave, attack after attack.

Harold looked up from the ground and through the veil of tears saw Kirima's little bare hand exposed between the folds of the blanket as she was wrapped in her father's arms like an injured baby bird. Amak rocked back and forth, back and forth, back and forth, like the gentle rocking of the waves, like the perpetual motion of a pendulum. He stared into his daughter's peaceful face, as if her closed eyes indicated she was only sleeping in his strong arms. That's all it was, right? She was sleeping. But Harold knew it wasn't so. Aga's trembling hands framed her daughter's peaceful face, caressing her tenderly. The snow and frost covered her black hair tossed by the wind and her bare arms impervious to the cold. Nothing protected her; nothing could alleviate this terrible cold. Aga's sobs had turned to whispers, whispers in her daughter's ear, as if trying to wake her with the sweetness of a mother's voice. Then, unconsciously, Harold covered Kirima's hand in his. He wouldn't let go, not this time, no matter how cold her skin was, even when it was colder than the snow and wind that lashed at them. Still, Harold's pain was nothing but a faint reflection of Amak and Aga's suffering. He looked again at Kirima in her father's arms and at the frozen tears of her brother. She was being wrapped in her mother's kisses and sweet, whispered words of love. With numbed hands, he removed his thick coat. His body shook uncontrollably. Then, gently, he covered Aga's bare shoulders.

Kirima

The funeral rites lasted several days, during which time the singing, weeping, and long silences delayed the march north. It never stopped snowing. The snow came down harder than usual, falling straight to the earth with no wind to change its trajectory.

They wrapped Kirima's tiny body in an exquisite caribou hide that was lovingly adorned by her mother with colorful threads, then placed her in the sled. Amak mounted the sled and drove down the mountain. The rest of the community followed in silent procession.

Amak and Ukluk picked up shovels and began to dig in the pristine snow. They dug until they hit the sapphire-blue of the ice field. Then Amak went to the sled and tenderly picked up the bundle in which his daughter rested. Aga and Ukluk went to his side, reaching out their arms to share the burden. Harold and Mary Rose stepped back with the rest of the mourners to give them privacy, but Amak's eyes found theirs, and he motioned for them to come forward. Mary Rose felt Harold looking at her, but she avoided his gaze. She knew if their eyes met, she wouldn't be able to hold back the tears. No one in the family or anyone else was crying, and she didn't want to be the one who did. They stepped forward to join the family. The rest of the camp was watching them, but Harold and Mary Rose were oblivious.

Mary Rose had to swallow the sobs that rose in her throat like bile; she wanted to shout, to cry, to run away, but she joined them, resting her hands next to those of Harold, Amak, Aga, and Ukluk under the dark caribou skin that held the lifeless body of the little girl. The impossibly light bundle made Mary Rose irrationally hope these were only blankets and that at any moment she would spot Kirima's vivacious little face among the onlookers. But she didn't see her; she would never see her again. Mary Rose would never hear her singsong voice waking them in the morning, she wouldn't laugh at her confused expression when she described the color of hydrangeas, she wouldn't see her running around in the snow with Nattiq, she wouldn't see that look that hypnotized her so and made her miss—she felt a wave of grief shaking her, increasing pressure in her chest and throat. She couldn't bear the thought of those brilliant eyes that seemed to devour the world around her with every blink now covered by the thick blanket and seeing only darkness.

She was angry and hated this life. The same questions that had tormented her for years resurfaced like the remains of an ancient shipwreck buried under dark waters and thick layers of algae. Why should a sad, broken old woman like her survive when this little one, so delicate and full of hope, would never get to grow, stumble, learn, mature, fall in love, follow her dreams . . . why couldn't she live? Now Mary Rose's pain was as fresh as on the night of the storm. Her body began to convulse; she couldn't control it. It was as if the little bundle suddenly was too heavy, and she couldn't hold it any longer. Was it Dylan she was trying to hold with all her strength? Mary Rose fell to the ground. No one noticed because, at the same moment, everyone knelt to place the small bundle in the grave.

Harold helped her up, and Mary Rose let loose the tears she could no longer hold back. Amak offered them a shovel. Harold was gripped with panic. Looking the broken man in the eyes, he saw his own pain and took the shovel without hesitation. Under everyone's watchful gaze, Harold scooped the immaculate white snow and approached the opening. Snowflakes piled on the shovel and seemed to weigh more than they should. He held the shovel full of snow over the deep hole for a few seconds, not daring to release it. The hole held something it shouldn't. Amak joined him and looked at him with sorrow. Harold felt a wave of guilt. Shouldn't he be comforting this father?

Amak placed his hands over Harold's and nodded. Then Harold finally rotated the handle and the snow, carrying the burden of the past, scattered over the bundle inside. Harold knew it wasn't just Kirima's body he was burying in that blue grave; it was also that of the son he had never been able to lay to rest.

The Old Woman

Harold and Mary Rose followed the procession to Amak and Aga's tent. Everyone entered and sat around the low flames flickering in the middle of the room. Despite the crowded space, it was cold, but no one added wood to the fire or stoked it with the metal rod. Harold and Mary Rose sat next to an old woman they had rarely seen around camp. The color of the ashes seemed to blend with her dark skin, which was so wrinkled it was difficult to see her eyes. She was hunched over, hidden under layers of blankets, her gaze so lost in the fire she didn't seem to notice the presence of anyone around her.

Everyone stared at the flames, especially Amak, Aga, and Ukluk, who were seated on the other side of the circle, facing them. Harold and Mary Rose knew the kinds of thoughts assaulting their minds. When Mary Rose relived the moment that precious bundle disappeared under the snow, the feeling she was drowning started to rise again from the pit of her stomach. They had not placed any kind of symbol over the grave, nothing that would indicate Kirima's body rested under the heavy layer of snow. They simply allowed the snow to fall and soften the tracks until the grave site blended with the rest of the flatland: white, cold, lifeless. As they left, Mary Rose had looked back, unable to see where they had buried her. Kirima simply disappeared, swallowed by the enormous sea of frozen water, the same sea that had swallowed their son. Mary Rose realized her fingers were squeezing Harold's hand, and she loosened her grip. Harold looked at her, but she turned away, her eyes resting on the turbulent chaos of the dancing flames as she concentrated on holding back the tears that wanted to spill all over again.

At that moment, she sensed a guttural, almost inaudible sound. At first, Mary Rose thought it was the sinister wind howling through the tent folds, but the sound was sustained, unchanging, then rising in volume almost imperceptibly. Mary Rose turned her head a bit. The old woman's lips were barely parted and remained motionless, but the sound was coming from her. Then Mary Rose saw a golden shimmer in her entranced eyes. Reflecting the fire, the tear seemed to hold a familiar flickering yellow light that slowly slipped through the deep canyons of her wrinkles. Her voice lifted and soon filled the space. Mary Rose felt all eyes turn to the woman, trained on her like loaded bows. The song was like nothing Mary Rose had ever heard. It was different than the sacred songs sung before; it was more resonant, a strange, primitive, and visceral cadence that rose from the depths of her soul. Mary Rose's mind was trapped in a sticky web, drugged by the hypnotic rhythm that reverberated over everything and everybody as if they were made of crystal. She felt the tough shell she had worked so hard to maintain begin to crack; inside, something solid and dark, rotted by time and resentment, was emerging. Her whole body shook, and she couldn't disguise the tremor. Harold tried to soothe her, but his touch on her skin only made it worse.

Suddenly, Aga's voice joined the old woman's. Her soft voice blended perfectly with the old woman's, which still sounded hoarse, guttural, rough, and dark. Amak's voice joined in, and gradually, the volume of the three voices swelled. Ukluk and some women next to him joined in. The sound continued rising, filling the room with the deep reverberation of the growing voices. The sound was suffocating, intense, and repetitive, like the beating of a giant heart pounding ever harder. It was the roar of the waves; it was the wind ripping the leaves off the trees; it was the rain hitting the windows; it was the thunder resounding over and over in their ears. Mary Rose felt dizzy, and a cold sweat broke out on the back of her neck. There was a building pressure in her chest. She felt trapped, cornered by the lament, by the voices that seemed like they'd break something inside her and push her into a dark abyss. She had to get out of there.

She let go of Harold's hand and jumped up, running through the folds in the tent to the outside. Her boots sank in the deep snow as if it were tar. She managed to get outside the circle of tents before her vision blurred and she collapsed again on the snow. Desperately, she unbuttoned her coat. She needed air. She needed to throw off everything that was crushing her. Looking up, she saw it. The house in the distance. As alone, as dark, and as empty as she was. And she screamed.

She screamed, her cry raking her throat and spilling out a darkness she could no longer hold in. A pain that crumbled like an old log burned to a crisp, shattered like the flowerpot that smashed against the tile floor. Her tears flowed uncontrollably, burning as if there were fire trapped in each one.

Her hands sank in the ice. Moisture and cold penetrated through to her bones, but nothing compared to the pain in her heart. She couldn't stop hearing the ancient echo of thunder from that night rolling through the windows in the apartment or seeing the brilliance of the blinding flash of lightning illuminating the floor covered in fragments of stone, dirt, and petals. She smelled the dirt mixed with the ocean—decaying, wet, and salty. Someone embraced her, like on that night when her world exploded. She felt the cold of his wet clothes and smelled the salt of the sea and tears. It was Harold, it was Harold again who embraced her. And suddenly she felt all the rage she had contained for years explode.

"Go away!" she screamed. "Let me be with him!"

Mary Rose tore at her husband's coat, swinging at him in fury.

"I hated you! I hated you for coming home without him!"

Harold stood still, just as he had that night in the apartment. Enduring her fists, her cries, and her pain like a port withstanding the violent waves breaking against it.

"I can't take it!" she said between sobs. "He was so young!"

Mary Rose had no strength left to lash out at him. It felt like their bodies were no longer on the snowfield but crumpled on the tile floor in their old apartment in San Remo. Her whole body trembled from the howling of the storm, from the sound of the song that seemed to tear through the darkness that had consumed her for so many years. The darkness that had steeped her in a deep, rotting resentment now ebbed away through tears of light that spilled from her eyes.

Harold tightened his embrace, feeling his wife's body finally yielding. Mary Rose went limp, her tears freezing in delicate, icy scabs. She closed her eyes.

The Firefly

Mary Rose tried to open her eyelids, but it felt like they were covered by a thick veil. All she could see was darkness. She noticed her body rocking gently, rhythmically. She heard a splash of water, and the creaking of the wood she was sitting on got louder. Mary Rose knew she was in a boat, headed to an unknown destination, but strangely, she wasn't panicked or anxious. She remained calm and confident, with no intention of taking off the blindfold.

The boat slowed and stopped. Someone moved around her, risking capsizing the boat. Then she felt a hand take hers and help her onto the dock. She felt solid ground, and a second later, hands untied her blindfold, leaving her blinded by bright light.

Slowly, her eyes adjusted, and she could see Harold's face. With a full head of black hair, he couldn't have been more than twenty-five years old. He smiled and looked at her with his deep-blue eyes that seemed to hold the sea. Young Mary Rose saw they were on an old dock. From where she stood, San Remo looked like a cluster of small mollusks clinging to a big black rock.

"Where are we?" she asked, marveling at a large, dilapidated structure at the end of the dock.

"It's the old shipyard," said Harold, taking her hand. "Come with me, I want to show you something."

Mary Rose allowed her young husband to lead her into the dusty building. In the middle of the shipyard, Harold stopped and showed her where to sit on a big pile of lumber while he went to get something. When he came back, he brought with him a huge scroll tied with a yellow ribbon.

Harold leaned forward and gave his wife a soft kiss on her lips. Mary Rose felt a shiver of pleasure. She loved how Harold always smelled of sea and wood.

"Happy anniversary, Rosy," he whispered as he gave her the scroll.

Mary Rose untied the knot gently and spread the paper over the boards. It was a large sheet full of detailed drawings, notes, and measurements. "They're plans for a ship," she mused.

"They are," he said, sounding pleased. "But it's not just the ship I'm giving you, Rose. It's the chance to fulfill our dream. The dream we've always talked about, the dream of leaving the island and traveling, exploring, taking a chance on the unknown."

Mary Rose saw the spark in his eyes that she loved so much, the look that said he could do anything. "You know I would love that," she said, gently grabbing his arm as if she wanted to hold him back. "But we don't have the money to build something like this, Harold."

"I know." He sat down next to her. "But my supervisor said that if I work extra hours, I can use this old shipyard and build our boat using surplus lumber."

"You're serious? We really could leave?"

"Well, it'll take a lot of work. But I don't think we're in any hurry." He touched Mary Rose's belly tenderly.

Mrs. Grapes looked down at the small bump outlined by her green dress. Her hands covered Harold's, and she felt a flutter inside. Mary Rose looked up, but the light had changed around her. Harold was no longer in front of her, nor was the old shipyard building; instead, there was a door with layers of old white paint. She opened it and entered a room illuminated only by a shadowy yellow glow.

"Be super quiet, Mom," a voice whispered from the other side of the room.

Mary Rose walked over to the boy sitting in front of the window and felt the soft ocean breeze of a hot summer night blow through the window, the mauve-and-fuchsia hydrangeas she had planted in the flower boxes a few days earlier swaying softly.

Mary Rose kissed the top of her son's head. He hugged her without taking his eyes off the large pompoms on which a dozen fireflies danced and glowed like embers.

"They like them," he whispered.

"What do they like?"

"The flowers," he said, looking at her like he was sharing a great secret. "Before, they would fly away as soon as I let them go, but since you planted the flowers, they stay all night, keeping me company."

Mary Rose smiled when she recognized the same excitement and innocence she knew from Harold's eyes. She sat down on the edge of the bed and showed him a big jar she'd brought.

"Just this morning your father finished the grape jam," she said, handing him the mason jar. "And I thought you'd want this, so you could catch more fireflies."

The boy's face shone with pleasure, and he very carefully took it, holding it like a priceless treasure. "I can fit twice as many fireflies in here, Mom!" he exclaimed, holding it above his head. "Tomorrow when I help Dad in the shipyard, I'll bring back a ton! And when we live on the boat, they'll light the way for us!"

Mary Rose smiled at the happiness radiating from her son's eyes. Then he placed the jar carefully on the small night table and wrapped his arms around his mother's neck, showering her with kisses.

"It's just an empty jar, Dylan!" she laughed.

He stopped kissing her and sighed. "I love you."

Mary Rose hugged him tightly, his brown hair tickling her cheek, and she wished she could hold on to the moment forever. "I love you too, Dylan."

Mary Rose closed her eyes and squeezed him tighter, but instead of feeling Dylan in her arms, all she felt was emptiness. An emptiness that was more than physical.

A cold drizzle that smelled like salt water was falling on her face, and when she opened her eyes, she discovered a crowd of people looking at her. She hardly recognized them as they filed past. She sensed their looks of pity and the black homogeneity of their funeral garb as they walked down the muddy hill scattered with dying grapevines and headed back into town. It was Dylan's funeral. A ceremony without a body, without anyone to say good-bye to.

Finally, she was alone, or at least she thought she was. But Harold was there too. Without even looking at him, she walked past him to the edge of the barren cliff. In front of her was the gray sea, devoid of the blue that had shone in her son's eyes. Mary Rose knew that Dylan lay at rest somewhere in the giant abyss. She felt her tears spill over, burning her eyes, and then a hand tenderly took hers. But instead of feeling consoled by Harold's gesture, she felt a stab of pain and condemnation. She yanked her hand away.

"We can't give up," she heard Harold say.

Mary Rose spun around, her face red from crying; she was blinded by the same rage that seemed to fuel the waves that endlessly beat on the island. "He's never coming back!" she yelled, the words tearing at her throat. "Never!" Her voice echoed like a knife on the cliff walls, and she was racked with deep sobs.

Harold tried to hold her, but she pushed him away hard enough to cause him to fall back into the mud and crush the vines underneath him. "It's your fault! Yours!"

She ran down the hill, trying to escape the echo of her poisonous words that seemed to follow her like a pack of hungry wolves. The rain soaking her body stopped, and she felt her rage bury itself in some deep, inaccessible part of her as she was overcome by the powerful smell of fresh dirt. When she opened her eyes, she saw dozens of mauve-and-fuchsia flowers encircling the large unpainted house like an embrace.

"What color do you want?" The voice came from behind her.

Turning around, she saw Harold holding several paint cans. He looked different; his eyes had lost their sparkle, and his dark hair was sprinkled with gray. Mary Rose looked at the paint colors: sky blue, olive green, and bright yellow. The last color was the same color that had been in Dylan's room, and it shone through the darkness like a lighthouse beacon. Mary Rose thought of the fireflies that flitted around the hydrangeas, the same flowers she had planted in this garden. She knew which color.

When Mary Rose touched the can of yellow paint, it burst into hundreds of fireflies that fluttered around her like nervous sparks. Mary Rose reeled back, dizzy. The little points of light disappeared and were replaced by a vast sea that seemed to be hers alone. A wild landscape, virgin and unexplored. She looked up and saw two large, white sails cut across the deep-blue sky, billowing like huge lungs filled with air. Mary Rose caught her breath, feeling the soft breeze blowing her long hair that was now streaked with gray. Under her bare feet was a long deck of varnished wood, and she knew where she was. She was in a place where she had never set foot, a place that wasn't part of her memories, but of her dreams. She was on the boat they had been building, the nameless ship that had never set sail. And even though it couldn't be real, she was happy. Mary Rose felt the power of the ship carrying her, and then a loud roll of thunder crashed over her body. She heard the old woman's lament, a sound that seemed to emanate through the boards, a force that wanted to break everything. Mary Rose saw the helm spinning back and forth a few feet in front of her, and a firefly danced between its spokes. She approached the wheel, and then, just as she was about to grab it, she heard laughter in the distance.

"Kirima!" she shouted.

The ship rocked violently, and water began to cover her bare feet. Mary Rose shouted again, but she couldn't distinguish where the laughter was coming from. The resonant lament and the sound of splintering wood consumed everything. A new crash of thunder made the ship creak, and a crack appeared between her feet. Thousands of bubbles gurgled through the gap, and the water level rose quickly. Then she heard the laugh again and couldn't move. It wasn't Kirima's laugh, it was—"Dylan!" she screamed. The ship started listing, and Mary Rose grabbed the helm.

"Dylan, I'm here!" she yelled again.

The firefly circled around her, and she felt a pleasant warmth spreading through her arms, her chest, and her face. It seemed to melt the ice, pain, and bitterness that shrouded her. She felt powerful, sure, and capable of anything. With the helm in her hands, she was free. Too much light, too much heat. A second later, she awoke.

Startled, Mary Rose sat up in the bed of blankets that surrounded her, not knowing if she was awake or asleep. A bright light blinded her.

"Forgive my intrusion," said a hoarse voice.

The light was lowered, and she could see Amak holding a torch at the entrance to the tent. His eyes were hidden in the shadows and were made even darker by the flickering of the flame.

"Is everything all right?" Harold asked, moving to the entrance.

"I know it's early, but I came to see if you wanted to go fishing with me."

Harold didn't hesitate. "Yes, of course I'll go with you."

Mary Rose was still muddled and had a terrible headache, but his words brought her back to reality like a slap.

"We'll leave in fifteen minutes," said Amak.

The flap closed behind him, leaving the room in absolute darkness.

"You can't really be going."

Harold sighed and sat down next to Mary Rose. The darkness hid their faces from each other. "I have to," he murmured.

"You have to?" she repeated indignantly. "It's only been a few days since—"

But she stopped, trying to control the pain she felt remembering Kirima's silent body covered in tiny snowflakes and wrapped in her father's trembling arms. In her head, she heard the laughter on the boat deck.

"That's precisely why I must go, Rose. It's the least I can do for a father who has lost his child."

He got up and a moment later was swallowed by the opening in the tent. Mary Rose was alone again, wrapped in a darkness that grew around her as the sound of the dogs' barking and the sled runners faded in the distance.

A Hole in the Ice

The dogs panted heavily, picking up speed as they pulled the sled farther away from camp. Harold looked back at their tent, which was obscured in the wake of snow and ice, and saw a figure emerge. It was nothing more than a grayish smudge, but he knew it was Mary Rose. A second later, the camp disappeared, swallowed by the snow, and Harold felt guilty for his abrupt departure.

He faced forward again and found absolutely nothing to help him get his bearings. Everything was covered in an infinite white glaze. The sky and land merged together in a blurry embrace, impossible to distinguish from one another.

The icy wind began to blow harder across the extensive plain, taking his breath away and stinging his face. The wind swirled through the dogs' thick gray fur and buffeted the sled with powerful gusts that made the wood creak. Harold huddled deeper under the layer of blankets that Amak had piled on their laps, but the cold crept in from all sides. Only a narrow strip of skin between his hat and scarf remained exposed.

Amak didn't seem terribly bothered by the weather. His face was set, eyes fixed on the blurry horizon. He was attentive to the depressions and cracks that occasionally appeared along the edges of the sled's blades and that the dogs avoided with surprising agility. Harold wondered what the man must be thinking. Over the last several days, he had not seen him shed a single tear, hadn't heard a word of complaint or regret. But a profound sadness was reflected in Amak's dark eyes. Harold wanted to say something, but Amak spoke first.

"We're getting to the thinnest part of the ice field," he said, gently pulling on the reins to slow the dogs down. "It's not far now."

At that moment, he saw the thin line of the sea. Almost black, it stretched out across the whole horizon. Amak shouted something, and the dogs veered right. The terrain was milky white, lined with cracks they had to negotiate.

"We're here," Amak called out, pulling firmly on the reins.

The dogs slowed to a gentle stop, and the sled came to rest next to a long, blue crack in the ice. Harold felt stiff. The scarf covering his nose and chin was hard, frozen by his own breath. Amak threw aside the blankets and jumped down. Harold followed.

"From here, we go on foot," said Amak, unharnessing the dogs.

Harold saw they were quite close to the sea, which was dotted with hundreds of sheets of ice and bergs that steadily broke away from the giant ice field on which they were walking. Amak went to the back of the sled and unloaded a couple of large bags, boxes, and plastic buckets. Harold picked up one of the heavy bags and put it on his back. They walked over the ice, accompanied by the dogs that ran around them freely.

The terrain felt different under his feet than the snow around the camp. The surface was much harder, with almost no snow. The strong breeze coming off the water snaked over the ice field, baring the slippery, polished ice below.

About a half hour later, Amak came to a stop.

"This is it," he said, striking the ice hard with his heel.

Harold felt vibrations pass through his feet and all the way up to the top of his head, and he shivered with the thought of what would happen if the ice broke.

Amak took out a small shovel and began to scrape away the thin layer of snow. Harold took off his bag. Inside, he found the same shovel he had used to help bury Kirima.

Soon the snow was cleared, exposing the ice underneath. It looked like a large slab of veined marble. Amak struck the ice again, producing a hollow sound, and a large air pocket trapped under the ice shattered into hundreds of pearly bubbles.

"Step back," Amak said as he got a small ax out of the bag. "This is the most dangerous part."

Harold moved back and stood with the dogs, who were resting in the snow. Amak struck the ice so hard the ground shook. The vibration disturbed the dogs, who began to whine nervously. Harold felt an icy sweat break out on his back. He realized he didn't know what to do if Amak fell in the water. He knelt to check the supplies in his bag and found a thick rope. He relaxed a little. The ice shattered again, and some loose fragments flew. Harold stepped forward, rope in hand. Amak swung again, and the ax penetrated the thick layer of ice. Water immediately rose through the hole and pooled around them. Amak continued working on the opening until it was a good three feet in diameter, providing a big enough area for both of them to fish. Harold set the rope off to the side and used his shovel to help clear the large pieces of ice floating in the hole.

"Now we fish."

Harold and Amak got the small fishing poles from their bags, and Harold thought about the tiny pole that had fallen from Kirima's basket the day they met her. The men sat on buckets at the edge of the hole and baited the hooks with thick whale blubber that Amak had brought wrapped in a cloth. Then they lowered their lines.

The hours passed slowly, dragged out by a stiff wind that battered them mercilessly as they tried to hold their poles steady. The water in the hole was so dark that Harold couldn't even see the bait. It was a gloomy, unknown abyss, a well in which anything could be hiding.

Harold thought about Kirima. He imagined her seated in the same place, on one of the buckets, searching the water and hoping for a gullible fish to swallow her bait. Harold remembered the first day he took Dylan fishing. He was not much more than five years old. Harold smiled slightly as he remembered how Dylan held the little pole Harold had made him for all of five minutes. After that, he'd just watched his dad. Harold remembered his son's little hands holding onto the side of the boat, searching the water with those eyes as deep blue as the sea, hoping to spot the silhouette of a huge fish.

Harold's pole jerked. He peered into the well but didn't see anything; it was just the wind. Harold felt the bucket under him shake. Or was it he who was shaking? He remembered the storm that pummeled the camp the day Kirima died and imagined the force with which the wind must have blown across the ice field with nothing to protect them. Harold didn't know how Kirima had died; he hadn't dared ask Amak. He had suffered so much himself when the whole town had subjected him to question after question, none of which he could answer without feeling even more guilty and miserable.

Then Amak spoke. "I was too late to save her."

Amak's eyes remained fixed on the imperceptible movement of the water.

"The whole way here, she pestered me about wanting to make the hole, saying she was old enough. I laughed and told her she still wasn't strong enough to break the ice."

Harold smiled faintly as he remembered the day she'd dropped the fish while trying to carry boxes like her father and brother did.

"After we let the dogs loose," continued Amak, "the snowstorm picked up strength, so we hurried and got out our supplies, hoping to fish at least a little bit. I realized I had left the bait on the sled and asked Ukluk to go with me to get it. As we started back to Kirima, I heard the dogs barking. We ran as fast as we could, but when we got here, she was already gone. There was a huge crack, right here." He pointed

202

to the opening where they had their poles. "The ice had cracked under her, and she was floating among the pieces of ice. I jumped in. But it was too late. When we pulled her body out, her heart wasn't beating."

Before Harold could think better of it, the words burst out like a buoy propelled by a wave. "I lost a child too."

Amak was startled. He looked up from the hole and stared at Harold. Harold saw his eyes were red and filled with the tears that he hadn't seen until now. He felt stupid, guilty for having uttered those words.

"I shouldn't have said anything," he said, looking back at the dark pool.

"What happened?" Amak's voice was hoarse.

Harold sighed, not daring to meet his eyes. He stared at the water, lost in the dark abyss. "It was so many years ago," he said, tightly gripping his pole, "but there's not a day I don't remember that night as if it were yesterday. Time and again, I feel the wave crash against the side of the boat, the cold water pulling me down, and most of all, the unbearable darkness that covered me when I came to the surface. It wasn't the sea; it was my stupidity for underestimating its power, my stupidity for believing my son would always be safe if he was with me—it was my fault Dylan died that night. And I can't stop torturing myself day after day, thinking about everything we lost. He never got to finish the ship we were building together; he never got to make the voyage he longed for."

"What about you? Did you and your wife?"

Harold looked at him, visibly upset. "We . . . we couldn't do it without him," he stammered.

Amak furrowed his brow, squinting. "Look around you," he said, looking to the sky. "The clouds moving above us, the constant blowing of the wind, the ice breaking, the sea silently slipping under our feet . . . nothing ever stops."

Amak lowered his eyes again and looked at Harold, who suddenly felt dizzy, terrified by all the movement around him. "Life is a nomadic journey, Mr. Grapes. A road without trees to shelter us from the rain, without shoulders on which to rest, without lighthouses to show us the way when we are lost. I can't waste the life I've been given by standing still and lamenting the past until my days run out. I must get up and fight; I must keep providing for my family. I must keep moving forward, not just for myself, but also for my daughter and for all those who are no longer with us. Because in the end, that's why we're here, right? The only reason we are given life is to live it."

A hint of light glimmered on the dark waves of the well. Harold saw the clouds break and a long shaft of sunlight reached down through the sky, free from its prison. Then Harold's pole jerked. The first bite.

Beyond the Horizon

It was getting dark when Mary Rose finally left their tent. She had spent the whole day wrapped in the warmth of the blankets and immersed in a state of semiconsciousness. Now she walked through the snow, leaving the camp behind to see if she could spot the sled returning home. She was haunted by the remnants of the strange dream she had woken up with that morning. She came to a small rise and stopped. Some of the fires in the camp were lit, and from up here, the glowing, yellow tents reminded her of the little fireflies. She wanted to see her son's smile again, feel his sweet hugs and soft kisses on her face. Mary Rose squeezed her eyes shut, trying to freeze the moment in her head, but no matter how hard she tried, the images slipped away.

Finally, she opened her eyes and turned her back to the tents, looking in the direction Harold and Amak had gone that morning. Her eyes swept across the enormous open plain as she wondered where they could be. Then she made out the yellow patch that was once her house; it was outlined against the pale purple horizon like a shadow puppet. She once again felt the wet rain on her face and saw the people of San Remo dressed in black on the day of the funeral. She heard her own voice echoing off the cliff, and then she thought of the dark fur they had wrapped little Kirima in—fragile, pale, unmoving as she was slowly lowered into the giant field of ice that surrounded Mary Rose now. She felt the weight of loss all over again, the emptiness of her existence. She looked to the sky to keep the tears from spilling down her face and saw the hazy clouds breaking up into little wisps that gradually cleared, revealing a moonless night sky in which the stars shone brightly. Then she heard someone approach, and she turned to see Aga huddled under her fur coat, hair tucked into her hood.

"Don't worry," she said, looking at the distant horizon. "They'll be here soon."

Mary Rose tilted her head to one side and furtively wiped her tears. She didn't want Aga to see her cry.

"There's no shame," whispered Aga.

"I should be the one comforting you," Mary Rose said, not daring to meet her eyes.

Aga sighed and gently touched Mrs. Grapes's shoulder. Mary Rose looked at her, realizing that, despite the dark circles, the woman's eyes showed profound serenity and strength. Mary Rose couldn't fathom it and wondered how Aga could even leave her tent. For months after Dylan died, she hadn't left her room. She could hardly get out of bed. She remembered how sleeping was the only peace she could find during that time, the only thing that took away the pain. All she wanted was to get lost in dreams in which her son's happy face appeared every afternoon at the door of the florist shop, hair disheveled as he asked for the sack with their dinner so he could then run off to the shipyard where his father was waiting for him. Her memories of those months were hazy and confusing, an incoherent, fragile time of tears, shouting, sobbing, and blame.

After a few minutes, Aga lowered the hand that had been on Mary Rose's shoulder and stepped to the edge of the rise.

"Tomorrow we will resume our preparations to head north," she said without looking away. "We must leave soon, but there's time for one last thing. Something we want to do for you before we leave for good."

Mary Rose didn't move. She remained a few steps behind Aga, waiting for her to finish.

"Tomorrow, Amak and my son will take you both to your house so you can retrieve anything important."

Mary Rose felt a cold that froze her even more than the biting wind. She was stunned by the offer. Until that moment, she had not considered the possibility. She thought of the hundreds of objects, furniture, and junk that filled the lonely, frozen rooms. She couldn't find meaning in any of it. The bottled ships in Bubble Wrap, the clothing accumulated in closets and dressers . . . suddenly, her heart beat faster. One small item hiding under her pajamas in the dresser. It was the only object in the whole house of real value, the only thing they still had of their son: the photo taken in the shipyard. But when she turned to see the dark shadow of the house in the decomposing ice, she knew that, no matter how much it hurt, she couldn't ask her friends to make the journey for a faded piece of paper.

"We are so grateful, but—" She had a bitter taste in her mouth.

"Accept it as a gift from us," Aga interrupted. "There won't be any going back later. It's your last chance to say good-bye."

Mary Rose turned to Aga and was surprised by how much she looked like Kirima. She felt her breath catch in her throat. How was it possible that, despite having lost her daughter so recently, this woman was able to comfort them by offering them one last trip to their home? Mary Rose knew they were already impossibly indebted to Amak and Aga for having saved their lives, for having cared for them, and now for giving them the opportunity to return to San Remo. Mary Rose moved forward to the edge of the slope, stopping at Aga's side and looking in the same direction. In a few months, all this would melt and return to the monstrous sea. The same sea that would swallow the house forever—the same sea that had taken Dylan so many years ago and that now had also taken Kirima.

For the first time, she was not ashamed to have Aga see her tears. Mary Rose wondered how it was possible that she did not see blame or hatred in Aga's eyes, only strength born from pain, like the old woman's lament or a firefly's light that fights to shine in the darkness. It was something she had never managed herself. Instead, she had been taken hostage by her pain. She had stopped fighting and taken refuge in her resentment toward Harold.

"How do you do it?" Mary Rose whispered, looking up at the twinkling dome of stars.

"There is nothing we can do about death. It's out of our control. As long as we are alive, the only thing we can do is live."

The power of Aga's words carried her away from the snowy hill and took her back to her son's funeral. She was looking at the ice field but saw the cold sea in front of their cliff. The sea that had taken her son. The son that Harold had not protected.

"But how do you not blame anyone?" murmured Mary Rose without thinking.

Aga turned and looked at her in surprise. "Blame anyone?"

A gust of cold air whistled between the two women, and Mary Rose realized she had spoken aloud.

"Whom should I blame?" Aga asked before Mary Rose could retract the question. "Amak for having left Kirima alone for a few minutes? Myself for having let her go fishing? The ice for breaking? My daughter for acting foolishly? No. Bitterness and blame only imprison us and prevent us from moving forward."

Her words struck with painful clarity, and Mary Rose began to feel the same tremor that had come over her when she heard the old woman's guttural lament. Images of her memories rushed forth like in her dream. She heard her own piercing cries on the cliff, the repulsion at feeling Harold's hand touch her, and her anger when she pushed him to the ground. Mary Rose felt sick when the question she had dreaded hearing came from Aga's mouth.

"What was your child's name?"

Mary Rose felt as if she had been struck by lightning. She remembered that, just before they heard the shouting and the dogs barking, she had been about to tell Aga about Dylan. She had been relieved she hadn't. Mary Rose never would have forgiven herself if she had told the story of her son's death moments before Aga discovered she had lost her own daughter. Mary Rose felt bare and defenseless, ripped open. She tried to speak but could not pronounce her son's name out loud. She was afraid that if she did, it would open a door impossible to ever close again.

"It's all in the past," she said, looking toward the house.

"The past can be a heavy burden," Aga said.

"How do you lighten it?" Mary Rose asked, turning to Aga, her eyes shimmering with tears.

"You can't," Aga answered firmly. "But we can become stronger, so the weight doesn't hold us back on our journey."

"Our journey," she mumbled to herself, the words tainted for her.

"Life is a constant journey. We move from one place to another," said Aga. "The journey is what makes a fish different than a rock, movement different from stillness, light from darkness, life from death."

Mary Rose remembered how the tall mast stuck out from the old shipyard the day they decided to take apart not only their dream but also their life. The day they decided to change the fish into a rock: the boat into a house. An icy breath of air blew off her hood and swirled her hair. Mary Rose was overcome by the same feeling of freedom that she had felt sailing on the ship in her dream. She remembered the yellow light of the firefly that flitted among the hydrangeas, her son's laugh in the shipyard, and the excitement in Harold's eyes when he first showed her the plans for the boat. Her whole body was shaking, but she took a deep breath.

"He died shortly before we were to set sail on the boat we were building."

Aga gave a long sigh. "And what did you do with the boat?"

"We took it apart." She paused briefly and continued: "We made it into—" Then Mary Rose nodded toward the shipwrecked house, barely visible in the pale light of the stars.

Aga followed her gaze and understood. "A fish that looks like a rock is still a fish, isn't it?"

Mary Rose knit her brow, but before she could speak, a flash of golden light appeared in the sky.

"Look," said Aga, pointing to the heavens.

After a few seconds, Mary Rose saw two supernatural shapes dancing between the hundreds of stars filling the sky.

"Do you know what the northern lights are?" whispered Aga, without taking her eyes off the sky.

One of the lights was a deep, fiery red and the other a familiar golden yellow. The chaotic dance of the auroras soothed her and reminded her of the moment of absolute peace she had shared with Harold when she saw them for the first time on the ocean. The two of them alone, drifting aboard their home. The two ribbons crossed and flashed, and suddenly she heard the old woman's lament in her head. The resonant voice no longer made her uneasy, no longer broke her from the inside. Now it wrapped her in warmth, protected her.

"According to our ancestors, the sky is an enormous dome made of the strongest, most resilient material in the universe," Aga told her. "Beyond the horizon lies eternity, the land of the dead. It's a place made of light that we see only when a soul slowly ascends to it, delighting us in its perfection, erasing our sorrow, and reminding us of the beauty in our world."

Mary Rose felt tears well up, but this time they were from contentment. She watched the two forms dancing with each other as their colors blended and freed her from all the sorrow, pain, and ugliness. She felt the ocean breeze blowing through her hair, the rolling of the deck as they moved over the waves, and the freedom of the unknown.

"His name was Dylan." Mary Rose smiled.

"I think Dylan and Kirima just met each other."

Return and Departure

Mary Rose had already been asleep for some time when a draft of cold air woke her. She felt Harold's body sliding over to snuggle closer to her under the pile of blankets. She didn't mind; in fact, Mary Rose was comforted by the touch of his arms encircling her. Harold warmed up next to Mary Rose; then, after he gave her a goodnight kiss on the back of her neck, they both drifted off.

The next morning, they got up and went outside carrying their backpack, the seal pup playing around their feet. The wind had scrubbed away the clouds and left a brilliant blue sky. They felt the sun warming their frozen cheeks on the walk to Amak and Aga's tent.

The preparations for moving the camp had begun again, just as Aga had told Mary Rose they would. Groups of people moved back and forth to the sleds carrying folded tents, but this time, despite the good weather, everyone seemed to move slowly. No one was running or shouting; even the children seemed solemn. They all knew that this move meant a difficult and definitive good-bye. A final farewell to Kirima.

Harold and Mary Rose turned toward the ice field where little Kirima's body rested, but the sunlight bounced off the softening snow so brightly it felt like they were looking directly at the sun. All they could see in the middle of the white was one dark spot. Rising in front of a thin line of dark blue so intense it could only be the sea was their house. Today they would say a final good-bye to it also.

They continued toward the center of camp, where they found Amak and Ukluk loading boxes onto a sled. The seal sniffed around the big dogs that were already harnessed, then scurried away into one of the nearby tents. Amak turned and smiled when he saw them.

Amak clapped his hand on Harold's shoulder. "Harold is one of the best fishermen I know!"

Mary Rose looked at him, wondering if Amak was joking and remembering how they had barely caught enough to keep them alive during their voyage. Amak pointed to the side of the sled, where half a dozen large crates were piled up, all full of fat, shiny cod.

"You caught all that?" she exclaimed, her mouth agape.

"I don't think we'll need to fish again for another month!" Ukluk added.

It had been a long time since Harold had felt so proud. He was happy not only to have caught enough fish to feed the group for a good many days but also to have accompanied Amak. The trip was important, and he had connected with Amak in a way that he hadn't been able to do with anyone for years. They had forged a bond of friendship.

At just that moment, Aga came out of the tent with a little bundle that steamed in the cold. Her hair cascaded down the sides of her face, shining like silk in the sunshine. Mary Rose was pleased to see the shadows that had darkened her eyes the night before were now less pronounced.

"This is for your journey to the house," said Aga, offering them the bundle.

Mary Rose took it from her and felt warmth coming through the cloth. She peeked in to find little loaves of bread.

"Thank you so much," she said.

Ukluk helped Mrs. Grapes get settled in the back of the sled, got up on the front, then waited for his father to do the same. Amak loaded one of the full boxes of fish. Before he mounted the sled, Aga held him. She buried her face in the soft fur of Amak's coat and breathed in deeply. Mary Rose's heart raced when saw them embracing each other like that, in front of them and the whole village. Slowly, they released each other, and before Amak made his way to the sled, he went back to Aga and kissed her on the lips. Harold and Mary Rose were surprised, having never seen such intimacy between the couple before.

Finally, Amak got on the sled, and after a brief good-bye to everyone gathered, he whistled sharply. With a mild creak, the sled began to move. The dogs quickly picked up speed. Even though the settlement was soon left behind, Mary Rose's thoughts remained there among the tents. She couldn't get Amak and Aga's embrace out of her head. They had lost their daughter, just like she and Harold had lost their son. Yet there was no hint of rebuke or resentment in their eyes. There was no bitterness or anger. She reflected on the venomous contempt with which she had treated Harold during those first months without Dylan and the silent distance that had come between them over the years. How, in disgust, she had rejected the comfort he had offered. How, seething with rage, she had pushed him onto the muddy ground. Again, she heard her angry words when she screamed that it had been his fault their son had died that night. Mary Rose realized that none of that had helped to ease her pain; it had only isolated her from the only person who truly loved her. More than that, it had prevented her wounds from healing. She felt her eyes fill with tears. Without even realizing what she was doing, she removed her mitten and tenderly took Harold's bare hand, the same way he had taken hers so many years ago.

House of Ice

"We're almost there!" called Amak.

Harold and Mary Rose had dozed off, and Amak's shout abruptly roused them from their sleep. When they opened their eyes, they saw the landscape and light had changed. The sun was completely blocked by the black mountain they had seen when they first arrived in that inhospitable land, and the ice and sea had turned the color of antique gold. As Mary Rose stretched, she was surprised to see how close they were to the house. The battered yellow paint seemed to glow in the afternoon sun and stood out in contrast to the white that covered the porch roof and deck. As they got closer, they saw that the roof was no longer formed by two steep slopes of black tiles. It had turned into a shapeless mass of rafters, with pieces of slate sticking out of the mountain of snow that had flattened it.

Finally, the dogs slowed down until Amak whistled, and the sled stopped a safe distance from the edge of the ice field.

"Ukluk!" called Amak as he jumped down onto the ice. "Stay here with the dogs. You can set up the tents for us to spend the night. We'll be back for supper."

Then he went to the rear of the sled and got out some empty bags, which he threw over his shoulder. Harold and Mary Rose got down also.

They were numb from the cold ride, but it didn't matter. After a quick good-bye, they left Ukluk and followed Amak across the fragile ice.

As they got closer, the sound of ice breaking and being pulled out into the sea grew louder. The front of the house appeared to be sculpted from the ice surrounding it. The porch steps were covered in rubble that had fallen from the roof, the posts showed scrapes and wear, the siding was a jumble of broken planks, and the doorknob was covered in a layer of ice that glittered like thousands of gemstones in the afternoon light.

Amak stood behind Mr. and Mrs. Grapes, his eyes wide at the sight.

They all stared in silence for a few seconds, hearing the ice cracking and slowly breaking off around them. Harold and Mary Rose looked at each other, unsure of whether to enter. It felt like they were about to desecrate the ruins of an ancient temple. Finally, Harold reached for the door and, with difficulty, managed to turn the frozen knob. The ice that covered the metal cracked and stuck to his hand like a sparkling scab. As he pushed on the door, the ice that sealed the edges broke and a cascade of crystals crashed to the ground.

Harold expected to feel warmer, stale air when he opened the door, but inside, it was just as cold. The floors, walls, stairway, and lamps were completely covered with the same ice as the exterior.

As he crossed into the front hall, Harold felt as if he were entering an enchanted house full of frozen memories. Amak crossed the threshold after Mary Rose and carefully shut the door. He walked slowly, his eyes roaming nervously, unable to focus.

"Amazing," he murmured as he ran his hand over the broken banister.

In Amak's face, Harold and Mary Rose recognized the curiosity they had seen in Kirima's as she listened to stories of their adventures. Mary Rose smiled as she thought of the millions of questions Kirima would have asked had she been there with them.

They went to the kitchen, and Amak set the bags on the table. Its surface was like a shiny sheet of metal under the light of the setting sun filtering through the broken windows. The whole kitchen seemed to glow with a brilliant, golden aura.

"Do you mind if I look around while you get what you need?" Amak asked, running his hand over the curve of the faucet.

"This is your home," answered Harold, repeating what Aga had told them a few days before. "And if you see anything of use, please take it."

Harold and Mary Rose headed down the hallway with their backpack. As they passed by the open door to the basement, Mary Rose glanced down the stairwell. The light barely shone through the portholes, leaving the last steps in the dark. She felt a draft coming up the stairs like a ghostly breath. Harold joined her, and a shiver ran down his spine when he felt the icy draft.

"Too dark to see much." Harold turned back down the hallway. "I don't think there's anything we need down there anyway."

Mary Rose followed Harold to the dining room. It felt like they were in a run-down antique shop full of damaged items. Mary Rose went to the ruins of the china cabinet and wondered why on earth anyone would own a piece of furniture whose sole function was to display decorative plates and glasses. The backpack Harold was carrying was almost empty, but he wasn't even tempted to fill it with anything he saw cluttering the spaces they walked through. He stopped in front of a painting hanging over the improvised fireplace they had made to fend off hypothermia. A thin layer of soot covered the glass, and Harold wiped it away with his hand. Looking at the painting as if for the first time, he realized the maritime scene bore no resemblance to reality. The color of the setting sun, the reflections on the waves, and the fullness of the clouds seemed extraordinarily dull and artificial, far from their true beauty. Harold thought about the color of the sky at dawn and dusk that they had seen as they drifted on the sea, the ethereal shapes of the northern lights as they danced over their heads, and the perfection of the dolphin's acrobatics. The painting disgusted him, and he left the room.

Mary Rose was waiting for him at the bottom of the stairs that led to the second story. Harold looked at her and saw in her eyes the real reason they were there. Careful not to slip on the frost-covered steps, they went upstairs to their bedroom.

They walked past the boxes stacked around the room without even glancing at their contents. The rugs, pictures, and books stored in them now seemed like junk taking up space and gathering dust. Silently they approached the window and studied the frozen landscape through the broken glass. The view had changed significantly since they had left in search of help. The ice field in which the house was stuck was no longer uniform but full of cracks and puddles. They clearly heard ice breaking all around. Darkness began to close in. Not far away, they saw a yellow light. Ukluk must have started a fire. They knew they couldn't delay anymore; they had to hurry and get the only thing in the house that still held any value for them.

When Harold and Mary Rose stood in front of the heavy dresser, it was like reliving the final night before their eviction. Mary Rose opened the top drawer and quickly lifted the layers of clothing, revealing the small, square piece of paper that had been protected amid the wool and cotton. Harold carefully retrieved the photograph. This scrap of paper was the greatest treasure they possessed, the only thing that remained of a time when they had been happy. Harold turned it over to see the image on the other side, and then he froze. A thunderous boom like that of the fateful lightning strike on the cliff shook the room. But it wasn't lightning. Suddenly, the house shook violently and tilted to one side, throwing them to the other end of the room. Then the house righted itself with another violent crash. They heard Amak roar up the stairs: "Hurry! The house is breaking away from the ice field!"

Harold slipped the photograph into the bag, and they scrambled down the icy stairs. Meanwhile, they heard water rushing through the dozens of cracks in the house. The steps creaked under them, and one snapped in two under Harold's weight. Mary Rose caught him, and they continued down the stairs. Amak was waiting in front of the open door with a lantern swaying dangerously. Without even a final glance, they ran across the porch. As they stepped onto the ice, they realized the whole ice field was oscillating. The sheets of ice grated and creaked. The light from the lantern bounced in front of them in time with Amak's steps as he nimbly jumped and dodged the spreading cracks. Finally, the ground stopped shaking, but sheets of ice continued to buck up and down, making them dizzy. Once they were a safe distance from the house, they looked back, expecting to see the enormous wooden structure dislodged from the ice field, but it clung on.

They arrived back at camp under the dark of night. Only a thin sliver of moon interfered with the hundreds of stars that sparkled in the sky like glowing silver embers. Ukluk was waiting for them by the fire he had built in front of two small tents. The dogs were milling about the sled nervously due to the commotion.

Harold and Mary Rose hardly touched the cod Ukluk had prepared. The camp was immersed in a tense silence broken only by the unsettling sound of ice creaking in the distance. They soon called it a night. The next day, they would get up early to return to camp and then start the journey north.

Just before entering their tent, Harold and Mary Rose took one last look at the house, knowing that, when they woke, it would surely be gone. It was their good-bye, the final farewell for which they had been preparing. The only thing left was for the house to break free from the prison of ice that had trapped it. A prison like the one that had trapped them for years.

Unfinished Journey

Sheltered in the makeshift tent and still wearing their coats, Harold and Mary Rose lit a candle and huddled around the tenuous yellow light.

"How long do you think until we reach San Remo?" murmured Mary Rose, her gaze lost in the golden flame.

"Amak said it's quite a journey to the Great Breach, but once we're there, plenty of ships pass that can take us back to the island fairly quickly."

Mary Rose nodded, lost in thought.

"Don't you want to go back?" asked Harold, observing his wife.

"No, it's not that," she said, watching the tent above them swaying in the wind. "I just don't know what it will be like to go back to our old life."

"I was thinking about that too."

"This afternoon," Mary Rose said, "I thought that going back to the house and seeing all our things again would make me homesick. I thought that, after so many months of sleeping on the ground and eating out of one pot, I would miss all our comforts. Instead, I felt indifferent. Why do we need all that silverware when we can live with one spoon? We could have filled that," she continued as she looked at their backpack. "We could have easily filled it with books, clothes, blankets, bottled ships, silverware. But it's empty."

"We can't do anything about that now."

"I'm not sorry it's empty, Harold. I'm happy! When we first got here, I thought they led such sad lives, always moving around, struggling to survive. But now I realize we were the ones with sad lives! I wish we had friends like Amak and Aga at home. I'm going to miss them terribly."

Harold nodded slowly. "I'll miss them too, Rose. I still can't believe that scary man who yelled at us is the same man who is now such a close friend."

"I'll never forget the day Amak and the other two escorted you back to the tent—you should have seen your face! You were terrified!"

Harold frowned. "If they'd yelled at you like that, you would have felt the same way."

Mary Rose laughed, hardly recognizing the sound. "Luckily, Aga made them listen to our story."

"Yes. Remember how they were so suspicious of us? The only person who didn't think we were crazy was Kirima."

As he said her name, a frigid breeze penetrated the tent, making the candle waver. Harold went to the entrance and tightened the flap while Mary Rose opened the bag and took out the blanket to cover their legs. As she did, the photo fell in her lap. Mary Rose picked it up carefully and turned it over to see the faded image. In the flickering light, it was as if they were seeing it for the first time.

"I don't think there'd ever been a summer as hot as that one," Mary Rose said softly, passing her finger along the edge of the photo.

Harold sighed and nodded in agreement. The cold seemed to ease as he remembered the sound of cicadas in the old shipyard, the sweat dripping off his forehead, and the pleasant ocean breezes that brought relief from the stifling air.

"I remember we spent all day varnishing the deck," said Harold.

"I didn't think we'd ever finish. It took forever!"

Harold focused on the small fragment of deck visible in the photograph. The afternoon sun fell on the wood still damp from the varnish, making it gleam like glass. "I can still feel the brush moving across the boards and smell the varnish," Harold said, more to himself than his wife. Then he paused, and a smile slowly spread across his face. "Oh, we laughed so hard when you accidentally sat on one of the wet boards!"

Mary Rose felt the memory, buried deep in her soul, bubble to the surface. "I had completely forgotten," she said, smiling.

"Really? We were laughing about the stain on your dress for days!"

They both burst into laughter in a way they hadn't for years. Mary Rose remembered the sound of Harold and Dylan howling in the old shipyard and her surprised shout when she realized they weren't playing a trick on her.

"I made it even worse when I tried to scrub it out with seawater," she added, unable to stop laughing.

"And we all ended up in the water!" Harold looked wistfully at their wet hair in the photograph.

Mary Rose remembered how the dip in the water had felt so good in the afternoon heat and how Dylan had splashed around, trying to catch the tiny fish that tickled their bare feet. Then her gaze stopped on Dylan's big blue eyes, which were smiling at the camera, full of life and excitement, and she thought again of Kirima.

"Kirima would have loved that story," said Mary Rose.

"If it hadn't been for her, we wouldn't be here now," Harold added.

Mary Rose nodded slowly as she thought about Kirima's smile. This time, instead of pain or sadness, she felt gratitude. She was grateful for the opportunity to have known Kirima and to have spent that time together.

"She gave us a second chance at life," she whispered.

Harold felt like those words might undo him, like ice weakened by the sun, but Mary Rose didn't notice. She was too engrossed by the image she held in her hands.

"Last night, I talked with Aga about Dylan," said Mary Rose. "She didn't know what happened, but she suspected. At first, I didn't know what to say. I didn't think I could tell a mother who had just lost her daughter anything about my own loss. But the way she looked at me was so different from how I felt. She looked serene, at peace—she didn't blame anyone or anything. She has already accepted the pain and emptiness that her daughter left behind."

Mary Rose paused as Harold studied her, observing the faint flickering of the candlelight in her big green eyes. "I was stupid and unfair with you, Harold," she said finally. "When I spoke with Aga, I understood that all the anger I built up over the years only served to isolate me in my pain. Without realizing it, I created an ocean between us." She looked up and into Harold's eyes. "Will you forgive me? I had no right to blame you for his death—as if you hadn't lost your son too. We both lost him."

Harold expelled the breath he had been holding and gently took the photo. "I blamed myself." He paused a moment. "Yesterday, while we were fishing, Amak asked me a question that threw me," he said softly. "He asked why we had decided not to embark on our journey. All those years, I told myself we had taken apart the ship because it was the right thing to do. Because without Dylan, our dream didn't mean anything." Harold paused again, taking a deep breath. "But now I know none of what we told ourselves was true, Rose. We built the house out of fear. Not fear of forgetting him, but fear of moving on with our lives, fear of realizing our dreams. We were afraid of being happy again without him."

Harold was crying, and Mary Rose held him, her own tears flowing. They began to shake, finally freeing themselves from the yoke they had placed on themselves for all those years. Now that yoke of pain, anger, blame, and fear crumbled under their tears like iron corroded by salty seawater.

"I feel like I've failed him."

Mary Rose let go of Harold and looked at him, her vision blurred by tears. "We both failed him, Harold," she said. "We failed him by allowing our pain to extinguish his light. We turned his memory into the anchor that put an end to all the dreams we shared."

Then a strong gust of wind ripped open the flap at the front of the tent, blowing out the candle. The small, pitch-black space was suffused with the smell of the snuffed-out wick. Harold felt around on the ground for the box of matches. He pulled one out and struck it on the back of the box. Immediately, a small spark blazed in the air as the match took, revealing the glistening trail of tears that ran down his cheeks. Mary Rose felt like something was breaking inside as she saw the small flame sparkle in Harold's eyes the same way the fireflies' had shone in Dylan's. It felt like she was dreaming again, remembering that summer night when she had given the mason jar to her son. She heard his laughter and felt his kisses on her face. *When we live on the boat, they'll light the way for us!* he'd said, bouncing happily around her. Finally, those words made sense, as if she had found the lost piece of a puzzle. It was an idea that she had never considered before. Now the words reverberated in her head with a lucidity that frightened her.

Mary Rose closed her eyes, trying to get the thought out of her head, but it was impossible. There was no turning back. Her whole body fought against the suspicion that flooded her mind and the pain in her heart. The wind shook the tent again, and when she opened her eyes, she saw the match flame flickering in Harold's eyes, as if begging her to say what they both already knew. Mary Rose took a long, deep breath.

"Maybe," she began as if threatened by her own words. The match flame danced, and its light became more tenuous, burning down little by little. Mary Rose gathered her strength. "Maybe we were wrong, Harold."

"I know we were," agreed Harold. "It's so obvious now." But then he paused and sighed, as if it took great effort to accept the truth. "We haven't been adrift these last few months," he continued, holding his wife's gaze. "We've been drifting through life since the day we allowed his death to put an end to our dreams. Since the day we allowed fear and resentment to fill the hole he left in our lives. From that day, we let the light that guided us go out. That night, we lost not only our son, Rose. We lost ourselves."

A tear landed on the photo.

"It wasn't our destiny to build that house," continued Harold. "Our destiny was to sail our boat." The tear slipped down the photograph and finally stopped on Dylan's smiling face. "Dylan wouldn't have wanted to see our lives lost in a sea of regret. We can't keep making the same mistakes we've made all these years. We can't remain grounded in fear and in the past. We must take control of the direction of our lives again. We owe it to him, and we owe it to ourselves."

Then the match flame flickered, and just before they were engulfed in darkness again, Mary Rose touched the wick to it and lit the candle. A stronger light filled the room.

Mary Rose noticed Harold's deep-blue eyes were observing her with an odd expression. A look she thought she had forgotten but recognized immediately. It was the same look that lit up Kirima's face every time they told her a story. It was the same look on Dylan's face when he set the fireflies free outside his window. It was the same look the three of them had in the old photograph they held in front of them. It was a look of innocence and courage, free of the weight of the past and the uncertainty of the future. A look full of a dreamer's hope and the belief of one who never gives up. It was a radiant, clear look, the look of someone who embraces life and everything that comes with it. A look full of light, the same light that danced in the glass jar Dylan held that night in the boat coming back from the shipyard. The same light that glowed over the hydrangeas in his window box and chased away the darkness that tried to overcome his bedroom.

A light that illuminated the smiling faces of the retired couple who, thirty-five years later, looked at each other once again as if anything were possible, as if they had been released from the pain, fear, and bitterness that had held them down. As if they were finally free again to sail through life with nothing to hold them back. Mr. and Mrs. Grapes intertwined their arms and melted into a deep embrace.

"It's time to start living."

The Thaw

The dogs began barking frantically. Amak's eyes flew open, and he saw only the darkness of his tent. He leaped out of the blankets. He felt his whole body trembling along with the ground, the tent, and everything around them. He quickly woke Ukluk and stumbled outside. Dawn was just breaking, and as he stepped on the ice, he knew what was happening. The ice sheet where they had set up camp was pulling away from the rest of the ice field.

"Get the dogs to the sled!" shouted Amak when he saw Ukluk tripping his way out of the tent, his eyes bulging in terror. "Hurry before it all goes under!"

Amak took a few steps and then slipped. The sheet of ice tossed under him like a ship rocked by the waves. He scrambled up and ran to the tent where Mr. and Mrs. Grapes were sleeping. Then the ground boomed, and a crack snaked along next to him as it sprayed water and threw up shards of ice.

"Harold! Mary Rose!" he yelled, his lungs about to burst.

He kept moving forward, but the ice tilted and twisted to one side, and he almost fell into the water that angrily churned around him. For a split second, he looked back to see that Ukluk had gotten the dogs harnessed to the sled.

"Get them out of here!" he yelled. "I'll be right behind you!"

Ukluk didn't look convinced, but he didn't waste any time. Amak leaped and landed in front of Mr. and Mrs. Grapes's tent. "Harold! Mary Rose!" he desperately yelled again. Without waiting for an answer, he grabbed the front flap and burst in. What he saw, or rather, what he didn't see, made him freeze. Harold and Mary Rose weren't there. Amak was turning to leave when he saw a scrap of paper among the blankets. He picked it up and found a note:

> *Thank you for helping us remember the purpose of our journey. We'll never lose sight of it again. Harold and Mary Rose Grapes.*

Amak turned the note over and on the other side was a photograph. It was of a man and woman and a little boy with brown hair and blue eyes standing in front of a ship under construction. The boy's hair was the same color as the woman's, and his eyes were just like the man's. Amak recognized the younger features immediately and ran out of the tent just as the ice on which it was pitched split. The tent was immediately swallowed by the cold waters. He ran, fighting to keep his balance and jumping to avoid the rapidly forming cracks. He fell face-first next to the sled where his son, Ukluk, and the dogs were waiting on firm ice. And there, while lying on the cold surface, he looked back and saw the house, covered in ice and glittering in the rosy light of dawn as it floated toward the open sea.

A Final Farewell

Harold and Mary Rose leaned on the railing of the battered porch, silently watching the dark sea widen the distance between them and the land sculpted out of ice they were leaving behind. All around them, hundreds of ice fragments peacefully flanked them like faithful sentinels as they left the safety of terra firma for the freedom of the open water. A faint light began to emerge in the sky, delicately erasing the stars that were still shining above them and turning the ice field a beautiful violet. They spotted the two small tents Ukluk had pitched, the sled with the dogs sleeping by it. It felt suddenly strange that, just a few minutes ago, they had been part of that world. A world they were slowly leaving behind forever.

Then the small figures of Amak and Ukluk emerged from one of the mounds. After a few minutes of uncertainty, they could be seen abandoning the temporary camp and moving farther onto the ice field. Finally, the two men stopped and turned toward the sea, looking in their direction. Harold and Mary Rose waved their arms wildly. At first, the two figures didn't move, but then they also started waving their arms.

The wind picked up, but Harold and Mary Rose didn't move from the porch. They kept waving happily with the euphoria of those setting off on a much-anticipated journey, even knowing this would be the last time they would see their friends. Then they heard a long, piercing whistle. It was Amak's unmistakable signal for his dogs to move. But this time, Harold and Mary Rose were also moving, towed by the wind and currents. Harold returned the whistle. The unceasing wind carried them quickly through the waves and followed the constant movement of the clouds. Harold felt a deep gratitude for Amak and for everything he had taught him. Knowing he would never see his friend again didn't sadden him. He knew that, no matter how different their journeys, no matter how many miles separated them, the bond of friendship they had developed was impossible to break.

Finally, the two figures were swallowed up in the distance in the tangled network of cracks that ran across the ice field. The reddish sun began to extend its fingers over the farthest mountain peaks, and behind one of the frozen mountainsides, they saw a wisp of smoke climb into the early morning sky. Harold and Mary Rose knew the smoke came from the camp where they had lived these last months. Where they had been given refuge and food, where their wounds had healed. Mary Rose's gaze followed the curling smoke and she thought about Aga. Her friend would have just gotten up to prepare the breakfast meal that they had eaten around the fire. Soon, she would take charge of organizing the camp's final preparations to move. Mary Rose felt some sadness that she hadn't gotten to say good-bye but quickly traded those feelings for the serenity and strength that Aga had shown her. And even though she knew it wasn't likely anyone in camp could see the house moving away, she waved. Mary Rose waved good-bye to Aga and to everyone carrying the final items to the sleds as they got ready to start their trip north. Mary Rose smiled when she thought of how surprised they would be when they found out the two odd strangers they had welcomed and sheltered had decided to take off in their tumbledown house instead of journeying with them north to return home.

"Home," Mary Rose repeated to herself as she watched the smoke disappear. She thought back to the trace of smoke they had seen months ago, when the house had been iced in. When their only objective was to be rescued and return to San Remo.

Finally, the expansive land of rock, ice, and snow faded in the distance. Harold and Mary Rose had stopped moving their arms, but in their minds, they were still waving. Saying good-bye to the ice field also meant saying good-bye to Kirima. Mary Rose no longer thought about the dark bundle that held her body. Harold no longer thought about the heavy shovelful of snow he scattered over her grave. Harold and Mary Rose only thought of her smile and her laughter as she ran after sweet Nattiq, whom they had also left behind. They thought about their morning walks to her parents' tent, about her voracious thirst for knowledge and her lively eyes. They thought about the first time they'd seen her, when she ran away from them. Harold and Mary Rose could feel nothing but gratitude for Kirima for having saved them from freezing to death under the snow and for giving them a second chance at life. It was a gift they couldn't waste.

The Mason Jar

Harold woke up to the tinkling of glass. Upon opening his eyes, he was momentarily confused. He expected to find himself in the dark tent made of animal hides in which he had slept for months. Instead, he saw the cracked ceiling of his bedroom. He closed his eyes again to better hear the murmur of the ocean and feel the gently rolling waves that rhythmically rocked him in his bed. He breathed deeply and then heard the soft tinkling again. He opened his eyes and looked to the bedroom window, which was still partially covered by a large blanket that waved in the breeze. He could hear the peaceful, relaxed breathing of Mary Rose at his side. When he turned to look at her, he was overwhelmed by her beauty. The rosy light of dawn fell on her, giving her a supernatural glow, exquisitely defining her slender nose, and painting her lips a deep carmine. Her chestnut hair intermingled with gray shone with golden highlights and fell in soft waves across her forehead and framed her perfect cheekbones. Harold leaned over and gently kissed her forehead, feeling the warmth of her skin. Mary Rose sighed deeply, and a faint smile curved her lips.

Careful not to wake her, Harold got out of bed and headed to the window. Pushing aside the blanket keeping the chilly air from invading their room, he peered through the jagged glass. He saw a gigantic red sun rise from the ocean like a burning ember. Both ocean and sky were stained a majestic orange-red that went on forever. Harold noticed there were no longer large sheets of ice, only small remnants scattered like spores from a dying flower. The house itself had lost most of its ice shell, and only a thin dusting of snow remained, sprinkled on the rock like sugar. As the snow had melted, the piles of rubble that now crushed the barren grapevines were laid bare. Harold heard the clinking of glass again and realized the sound was not coming through the broken window, but from somewhere downstairs.

He carefully made his way down the broken steps to the first floor. There, the sound was more noticeable; a fragile reverberation that reminded him of chandelier crystals. He followed the sound to the half-open door to the basement. Harold opened it fully and was confronted by a musty smell. He stepped onto the landing and slowly began descending the stairs. Icy water wet his bare feet. The feeling took him back to the first day they woke up floating in the middle of the sea, when they came down these same stairs and saw they were sinking. But unlike that day, Harold continued down the steps, feeling none of the anguish and terror of that moment. He thought about how Mary Rose had pushed on the board as he drove the nails. He remembered resurfacing and filling his lungs with air, pleased with a job well done. He recalled the love he'd felt as they had worked together.

Harold reached the flooded basement floor. In the faint light coming through the portholes, he discovered where the tinkling sound was coming from.

Dozens of bottles containing the tiny ships he had made were floating around and knocking into each other, submerging and reemerging like jellyfish. Harold felt one of the bottles bump into his side and gently picked it up. The rosy light coming through the round windows illuminated the cracked glass, and he saw it wasn't a bottle, but the old mason jar his son had used to catch fireflies.

Harold remembered when he'd begun to build this miniature ship, the first of many. He looked closer and smiled at the faithful reproduction of its hull sailing in a sea of blue resin, at the sheets in the tiny pulleys, and the sails billowing full in an imaginary wind. But then his smile faded. Suddenly, he felt suffocated by the glass surrounding the ship, as if trapped on the vessel eternally frozen in a plastic sea. Looking down, he saw that bottles floated around him like dying fish gasping, fighting for their last breaths. For a long, terrible moment, Harold fought to breathe, overwhelmed by the hours he had wasted enclosed in that dark basement as he built fictitious worlds protected by glass to isolate himself from the real world.

Harold removed a drawer from his old work desk and filled it with the bottled ships. With utmost care, he took them up the stairs and outside. He sat on the only intact porch step and rested the heavy drawer on his lap.

Thoughtfully, he took the bottle perched on top of the mountain of ships and set it in the water. The bottle was swallowed by a wave, but a second later, it popped up again, spinning like a real boat about to capsize.

Harold launched another and then another, until there was just one left. Just as he was about to pick it up, he heard the creak of wood behind him. He turned and saw his wife. Without saying a word, she sat down beside him. Mary Rose ran her fingers over the gleaming glass jar and smiled when she saw the tiny replica of their ship.

"Let's do it together," Harold said softly.

Each of them took one end of the cracked jar and, with one last look, launched it on the open sea. Like the bottles, the jelly jar sank, only to reemerge with a little skip over the surface. Harold took Mary Rose's hand in both of his, and they sat together in silence, watching the ships float away. Harold filled his lungs again with fresh morning air and felt free. He was free not only from the choking feeling that had come over him in the basement, but, more importantly, from the glass bubble in which he had been encased for years. He had tried to protect himself from the pain but had only trapped himself deeper inside. Harold had bottled up his dreams and his freedom. A freedom that, like the little ships now slowly floating away, would never again be limited. Because Mr. and Mrs. Grapes had decided to be free.

Grapevines and Hydrangeas

Mary Rose got up from the chair she had put on the back porch and went to the railing. Her gaze passed over the dark storm clouds beginning to turn the ocean gray. She could feel the rocking of the waves and the boards creaking beneath her feet. The breeze was cool, but not cold. The temperatures had climbed slowly as they'd floated south, and the fur parkas Amak and Aga had given them were no longer necessary.

A flash of light lit up the thick bank of clouds, and a second later, Mary Rose heard the rumble of thunder roll over the silvery sea. She thought back to the night of the storm in San Remo de Mar, the night the house plunged into the sea. But this time, Mary Rose wasn't worried or nervous.

A cold raindrop hit her cheek. She took in a last breath of fresh air as the wind tossed her hair, and then she went inside.

As she closed the door, she heard the wind howl like a restless ghost through the cracks and chinks in the house. Mary Rose walked through the dimly lit living room, bits of broken ceiling plaster crunching under her feet. When she arrived at the threshold to the hallway, she stopped. Mingling with the pure, moist air brought in by the storm was a strange, unpleasant smell. Mary Rose started toward the kitchen. As she entered the kitchen, the odor became stronger, almost tangible. The stench led her to an unused set of shelves lying facedown on the floor.

The smell was coming from underneath. Mary Rose struggled to raise one end of the unit and turned it over. She was hit by a strong rotting smell. For a few seconds, she stood frozen at the sight of the hydrangeas she had transplanted into pots after the fall.

It was clear the plants had been dead for a while, killed by the glacial cold. The same cold had then preserved them for months like mummies. Now with the warmer temperatures, they had begun to rot. Mary Rose went closer and saw that the normally thick stems were wrinkled and bent like old scarecrows, unable to bear the weight of the lush pompoms that once had graced the tops. They were now colorless blooms, covered with a layer of fuzzy gray mold that was growing on them clear down into the dry, cracked soil. Mary Rose reached out to the base of the flowers, and the stems broke easily at her touch. The flower fell, and its black petals disintegrated like fine soot.

Mary Rose left the rest of the decomposed bloom on the infertile soil and remembered the day she had first begun to plant hydrangeas around the newly constructed house. Hydrangeas she had moved from outside Dylan's window. For years, she had thought the vibrant color had helped make her loss more bearable, that it had helped her remember his golden, lively glow, but now she knew it hadn't. As she looked at the flowers, Mary Rose felt the weight of the past pressing down on her again, squeezing out the last drop of life, compressing her like the withered vines. The hydrangeas had never smelled of anything but death; they were funeral flowers she had planted over and over again in front of her son's grave—in front of the sea. But Mary Rose wasn't upset about the three dead plants or about all the lost hydrangeas she'd planted throughout her life, because now she understood that what had really killed those flowers wasn't the cold or the lack of water and light. They had died because they no longer were feeding off the pain, longing, and bitterness that had kept them alive for thirty-five years.

She looked at the plants one last time, then yanked them out by their roots. One by one, she felt the stems crumble in her grasp, the dark petals turn to dust. The fetid odor coming from the dry bundle in her soil-caked hands was unbearable. She turned and looked out at the vast gray ocean that was framed by a broken window, then hurled the flowers through the opening.

The bundle of rotten flowers fell on rubble, crumbling into dust that the storm scattered across the sea. A light, fresh rain began to fall, washing away the last traces of them and revealing two tender green shoots that were fighting to emerge from one of the crushed grapevines. Harold and Mary Rose weren't the only ones who had waited thirty-five years for new life.

The Adventure of a Lifetime

Harold and Mary Rose hadn't slept all night. A late-afternoon shower had quickly changed to a violent storm. They had spent their sleeping hours trying to prevent the remaining furniture from smashing into them as everything rolled around like marbles in a cardboard box. Finally, when the morning sun began to peek out from behind the thick storm clouds, the rain let up enough for Harold and Mary Rose to fall into bed. They fell asleep immediately, worn out from the long night.

It was noon when Harold and Mary Rose finally woke, their aging bodies registering the previous night's activity. It was hot in their bedroom, so they began looking through boxes for summer clothing, each movement revealing stiff joints and producing stabs of pain in their fatigued muscles.

Harold found a pair of shorts and an old short-sleeved shirt. He stood in front of the cracked mirror to button it up, then stopped short.

"I didn't know you still had it," said Harold, looking at Mary Rose in the mirror.

Mary Rose smoothed out the sheer fabric of her yellow-flowered dress and smiled at him.

"I didn't either." She turned around and held out the hem of her dress. "Look, you can still see the stain."

Harold smiled as he remembered that day in the shipyard. *A day just as hot as this one,* he thought as he opened the bedroom door and felt the air rising up the staircase. They headed down to the first floor, and through the sagging front door hanging ajar they saw the porch was flooded, submerged about an inch underwater. Harold and Mary Rose walked barefoot through water to the edge of the porch, where they took in the scene in front of them.

There was no trace of the storm, not a cloud in the sky. The sea was a polished mirror that clearly reflected the blue sky and brilliant sun. As if the ocean and sky were two halves of the same entity, it was impossible to distinguish reflection from reality.

Looking over the edge, Harold and Mary Rose saw themselves perfectly reflected in the water. Harold, in his old shorts and sky-blue shirt, and Mary Rose, in the same summer dress she had worn the afternoon they had taken the photo in the shipyard. Except for the dress, nothing matched the image of the young Mr. and Mrs. Grapes. Messy white hair concentrated on the sides and back replaced Harold's former thick mat of shiny black hair. His smooth skin, once brown from the sun on the docks, was now covered by deep wrinkles. The muscular physique of a shipbuilder had lost its tone and strength; instead of callouses from hard labor, his hands showed age spots. Mary Rose also showed signs of the passage of time. Her thick long brown hair had lost its brilliance and was sprinkled with a powdery gray. Her svelte figure was less defined, and even though she didn't have many wrinkles, her cheeks had lost the blush of youth.

More than thirty-five years separated the image of the young Mr. and Mrs. Grapes and the version of themselves they saw now. Thirty-five years during which they had barely noticed the inevitable passage of time as it had silently slipped through their fingers.

"We've wasted so much of our lives focused on an image of the past," Mary Rose said as she trailed her foot over the water, distorting their reflection.

Looking up from the warped mirror, Harold turned to her. "It's not about the time we've wasted, Rose, but about what we do with the time we have left."

"You're right," she said, the cool water caressing her leg.

"So let's enjoy what we have here and now."

Mary Rose's face registered alarm as Harold picked her up. "Harold!" she cried. "Don't even thin—!"

They both plunged into the water. For a moment, Harold and Mary Rose were stunned by the cold. But shock quickly changed to pleasure as bubbles tickled their faces and their clothes oscillated gently around them. Seconds later, their heads broke through the surface, and they filled their lungs with air, letting out the breath they had held for years.

Harold smiled at Mary Rose as the refreshing water dripped down his face. Mary Rose shook strands of wet hair out of her eyes. She frowned at Harold and splashed him.

"That's for throwing me in with my clothes on!" she said.

And then, before Harold could reply, Mary Rose found his lips and kissed him. "And that's for making me feel alive again. Thank you for saving us."

"I didn't save us," he said, instinctively thinking of Dylan.

"Yes, you did," she said, pulling him closer. "Without your perseverance, we would have died of thirst almost before our journey had begun. Without your courage, we would have frozen to death before we could meet Kirima. Harold, without you, we would never have freed ourselves. We couldn't be where we are now."

Her words pierced his heart. His eyes filled with tears that blended discreetly with the waves splashing against his face. He felt the last remnant of guilt cut loose like a heavy anchor that sank forever into the depths of the sea below them. Then they both looked up toward the house and saw last night's storm had carried away the last of the tiles and rubble from the roof. The bare attic was now a flat deck from which the blackened support beam rose, looking once more like the mast it was. Harold and Mary Rose gazed in wonder at their beat-up house, full of scars. Scars that, like the ones on their bodies, told the stories of their adventure. They could still picture the dolphin that had saved Harold from drowning and the reflection of the northern lights dancing in the night sky. In the broken windows, they could see the house passing through the giant iceberg and the polar bear bellowing on the ice field. In the hallways, now littered with rubble and swollen with water, they could hear the stories Amak and Aga told them around the fire and Kirima's laughter as she played each morning with Nattiq.

Harold began to smile, and his smile turned to laughter. Then he gave Mary Rose a kiss. A long, passionate, deep kiss. Time stood still as Harold wrapped his arms around her, and their kiss seemed to last forever. When their lips finally separated, their faces no longer seemed so old. They treaded water with the same strength as in their youth, and their eyes shone with the same radiance as the sun bouncing off the liquid mirror. They felt alive in a way they hadn't for years. Again, they looked at the tall mast rising from the structure in front of them and smiled as they realized it was no longer a house, but a ship. No matter how many wrinkles they had or how many years they had lost, now, at this moment, everything had been restored. They had finally realized their lifelong dream.

Lights on the Sea

The sun was setting on the horizon when Harold and Mary Rose took the last flight of stairs up to the attic. Debris was piled high on the top steps, but they were able to move it aside and get to the door. Harold rocked his weight back, then rammed his shoulder into the damaged door. It broke off its rusty hinges and crashed to the floor.

They entered what used to be the attic. Only a flat deck remained. The gambrel roof, the large round window, and the rafters had all collapsed under the weight of the snow. The storm had taken care of the rest, clearing away all traces of the slate tiles and timber. The bare wood floor gleamed as if it had been treated with the same varnish they had used years before.

As they crossed the deck, they were momentarily blinded by flashes of the sun's bright-yellow reflection as it slowly sank into the sea. From that height, the ocean seemed bigger and deeper than ever. There was nothing but water as far as they could see—no mountains or city lights in the distance. Only an infinite sea, unfathomable, and as full of mystery as life itself. Harold and Mary Rose felt a warm breeze on their backs that dried their clothing and pushed them toward the light of the setting sun.

They stopped in the center of their new rectangular deck alongside the imposing mast. Mary Rose ran her fingers gently over the rounded surface, feeling the rough bumps of the blackened veins on the hard wood. Harold observed her, remembering how difficult it had been to transport the mast from the old shipyard to the highest point on the island.

Then Mary Rose saw something strange in those scorched cracks. She cocked her head and leaned closer for a better look. She felt again with her index finger and realized the markings weren't natural; someone had carved letters into the wood. They had gone unnoticed all this time and now were worn after so many years.

"Our home," she read slowly.

"What?"

"Our home," she repeated, almost to herself.

Harold moved closer and followed his wife's gaze. At first, he didn't see anything, but then he made out the tiny writing running across the grain.

"I never saw it before," said Harold softly when he recognized his son's childish handwriting. "He named our ship."

"Dylan always knew this was our real home," said Mary Rose as they walked to the edge of the deck.

The sun that guided their way like a lighthouse was now barely a glimmer of yellow light sinking below the waterline.

"Yes," said Harold, moving closer to his wife. "He never stopped believing in our dream. Or in us."

Finally, the last remnant of light was swallowed by the sea. Night began to fall over them like a soft blanket. In the sky and reflected on the sea, the first stars were visible. Then, under the darkness that was enveloping the world, appeared a strange luminescence. A light so tenuous and diffuse that it didn't seem real. It expanded like the warm, yellow light in Dylan's jar, the lantern that guided his childish dreams in the night.

Mary Rose recognized the brilliant light in the sky as the lightning that had struck the mast and opened holes in the yard, breaking the house away from the cliff side. It was the same light reflected in the old woman's tear and in the candle of the small tent. It was the light of the aurora they had seen from the dark porch and that had reflected off the dolphin's back. The same aurora she had seen dancing over the ice field. Mary Rose thought about what Aga had said when they watched the ethereal lights together.

"It's Dylan," she sighed.

Then a subtle vibration began under Harold's and Mary Rose's feet, working its way through their entire bodies and making the wood creak and the water bubble. The tremor was caused by the light that now filled them, expanding over them like a supernatural sail, like the missing sail from their boat. It was a light that seemed to call them from the depths of the golden sea and weakened the rock surrounding them. Harold and Mary Rose looked deep into each other's eyes and smiled with understanding when they saw the luminescent yellow blending and dancing with the green and blue of their eyes.

Mr. and Mrs. Grapes held each other tightly, feeling a new light rise from inside them. A light that freed them from fear and pain, a light that gradually melded with the light shining in the sky and on the water. Light that appeared each night in the little fireflies. It was Dylan's light. It surrounded them with warmth and tenderness. Harold and Mary Rose knew they weren't alone. They felt their son's embrace again, his tender kisses, and the warmth of his little hands in theirs. The three of them were together again, happy and looking toward the horizon they had finally reached. They were sailing on the ship they had built, on the dream they had finally realized, on the immense sea that was their home. Their true home.

"I love you, Rosy," whispered Harold.

"I love you too, Harold," answered Mary Rose.

From a distance, if anyone had been there to see it, Mr. and Mrs. Grapes's house no longer looked like a house floating aimlessly. It was a ship. An amazing ship, guided by a light that shimmered on the horizon. A ship that slowly sank in the hazy line where the sky and sea are one.

If anyone had been there at that moment, they would have felt the wind drop and observed the twinkling starlight go dark for a fraction of a second. In the bright night sky, shimmering above the golden sea, they would have seen two new lights appear: one green like freshly cut grass and the other blue like the ocean.

It was the light of those who have embraced life in all its wonder. Of those who have enjoyed their time and the people they love. It was the light of those who accept their own mortality at the end of their journey. Lives no longer filled with regrets but with the certainty of having fulfilled their destiny and faithfully lived out their dreams. It was the light of Harold and Mary Rose, known to all as Mr. and Mrs. Grapes.

ACKNOWLEDGMENTS

Many of you have spent years (yes, years!) following the development of this book, an arduous process in which sometimes even I lost faith. Thank you all for always being there. A special thank-you to my mother. She was the first to read the drafts of this story and to believe Harold and Mary Rose's extraordinary adventure deserved to be told.

Thank you to my father for giving my childhood a soundtrack. Without the music of Mike Oldfield, I never would have been the boy—or the man—who believed that anything was possible.

Thank you to my sister, for her unfailing support and boundless energy. Even though I never tell you, you are my idol.

Thank you to all my friends for being my guinea pigs with the first versions of this book. Your opinions were invaluable. My sincerest thanks to Marta Vilaspasa, Nuria Briz, Mireia Mercadé, Marta Lluch, Lorena Pedre, Marco Sansalone, Rebeca Canedo, Nuria Arnau, Alicia Jerez, Xavier Gumara, and many more that I'm sure I'm leaving out.

A special thank-you to Jonathan Sanz for supporting me and putting up with me every day, which is no small feat.

I also owe a great deal to Daniel Hareg, who, with his infinite patience and amazing talent, helped bring out my best writing. To Mónica Carmona, my literary agent, thank you for making it possible for *Lights on the Sea* to reach an ever-increasing readership. Thank you to my editors, Belén Bermejo (Spain), Daniela Thiele (Germany), Cristina

Prasso (Italy), and Elizabeth DeNoma (US), for believing in this story. Their talent and passion for literature transcends the months of phone calls, emails, and videoconferences so that today, you may have *Lights on the Sea* in your hands. And thank you to all the translators whose excellent work allows this story to be read in so many languages. For this edition, I want to especially thank Catherine E. Nelson.

I also want to express my appreciation for writers like JRR Tolkien, Yann Martel, Anne Rice, and Viktor Frankl for inspiring me with their wonderful stories and their ways of understanding the world.

Lastly, I want to thank you, the readers who have bought this book. *Thank you!* I hope with all my heart that the story of Mr. and Mrs. Grapes has inspired you and motivates you to stop living the life others expect of you and begin living the life you have always dreamed of. Although sometimes things happen that we don't understand, and sometimes it all seems too hard, we can never give up. Because in the end, life is a journey that should be lived fully and if not, well, go ask Mr. and Mrs. Grapes.

Miquel Reina
Barcelona/Vancouver, October 3, 2017

NOTE FROM THE AUTHOR

I began writing *Lights on the Sea* during my last year of university—and that was a few years ago! The truth is that the project has always been there, like an old friend you don't see for long periods of time, but when you get together again, you feel like time hasn't passed at all. And the thing is, when you work in publicity, time is not something you have a lot of. Over the years, I had developed a more or less "respected" reputation in the creative world. Despite that, I felt like something was missing. Then, like lightning out of the blue, this old friend reappeared: the story of Harold and Mary Rose.

So, after a lot of reflection, I decided to leave my job so I could consider what I wanted to do with my life and what projects I wanted to dedicate my time to. I took a risk, and then everything began to make sense. During the last year, I moved to another part of the world, changed professions, and finally, after all those first drafts that I read every night to my mother, I'm publishing my first book!

I only want to say that I hope this novel you now hold in your hands has served to light a spark in you, no matter how faint or if you don't know where it comes from. Because even if it takes years, in the end, if you don't give up, dreams can come true.

Discover more at:

www.lucesenelmar.com

www.miquelreina.com

BEFORE YOU GO

If you think one of your friends or family members would be interested in this story, I would be honored if you would share it with them. And if you feel this book has benefited you in any way, I would be eternally grateful if you would write a review on Amazon or social media.

Thank you again,
Miquel

ABOUT THE AUTHOR

Photo © 2018 Jonathan Sanz

Barcelona-born Miquel Reina defines himself as a dreamer and a fighter; from a young age, he was drawn to the creative life, studying design and cinema before building his reputation as a filmmaker and graphic artist. His work in advertising won him several awards, including the prestigious Bronze Sun at Spain's Festival de San Sebastián in 2011, and in 2014, his music video "Dead in the Water" was screened at the Tribeca Film Festival. Reina has lived in Vancouver, Canada, since 2016, working for a video-production studio and dedicating his free time to his most gratifying passion: writing. *Lights on the Sea* is his first novel. Visit Miquel at www.miquelreina.com and www.lucesenelmar.com.